KEEP HOLD

By the Author

Getting Lost

Keep Hold

Visit us at www.boldstrokesbooks.com

KEEP HOLD

by

Michelle Grubb

2015

Credits
Editor: Cindy Cresap
Production Design: Stacia Seaman
Cover Design by Sheri (graphicartist2020@hotmail.com)

Acknowledgments

Many thanks to Monique Gorham for her amusing medical stories and friendship—I've never looked at an eggplant quite the same.

Thank you, Alanna Cannon and Jean Cooper for the missing commas, corrections, thoughts, and feedback.

Bold Strokes Books—Radclyffe, Sandy, Cindy, and team, once again thank you for the opportunity to write for such a renowned publisher.

Finally, to Kerry Grubb-Moore, thank you for your endless support and encouragement and for putting up with me. You have the patience of a saint.

For Kerry.
My everything.

PROLOGUE

Claire wasn't night shift's biggest fan. For the past few months, she'd switched to autopilot and been running on empty, with no idea what she was doing with her newly apparent shambles of a life.

There was something about being an emergency department nurse—responsible for the welfare of patients ranging from the acutely ill to the downright stupid—that caused your closest friends to glare wide-eyed at even the slightest suggestion you may not be firing on all cylinders. Everyone wanted to believe nurses were the epitome of good. If doctors were God, then a nurse was his right-hand man, right?

Wrong.

Claire trudged from the labour ward at three in the morning after fetching a pair of industrial strength forceps. She felt so far removed from God she might as well have been in another realm of reality.

She clocked her reflection in a one-way mirrored window and shook her head. She was convinced she began her shift looking professional and capable. Now she resembled a drunkard pretending to be a nurse at a fancy dress party.

Stalling beyond the ED threshold, she cursed and inhaled deeply. The acutely ill, she was happy to treat. The downright stupid though? Really? Of course they received the same level of professional care, but her snide attitude came free.

Claire swung the curtain open, far wider than necessary, to reveal a massive, hairy rear end. She knew it was going to be there, yet was still shocked at the sight.

Unable to resist, she gave the closest cheek a little tap. "All right, Mr. Sullivan?"

No, tonight God wasn't enough. Tonight she needed Jesus, Mary, and all the bloody saints for this delightful patient.

Mr. Sullivan, a large man in his fifties, groaned. The only comfortable position he could sustain was on all fours.

The look Claire exchanged with Dr. Murray, whilst handing her the forceps, suggested they'd be groaning, too, if they had a massive eggplant stuck up their rear end.

Upon arrival in the ED, the cranky Mr. Sullivan had requested a male nurse; bad luck, Mr. Sullivan. He'd also requested a male doctor. Lucked out there, too. And when he demanded the entire hospital staff lie to his wife about his self-inflicted condition, Claire simply smiled. His wife was already on her way, and even the great Houdini himself couldn't conceal a sizeable vegetable firmly lodged up his behind. On all counts, Mr. Sullivan was buggered.

Claire had long since stopped trying to figure out why humans harboured an unnatural desire to force large objects into relatively small holes. She'd seen kids with coins up their noses, buttons in their ears, Lego men heads in belly buttons, and now a grown man with an eggplant up his bum.

"I have to admit, Dr. Murray, this is the first eggplant extraction I've assisted in."

Dr. Yvonne Murray, affectionately known as Murray, was Claire's favourite ED doctor and a good friend. The petite doctor from outback New South Wales said it like it was, earning respect for her fairness and never ending repertoire of crude jokes.

They stood at the foot of the bed, bewildered. Dr. Murray set her hands firmly on her hips, sporting a deep frown, staring in awe at the severely stretched anus before them. "No moussaka for a while then."

Claire sighed. *Damn. I love moussaka.*

"Right, now, Mr. Sullivan, this might tickle a little." With great care and precision, Murray aligned the well lubricated forceps and gently inserted them into his rear end.

"Shouldn't you give me something for the pain?"

Claire suspected panic and a strong sense of vulnerability had finally overridden Mr. Sullivan's previously smart tongue.

"No time for that," Murray lied, applying pressure and slowly edging the forceps deeper. "And anyway, you managed to get it in there without painkillers; I'm sure you'll be a big brave boy for me now." Taking pity, Murray turned to Claire. "More lubrication, thank you, Nurse."

Claire liberally applied lubrication, the vision before her momentarily causing her stomach to lurch—the sight was so horribly unnatural—and Murray continued to slowly insert the forceps until they sufficiently encased the entrapped vegetable.

It was when Murray began to explain how Mr. Sullivan should assist in the extraction by pushing gently, that Mrs. Sullivan made her grand entrance into the emergency department shouting loudly. "Young lady, I am the unfortunate wife of the idiot you have in there. Do not block my way!"

The short, sharp clacking of heeled shoes echoed on the polished floor, even over the hum and bustle of the emergency room. A brief look from Murray told Claire to intercept and prepare the unfortunate woman.

Claire slipped through the curtain and promptly collided front-first into an attractive older lady, mid-fifties, perfectly made up, wearing a black velvet tracksuit and bright red stilettos.

"Mrs. Sullivan, I presume?" Claire attempted a light and friendly inflection.

"Don't *Mrs. Sullivan* me. I don't care what state that prick of a husband of mine is in. I want to see him immediately."

Claire shrugged. She didn't care either. She ushered the poor woman in.

"Not again, Garry, I'm fucking sick of this!" Mrs. Sullivan screamed at her husband's exposed and violated backside. Then, moving to berate him eye to eye, she continued, "You promised me, you selfish shit. You're damn lucky I don't rip those tongs out of your ass and ram that fucking thing right up to your eyeballs. This is the last time, Garry. Do you understand me?"

The previously arrogant Mr. Sullivan nodded in agreement and began to sob.

Claire rolled her eyes. *You're kidding me?* She couldn't wait for this to be over so she could read his file, see what else poor old Garry had been up to.

Sighing to indicate she'd had enough, Dr. Murray appeared keen to end the freak show. "Okay, let's get this veggie out of you. Mrs. Sullivan, do you want to hang around for this or can I get a nurse to call you when I'm done?"

"I'll stay, thank you." She curtly eyed her husband.

"Righto, now just try and relax, Mr. Sullivan."

Relax? Murray must be kidding if she thought Mr. Sullivan was even capable of relaxation, especially now his wife had arrived. Claire watched as Murray braced herself to remove the foreign object. It wasn't going to be easy.

It took over a minute to reach the halfway mark. Murray struggled over the wide girth of the eggplant and beads of sweat emerged on her brow, although it was nothing compared to the state of poor groaning Mr. Sullivan.

"Claire, you'll have to get behind me and help pull."

She shot Murray a look. *What?*

Murray shrugged.

It was stuck.

Although only slight in stature herself, Claire's arms could easily encompass the doctor. She stood behind Murray and grasped her wrists.

"Don't enjoy this too much, Nurse."

"I was just about to say the same to you." Claire deliberately pressed her whole body against Murray's.

"That's not helping, Nurse."

"Well, it's certainly helping me, Doctor."

Murray ignored her and turned her attention to the task at hand. She encouraged Claire with cries of "pull," and Mr. Sullivan with cries of "push."

Claire wasn't sure she could eat eggplant again.

With Murray's encouragement and an enormous cry from Mr. Sullivan, the slippery eggplant shot out with a slurping suction noise best described as revolting.

Holding the eggplant aloft, Murray exclaimed, "It's a boy!"

CHAPTER ONE

Moping wasn't Claire's style, which is to say she was disappointed to find herself lacking motivation—no extra shifts at the hospital, no running, no t'ai chi, and she couldn't shake the feeling that the last four years had been a complete lie and a waste of time.

The thumping rap at the door offered a welcome distraction.

"Hi, Claire." The deep velvet voice of Jess Mercer was still, to this day, one of the sexiest sounds to Claire's ears. She affectionately cupped Claire's cheek with one hand, kissing her softly, carefully balancing coffee in the other.

"Hey, yourself. Thanks for bringing coffee. The thought of instant is dreadful on any day, let alone a Saturday."

Familiar with her surroundings, Jess walked the length of the hall, through the compact kitchen, and into the tiny but immaculately manicured back garden. "What's wrong with your machine?" She set three coffees on the outdoor table beside a neatly stacked fruit platter. "And where's Victoria?"

Claire mumbled incoherently about the coffee machine that used to occupy extraordinary space on the bench. Agitated, she set down a jug of water and two glasses. "Berlin."

"Pardon me?" Jess glanced at the third coffee she'd bought.

"Victoria's in Berlin. Left in June."

"June? Wow!" The smile disappeared from Jess's face. She swiped long, straggly strands of blond hair from across her sunglasses, and when they refused to stay in place, she rested her glasses on her head, keeping every strand restrained. "You should have told me. I'll miss you." Jess smiled before her face contorted. "Shit, Claire, this is huge. How am I going to break it to Alex? I assume things have improved between you. Let me guess; you get the fun job of staying behind until everything's finalised?" She eyed Claire. "You loved Germany, didn't you?"

"I'm not going."

"What? How come? Has something happened?"

"Nothing happened, other than the fact that she didn't ask me."

Jess's eyes widened, rendering her uncharacteristically speechless.

"I'm not moving to Berlin with the woman I was convinced was the love of my life, Jess, because she didn't fucking ask me to go with her."

A red splash of anger coloured Jess's cheeks and her voice lowered to a protective growl. "I beg your pardon?"

"She doesn't want me there." Frustration filtered through Claire's attempts to remain calm.

"So, what does that mean for you two? I know it's been a bit rough this last little while, but moving to Berlin sounds so drastic."

"Means we're over. Done and dusted." Claire choked back tears.

"No? Really? Surely there's something you can do?"

"I fucked it up."

"That's not true."

"Well, I must have. Berlin is a long way to go to get away from someone. To get away from me. Ballarat I can understand, but Berlin."

"Be honest. You'd have followed her to Ballarat. It's only three hours away."

"You're not funny and you're not helping."

Jess patted her arm. "I'm sorry, but seriously, after four years, there must be something—"

"Just leave it, Jess. It's finished for good. And we both know it wasn't really four years."

"You had some good times."

"Yeah, and I ruined it all."

"For God's sakes, you didn't ruin anything. It takes two. What did she say to you when she left?"

"It's not what she said." Claire couldn't relive the day again. Not yet. "She's gone and she's not coming back. I drove her away and that's all there is to it. I know what you're thinking. I know we were considering a break, and I know things had been better, but..."

Jess shook her head, bewildered. "Ah, Jesus, Claire. I don't know what to say. I'm so sorry, honey."

Claire's voice crackled, but she held it together. "What can you do, eh?"

"You should have told me, honestly, Claire, she's been gone months."

"You've been so busy and you were in Europe for six weeks. You weren't even here."

"I had my phone. I was only a phone call away."

"You and I both knew it was a possibility."

"Well, I don't know if I'd have predicted a move quite that far. I can't believe you didn't even send a message."

"I was fine." She lied. "Shit happens."

"*Was* fine? Are you sure you're okay now?"

Claire couldn't face the truth. "Yes, perfectly fine."

"So, where's the coffee machine? *Berlin?*"

"Her mother took it."

"Oh for Christ's sake, she couldn't even leave the fucking machine?"

Claire shrugged. She loved that machine. "It's karma. That's what it is. What goes around comes around, you know?"

Jess shook her head and lowered her voice. "It's nothing like us, sweetheart."

Claire fetched the shade umbrella from the neatly organised garden shed. "So, Madam Crown. For the benefit of the jury, please explain why, seven years ago when your girlfriend, Claire O'Malley— hot, sexy, and six years your junior—asked you to accompany her to Europe, you declined?"

"Claire, don't do this."

Claire sighed. "I know my leaving effectively ended our relationship." Claire shoved the umbrella through the hole in the table. "I believe Ms. O'Malley is well aware that you were busy establishing a career as one of the most respected Crown solicitors in Victoria—a far wiser option than pissing your life up the wall in Europe."

"Is Victoria six years younger than you?"

"Four. Same difference. Don't worry, you win."

Jess frowned disapprovingly.

"Either way, I asked you to run away with me when I was young and stupid, and you turned me down. I was willing to go with Victoria, and she didn't want me there. Just bloody perfect."

"Do you really want to go to Berlin?" Jess asked.

"Yes, of course."

Jess raised her eyebrows.

"Well, I at least would have liked to have been asked."

"So you could turn her down?"

"No! Well, maybe."

"Is it your ego or your heart that's broken?"

Claire wasn't sure she knew the answer. She felt like her heart had been breaking for months now, long before Victoria left. As much as she tried, nothing was ever good enough for Victoria. She walked on eggshells around her, trying not to upset her and bear the brunt of yet another bout of silent treatment or ranting. Something in Claire felt broken, but she wasn't convinced it was her heart or her ego. Perhaps *she* was broken.

Jess kicked the umbrella into place under the table before pulling Claire into a warm embrace and, like old times, Claire's head rested perfectly in the hollow of her neck. "Come round for dinner tonight?"

"Hey." Claire playfully pushed her away. "It's too late to rescue me now, thanks all the same. I've already stopped sniffing her pillow, and I actually changed the sheets months ago. I don't want you inviting me to dinner so you can take full credit for my miraculous recovery."

"But you still seem a little…"

"Go on. A little what?"

"Well, sad I guess. You look exhausted."

Claire was beyond exhausted, if that were possible. Half the reason why she hated instant coffee so much was that she drank too much of it. She couldn't afford a new machine.

"Alex would love to see you. She's sick of me whinging every time she touches me." Jess wiped a tear from Claire's cheek. "You'll get loads of cuddles. She needs *someone* to cuddle."

Claire sighed. "What's wrong with this picture? My pregnant ex-lover invites me to dinner with her gorgeous wife, my ex co-worker, who is possibly feeling neglected because your hormones are going mental, so my ex-lover offers me up as a cuddle substitute. Seriously, can my life get any weirder?" The truth was, even before Victoria had left, it had been months since they had been intimate, and she couldn't even remember when they had last hugged or kissed. Some personal contact with someone other than her patients was tempting.

Jess simply shrugged and smiled. It obviously didn't seem weird to her at all.

Claire ducked inside to switch off the radio; some old seventies song about a jilted lover was cutting a little too close to the bone. She froze. The penny dropped. Since becoming pregnant, Jess had been ill and called less frequently. Claire sensed trouble.

"What's up?" Claire emerged from the kitchen, straight to the point.

Jess frowned.

"Come on, Madam Crown. Spill."

Jess drew a deep breath. "You know me too well."

Claire smiled.

"We're having twins."

"Wow. Twins is huge. Congratulations!" Reality dawned on Claire. "Jesus, that's a lot of nappies."

"And very little sleep, I presume."

Sensing there was more, Claire waited patiently.

"The ultrasound showed there's a strong possibility one of the foetuses could be abnormal." She shrugged. "Happens at my age."

Claire squeezed Jess's shoulder. "Oh dear, Counsellor. You just used the words 'possibility' and 'could' in the same sentence. *And* you referred to your babies as foetuses. You'd better tell me all the facts."

Jess finished her coffee, massaging her forehead. Claire could see by the deep crease of her brow that she was worried. She allowed Jess time to gather her thoughts. Jess Mercer was *always* in control. She was strong-willed and fearless. She processed information at an alarming speed and her sharp tongue never failed her.

Claire had long suspected Jess became a lawyer to justify her argumentative personality. Why simply argue and prove your point for fun? Crown Prosecutor Jess Mercer was paid handsomely to do what she loved most—arguing and winning. She would research a topic then regurgitate the cold hard truth, void of emotion or feeling. Her love of facts made her perfect for the job.

Claire had left Jess to travel the world and find herself. They both knew she needed to lose Jess before she could become the real Claire O'Malley. At thirty, Jess was the hottest new solicitor in Melbourne, and dating a twenty-four-year-old nursing student with grand travel plans had been destined to come to a head.

Now, knowing her strong reliance on facts, evidence, and proof won her an alarming percentage of arguments, Claire knew Jess appreciated the opportunity to put forward her case, her way.

"The obstetrician reeled off some statistics about Down syndrome, spina bifida, and cystic fibrosis, but I don't remember them; it all seemed to happen so quickly. One moment we were elated about the babies, next it all seemed to come crashing down. The doctor made it clear she wasn't making a diagnosis, just informing us of the facts."

"At your age, the chances increase from around one in two thousand to one in just over one hundred for having a baby with Down syndrome. I don't know statistics for the other conditions," said Claire.

"She said there were tests, an amniocentesis. Apparently, it comes with risks." Jess was barely holding it together.

"I think the risks are small, but the consequences can be pretty bad."

Jess nodded. "That's what the doctor said."

"Will you have the amniocentesis?"

Jess half shrugged and half nodded.

Claire cleared her throat, finding courage to ask the question that Jess really wanted to discuss. "Will you terminate if it's positive?"

"It sounds horrific, doesn't it? *Terminate.*"

"It's okay to talk about it and think about it, Jess."

"I feel like a monster."

Claire took a different tack. "So, what are your options?"

Jess thought for a moment. "Okay, I have the test and I know for sure if the baby has Down syndrome at least. I don't have the test and I let the pregnancy run its course, essentially mitigating any risk of losing the baby, or babies, from unnatural causes." Jess paced the small grassed area. "But will finding out alter my decision? If not, then it's reasonable to deduce that the test is unnecessary. If *yes*, then is the risk involved in the test of lesser or greater consequence than not having the test at all?" She looked Claire in the eye. "Can I live with insisting on an invasive procedure and possibly losing my babies? Or can I live with raising a disabled child?" Jess hesitated. "Or should I terminate if the test is successful and positive?"

"It's a tough one."

"It's impossible."

"What would your advice be to me, if I were in your shoes?"

"I really don't know, Claire. That's the problem. On this one, I just don't know."

Claire yanked Jess into the chair closest to her. "Yes, you do know. You'd give me your best advice based on all the facts because you love me. So, say you have the test. Say it's positive. If you have the baby, it will be disabled. Given that it's difficult to know what any of us would do under any circumstances, what do you think *you'd* do with this knowledge?"

"Shit. I'm not sure I know."

Claire waited for her to analyse and compartmentalise her thoughts.

Jess focused. "I've had the test?"

"Yep. It's not the best news. It's positive."

"My baby will have Down syndrome or some other chromosomal disorder?"

"Ah-huh, ninety-nine percent certainty."

"But it's still *my* baby?"

"That's true. Your flesh and blood."

"And there's every chance I will give birth to another normal child."

"Correct. Scans show your other baby is fine."

"So, either I take my baby's life away, or I give it a fighting chance?"

"That's certainly one way of looking at it."

"The average life expectancy for a person with Down syndrome is over sixty these days."

"That's not a bad innings," said Claire.

"I can give my baby nothing or, on average, sixty good years."

Claire nodded.

Jess met her eyes. "I don't think I need the test."

Claire leaned back. "Good decision. Brave decision."

CHAPTER TWO

Alex was *exactly* the type of woman Claire had expected Jess to fall in love with—same age, equally intelligent, and perfect to remain at home and raise their children. She was possibly one of the nicest people Claire had ever met. Jess was good-looking, but Alex was a stunner.

An air of self-assurance surrounded Alex, and contrary to Claire's first impression, it had nothing to do with her looks. Her confidence and energy was addictive, and Claire loved it, envying her enthusiasm and warm heart.

If Alex had ever been afraid of losing Jess to her ambitions, she never showed it, and that was why, Claire suspected, Jess worshipped the ground she walked on.

Claire rang the bell and ripped the wine from the tacky brown paper bag Jess had taught her never to arrive at a dinner party holding. Although relieved she was no longer twenty-four and lost, she found little comfort in the fact she was now thirty-one and recently jilted.

"Here she is." Alex engulfed her in a warm hug. "I think Jess is right; you do look a little forlorn."

"I *am* forlorn." Claire went along with it. Surely tired and forlorn could be interchangeable in these circumstances.

"Bloody Victoria, I never liked her."

"You said you thought she was lovely!"

"And she was, until she left you. Now I've hated her all along."

A delicious smell wafted from the kitchen, and Claire handed over the wine. She'd never walked into this house and been greeted with normal cooking smells like a roast lamb or casserole. For all of Jess's lack of creativity in anything other than the law, she could cook. The fact astounded everyone except Claire. It was the single thing, besides amazing oral sex, that Claire had given Jess—encouragement in the kitchen and a license to mess up.

"You've got her to cuddle all night," Jess said from the other end of the hall. "Can she at least come in the door?"

While it took Claire about ten paces to walk the entire length of her own apartment, Jess and Alex's place felt like a school dorm. The front rooms were spare bedrooms, a study, and a bathroom, while the rear was an expansive kitchen and living area. Upstairs was the master bedroom, en suite, and another living area. Alex had decorated of course, light and airy, and with Claire's rough estimate, she guessed her two-bedroom place would fit upstairs with space to spare.

"What's for dinner?" Claire accepted a glass of red and stuck her nose over the stove for a sniff.

Up to her wrists in batter, Jess leaned forward to kiss her on the cheek. "Your favourite, honey. Something to cheer you up."

Claire didn't recognise the dish and wondered how it could be her favourite. But then she spied a bowl of prawns and her mouth watered in anticipation—Jess knew how to make her feel better.

"Throw your keys in the bowl, Claire. Relax and have a few glasses of wine tonight. I've made up the spare bed for you," said Alex.

"For me? You have two spare beds and they're always made up."

"Well, perhaps we're always hoping you'll stay." Alex mimicked Claire's tone. "Keys in the bowl, please."

"I thought I was here to be cheered up and nutritionally sustained, not participate in one of your dirty swingers parties."

Jess looked up. "Come on, Claire. The cat will be fine for one night."

Claire raised her eyebrows.

"You're kidding me? She took the fucking cat? Let me guess, her mother?"

She didn't even like the bloody cat. But four years together was four years.

Alex emerged from the linen cupboard and against all protests, took Claire to the couch to talk. "Come on, I want to know all about it. Bloody Jess came home with no details this afternoon."

"I just feel so stupid. I knew she'd applied for the damn job. I knew she was short-listed, and the day I found out she'd already had an interview was the day she told me she'd taken the job and was leaving. We didn't even get a chance to talk it through or have an argument about it. Nothing. Her bloody mother came charging through the door and started taking things almost straight away. It was just fucking awful."

"Murray said you were good at work for the most part, but in the last few months, she's been worried about you."

The week after Victoria left was horrendous, but she'd worked nights, had a couple of days off, and although the process was slow, she'd made commendable improvements and was nearly back to normal. That was until a few months ago. That was when it all began to go tits up. Twice now she'd been pulled up by the Nurse Unit Manager on careless mistakes, and on top of being caught sleeping on the job, she was struggling. It wasn't like Claire to struggle. Claire cracked on with things, that was her nature, that was what made her an outstanding nurse, yet what she was going through now had snuck up on her, and it was frightening.

"I know Murray's worried, but it's just a glitch. Honestly, I'm fine."

"And what's causing the glitch?"

Claire had no idea what was causing the glitch, but the aftermath was horrendous. She just wanted it to end, and tonight she wanted to enjoy the evening and forget about it for a while. She dodged the question. "Dealing with idiotic patients with eggplants up their arse is enough to cause any nurse the odd malfunction."

"What up his arse?" Jess called from the kitchen. "I think I need to hear this."

Delighted her deflection had worked, Claire provided an in-depth synopsis of Mr. Sullivan's sordid tale of painful extraction.

"Look on the bright side," offered Alex. "It could be worse; you could be Mrs. Sullivan."

She had a point.

The phone rang, piercing the air with an intrusive clangour.

Alex shot up to answer while Jess stared at Claire. "You haven't been sleeping, have you?"

Claire knew better than to lie. "Barely."

"Alex and I have talked, and we think you should come and stay with us for a while."

"Jess, I'm okay. I've been perfectly okay for the past four months now. My shifts are all over the place, I just need a few day shifts to get a decent night's sleep."

"I know, but I'm worried about you. Worse than that, Murray is worried about you, and we all know it takes a lot for Murray to even bat an eyelid at mild inconvenience, let alone taking the time to be bothered to actually be worried."

"You're barely making sense, Madam Crown."

Jess sighed. "Look, why be lonely there, when you can come and get over all this here?"

"I'm over it Jess, honestly. I was dumped. I'm not dying. Not even of a broken heart. This shit happens every day. I'm not special. I'll be fine."

"You're special to me, to us both. I don't want you to hurt."

Claire moved to kneel in front of Jess. "You can't fix this, Madam Crown. I know you fix things and you make them better. You both do"—she gestured toward Alex in deep conversation on the phone— "but I'm not one of your clients. Whatever it is I'm going through, I *have* to go through, Jess. This process has to happen, otherwise Victoria was a waste of time, and I can't deal with losing her *and* the past four years of my life all at once."

Jess sighed.

Claire knew she understood because it was Jess she had reached out to when things with Victoria began to go south. She couldn't pinpoint the day things began to change, but one day Victoria stepped back from her, not literally, but emotionally. Claire had no idea what she had done wrong. She still didn't.

"That was Kathryn." Alex returned to the couch and pulled Claire from the floor to snuggle with her.

"Kathryn who?" Jess looked on blankly.

"Your sister! How many Kathryns do you know?"

"What did she want? How come I didn't speak to her?"

"Oh, you will." Alex was amused.

"I will?"

"Yep. She's on her way."

"What?"

"She said she hoped it wasn't an intrusion."

"An intrusion? I haven't seen her for three years, barely even heard from her."

"Regardless, she apologised for not phoning ahead, but called as soon as she landed. She's in a cab as we speak."

Jess was flabbergasted. "But she doesn't even like prawns!"

CHAPTER THREE

Claire wasn't even sure she remembered what Kathryn looked like. Absolutely nothing like Jess was all her memory told her, although lately, Claire's memories were a jumbled, fragmented mess. She struggled to remember a time when she and Victoria had been happy. It occurred to her that the human brain could fool you into not missing something you no longer had, just to make the pain bearable. Had she fooled herself into happiness all those years, or was she fooling herself out of it now?

Alex cornered her in the kitchen as she poured another round of drinks. "Talking about it will help, you know."

"You know all there is to know."

"I doubt it. What did she say when she left?"

"It wasn't so much about what she said, it was what she did. It was truly awful that I was in love with someone capable of treating me so badly."

Alex waited. It was her special skill.

Claire knew she'd have to tell them sooner or later. Later was her preferred option, but Alex didn't seem on board with that. "We watched a movie together the evening before, slept in the same bed, and in the morning discussed our plans for the weekend." Saying the words sent her right back to that morning. It hurt. "She was eating toast and simply announced she was leaving."

"What did she actually say?"

"She said our relationship had run its course, she no longer loved me, and she had taken the job in Berlin." Alex patted her shoulder.

"Do you know what's sad though? I actually laughed. I thought she was joking. I'm so fucking stupid."

"You're not stupid, honey. You need to stop beating yourself up over it."

Claire wasn't so sure. She felt as thick as ten planks. Not one living cell in her body saw it coming. "She took her phone from her pocket, typed what could have only been one or two words, and within a minute, the front door crashed open and her mother charged in and began disassembling the coffee machine."

Victoria's mother neither greeted nor acknowledged Claire and only provided a cursory glance when she yelled at her to leave things alone and get out.

"I hate myself for it, but I actually begged her to stay."

"That's natural," said Alex. "You're human, like the rest of us. It was a shock. It was a shocking thing to happen. I actually think you handled yourself well."

"She walked out without a second glance." Claire sighed.

"And you'll be okay. It might not feel like it now, but it doesn't seem like you were meant to be with her. You deserve someone who loves you for who you are and who will treat you with the love and respect you deserve."

"That's just it, Alex. Maybe she did exactly that."

Claire couldn't imagine what sort of person would drive their partner to leave the country with barely a second thought. What sort of useless, horrible person would do that? She would. Claire Patricia O'Malley not only drove her partner away, she drove her to the other side of the world.

They left the kitchen as a barely audible rap at the door stopped them in their tracks.

"Don't look at me." Claire shrugged. "I don't live here."

Jess and Alex stared at each other.

"Oh, for Christ's sake." Claire marched toward the front door.

❖

Kathryn hated arriving unannounced, but it was the right time to leave Queensland, and she needed to judge her sister's reaction to her intended move to Melbourne for herself. It was time to come home. She might have kicked Andy out two years ago and rebuilt her life and self-esteem, but now it was time to let go of the past. Moving to Melbourne, cosmopolitan and vibrant, was the first step; rekindling the potholed relationship with Jess was the second.

She hadn't given a second thought to how she might feel standing at the doorway of her sister's home. A wave of childhood nausea swept over her remembering the time she was ten and had been sent to their neighbour's house to confess a crime her neighbour hadn't even been aware she'd committed; *Sorry, Mrs. Rogers, I picked all your roses because I thought you were dead, not sick. I've made them into a perfume. It's for you. Well, it is now*. Mrs. Rogers's budgie had died. Mrs. Rogers remained very much alive for another thirteen years, and the bout of flu that had seen her indoors for a week coincided with her pet budgie's full speed kamikaze flight into a window.

The door swung open, and everything she'd rehearsed disappeared. "Claire?"

By the look on Claire's face, she was taken aback, too.

"I am at the right place, aren't I?"

Claire looked her up and down before blushing as their eyes met again. "I'm sorry. You just look, um, different." Kathryn smiled and stepped into Claire's open arms. "Hi, Kathryn. It's lovely to see you again."

"And you, too, Claire. What has it been now, nine years?"

Before the conversation could progress, she looked over Claire's shoulder to see Jess and Alex approaching.

It never ceased to amaze her how consuming Jess was. She had a presence like no one she'd met, and even growing up as her older sister, Kathryn knew she would one day achieve something great. Not surprisingly, others felt it, too. "Jessica, how are you?"

"Well this is certainly a surprise." Jess reached for her and drew her into a tight embrace. "I can honestly say I didn't wake this morning expecting you to arrive on our doorstep."

Alex pushed forward. "Welcome, Kathryn." They kissed on the cheek. "How are you?"

Kathryn didn't want to announce on the doorstep that she was unemployed, single, four stone lighter, and divorced. Although by the look on Claire's face, the weight loss hadn't gone unnoticed. Was the rest so obvious?

Jess ushered her in, and Claire dragged her suitcase over the threshold. She had no idea Jess was even in touch with Claire, let alone friendly with her.

The first time she'd met Claire, she remembered feeling jealous. Not of her looks or the fact she was sleeping with her sister, but because she seemed limitless. She saw no obstacles and nothing constrained her, especially not the ideals of parents or anyone else influential in her life. Claire liked fixing people, so she became a nurse. She liked older, stylish women, so she dated Jess, and she wanted to travel the world, so she did. Kathryn had married the first man who'd asked her. The first man she'd slept with and possibly the most boring man on the planet.

As the memories came flooding back, she recalled just how much Claire had disliked her. Perhaps Claire sensed her jealousy. Perhaps now, nine years on, they could just get over it.

"Wow, something smells great," said Kathryn.

"Shit!" Jess hurried back to the kitchen to stir various pots on the stove. The others followed.

Seemingly satisfied dinner was on track, Jess poured more wine. "A toast to my unexpected sister." She turned to Claire. "And my dear forlorn friend."

Everyone clinked glasses. Kathryn was about to enquire why Claire was sad, when she noticed Jess was drinking mineral water. "So, little sister, you're either an alcoholic or you're pregnant. Which one is it?"

Jess grinned, cuddling up to Alex. "We're pregnant. Twins."

"Oh, my God!" The hugging began all over again. "Congratulations, that's fabulous news."

Few things Jess did surprised Kathryn. She was older than Jess by two years, but still managed to live in her shadow. What *was* a surprise was that it was Jess carrying the babies. "Good for you, but I never knew you wanted children."

"Neither did we."

"Until now," added Alex.

Kathryn turned to Claire. "Were you surprised?"

Claire shrugged. She'd seemed preoccupied by the framed photos, sparse as they were, in the living room. "I think I was initially. I mean, look at this place. It's hardly your average child friendly nursery, but I'm sure the littlies will appreciate the polished peppercorn hickory floorboards, the white walls, and the pale granite worktop when their Aunt Claire buys them crayons."

Kathryn had forgotten Claire's wicked sense of humour. It was probably the only thing she'd liked about her. She joined Claire in front of the only three black-and-white pictures in the room. "Jessica Mercer!" She held aloft a photo taken years ago. "I can't believe, of all of the photos you must have of me, you choose to frame this one?"

She was mortified. In the picture, she must have been in her early thirties. Her hair was shaped into a blunt bob, and she was wearing the most hideous floral dress. She'd worked hard in the last two years to find her own identity, and with the help of a few good friends and a great wad of cash, she'd made external improvements as well as the internal ones. Nothing surgical, just a personal trainer, a new wardrobe, and a great hairdresser. When Kathryn looked in the mirror these days, she shocked even herself but was proud of her transformation.

"You can't complain. It *is* you. That's exactly what you looked liked back then," said Jess.

"Yeah, well, I've made some improvements since then."

"I can see that. You look amazing."

❖

Claire couldn't get over Kathryn's transition from frumpy housewife to hot, sexy woman. More importantly, she enjoyed the fact that she could recognise Kathryn in that way. Until now, she'd been wondering if her experience with Victoria had numbed her senses. She smiled, pleased to know all her lesbian bits remained in working order. She stole one last look at the picture before following everyone back to the kitchen.

After what she'd been through in the last few months, the intrigue and mystery surrounding Kathryn's arrival was a welcome little drama to keep her distracted for the evening. Like an excited puppy, she joined them, desperate not to miss a thing. She was surprised no one had asked about Kathryn's husband yet, but in case everyone else knew something she didn't, she refrained from prodding.

Kathryn had lived in Brisbane when Claire last saw her. She had been married to Andy, and since she was an accountant, her life was as exciting as a dead ant compared to Claire's, whose priorities had been drinking, studying nursing, and intimately studying Jess.

From what she could remember, Kathryn had married young, worked hard to establish her career, and had seemingly become trapped in a mundane time warp. Alarmingly, she didn't even have children as an excuse. When Kathryn turned thirty, Claire remembered thinking that she must have been thirty for years, she was so good at it. Being young and immature herself, Claire had written Kathryn off as a boring waste of space.

Dinner was delicious—the Andy subject remained untouched—and the prawns were exquisite, and Kathryn couldn't believe Jess even knew where the kitchen was, let alone her way around it. As always, Claire and Alex tidied up, leaving Jess and Kathryn to tour the garden.

Claire eventually snuck off to the bathroom. She took two pills and hoped they'd counteract the sleepy effects of the wine. She knew it was probably a bad idea, but the truth was that she couldn't think of a better one. She was out of options. Riding it out was her only choice. The last thing she needed was to fall asleep on the couch and scare everyone half to death.

❖

It had occurred to Kathryn to tell Jess about Andy in the garden, but she only wanted to have to tell her story once. There were the inevitable questions that followed such a revelation, and while she'd heard many of them before, she was comfortable holding an audience with Jess, Alex, and Claire. Months of therapy left her confident to talk about that devastating period in her life.

After filling empty glasses, Alex patted the couch, gesturing Claire to her. What the hell was going on? Claire had been dumped, that much she could tell, but it must have been a while ago now because she didn't really appear too upset, just perhaps vague and distracted. Her best guess was that there might have been issues at work, but it was only a guess. It was odd, though; Claire with Alex and Jess sitting alone in an armchair. She set her confusion aside to tell her story.

"Andy and I aren't together. Three years ago, he had an affair." She saw a wave of sadness wash over Jess. "I'm sorry I didn't tell you, I just needed some time for me."

Time *or* space. The words felt interchangeable in relation to how she had felt amidst the misery. The time was to heal and the space was to find herself. The role of the jilted wife was the same the world over, played by the same actors with the same script and the same ensemble cast. She had been the star of her own banal discarded-wife movie.

"Do you remember his crush on Diane Keaton?"

"The actress?" asked Alex.

"Besides her husband and loads of granddads around the world, does *anyone* actually have a crush on Diane Keaton?" asked Claire. "I mean is that even possible?"

Jess nearly choked on her mineral water. "My God, he was insufferable."

"Well, he found the real deal. Well, not exactly the real Diane Keaton, but the next best thing. Diane Bloody Pembroke." Kathryn waited for Jess to recognise the name.

"Did I meet her once?" Her eyes widened. "You're kidding? Diane his boss?"

Kathryn knew the way she told the story lightened the weighty conversation. It would even be amusing if it had happened to someone else, but it happened to her, and no matter how many times she retold her sordid tale, it was rarely amusing.

Both Alex and Claire looked to each other for clues.

"Diane Bloody Pembroke was Andy's boss of four years. She was sixty-two when they first began their affair."

Claire whistled and kicked her legs off the end of the couch, placing her head in Alex's lap. "Whoa. What was he, thirty-five, thirty-six? I thought that kind of thing only happened in the fantasy life of hetty women in chick flicks."

Kathryn frowned at the closeness of Alex and Claire. The relationship between Jess's wife and her ex-lover, in her opinion, shouldn't look anything like what she was seeing. Jess was seeing it, too, and it troubled her why she wasn't intervening. "Hetty?"

"Heterosexual," said Claire.

"So, similar to me calling you a lezza?" Kathryn smiled, but it lacked conviction. She had watched Andy and Diane behave as close friends, she had even thought they shared a familiarity resembling a mother and son relationship, but then right under her nose, they began shagging like rabbits. Naturally, it had left her wary of blurred lines and crossing boundaries. Jess looked sad for what Kathryn had just told her but oblivious to what was happening in her own backyard.

"I'm so sorry, Kathryn. I really wish you'd told me," said Jess.

Kathryn didn't tell anyone, not for the first year after she found out.

"We tried to make it work. Andy lied and said he'd ended it with Diane, but the truth was she fired him. He'd served his purpose and he was in love with her. She didn't want a love struck puppy, she wanted a toy boy."

"Funny, isn't it? I thought you and Andy were so well suited. You seemed to just gel as one. I honestly thought you'd last."

"We were boring, that's all. Comfortable being boring, too, that's the sad thing. I thought that's what Andy liked. I thought he liked my boring clothes, my terrible hair, and our placid lifestyle. It was as if I was trying to please him, but I was only guessing how. Turns out dressing and acting like I was bloody sixty-two just wasn't enough."

What Kathryn regretted most was holding on. Their parents had taught her and Jess well; you put up with the lot you were given and you made it work. The difference between them was that Jess only pretended to live by that philosophy. Kathryn took it for gospel.

"For a year, we lived in the same house and ran separate lives. It worked for Andy. He got a new job, a better job, and a new girlfriend."

"And what did you get?" Jess was close to tears.

"I got an extra fifteen kilograms and depression."

"But you're okay now?"

"I'm fine now." She smiled warmly to reassure Jess. "Honestly,

I'm fine. Look, it was a process. It's always a process. After he left, I realised I'd spent a year wanting him to want me again, but behaving like someone who wouldn't piss on him if he were on fire." Claire stifled a giggle. "I spent the next two years looking after *me* and only moving forward."

"Is that why you couldn't tell me or come and stay?" Jess looked hurt.

"I didn't feel strong enough to be around you. I'm sorry if that sounds harsh, but it's not a reflection on you. It's about me and how I was feeling."

"But you're better now?"

This time Kathryn went and hugged Jess. "Yes. I promise. I'm all better now. I could do with another drink though." Telling someone your fifteen-year marriage was over never became any easier, and she'd done it more times than she cared to remember now. Jess handed her the bottle, and she filled her glass before draining it again, waiting for the sensation of frayed nerve endings to dull with the alcohol.

"So, the upshot of my tale of destruction and renewal is that I'm moving to Melbourne."

"What? As in now?" asked Jess.

"Sometimes it's difficult to believe you're a stern-faced lawyer."

"You're moving down here now?"

"Yes, Jess. I want to come home. Is that so bad?"

"No, of course not. I think it's great. It's just a big move."

"You'll stay with us until you get settled, Kathryn. We'd love to have you," Alex said.

Kathryn gave Alex her full attention, her eyes flicked down to Claire, lying with her head in Alex's lap. It wasn't right, but once again, she glossed over the sight before her. "Thank you. I hadn't presumed you'd offer, but it would be wonderful if I could stay with you both for a little while, just until I sell the Brisbane property and can purchase down here."

"Did you do well in the settlement? You should have called me. I could have taken a look at the finances for you," Jess said.

"You're not even a family lawyer. But don't worry. My lawyer made sure the split was equitable. I didn't miss out."

"I would have liked to have helped."

Kathryn knew it was Jess's way of reconciling her absence for the last three years. Three years of not helping Kathryn through a hard time, but Kathryn had chosen to rebuild her life alone. Jess didn't need to feel guilty. "I fixed myself, my way. I was hoping you'd be proud of me."

Jess kissed her cheek. "I always have been."

❖

The heavy topic of infidelity and divorce had taken its toll, and had Claire been honest with herself, she would have admitted that the subject cut a little close to the bone. For a while, however, it had been nice to hear that she wasn't the only one to struggle her way out of a relationship. It took time. That's what everyone kept saying.

"So, Claire, you're single again?" It was a statement rather than a question, but when Claire met Kathryn's stare, she knew an answer was expected.

Claire nodded forcing her eyes open. "Sure am." Alex stroked her cheek.

"How long?"

For the first two weeks or so, Claire knew exactly how long, almost to the minute, since Victoria had left her. Now, she was pleased to realise she had to stop and work it out. "Just over four months, I think."

"I was a mess at four months," Kathryn said. "And eating myself into a heart attack if I remember rightly."

"I've come to realise my breakup was inevitable."

"Aren't they all?"

"I just think there's a right and a wrong way to finish with someone. I copped the wrong way and so did you by the sound of it."

"But four months isn't that long." Kathryn frowned. "You're doing incredibly well."

"When I finally began to feel better, I realised she wasn't worth feeling shit over any longer."

"Lucky you."

Claire shrugged, not sure how to respond, but she stiffened at the tone in Kathryn's voice. "Well, it is what it is, I guess."

"I'm sorry, and forgive me if I'm out of line, but do you always cuddle up to my sister's wife like that?"

"Kathryn." Jess's tone was firm.

"I'm just saying. I have a little experience in this matter, so don't discount me offhand. Doesn't it worry you? I mean your ex-lover and your wife, all snugly on the couch. This is how it starts." Kathryn's voice wasn't raised, and her tone was even and polite, but if Claire were a betting woman she'd have put her house on the fact that Jess was insulted and not about to stand for the sudden change in direction of the conversation. Claire suddenly felt wide awake. The evening had taken yet another strange twist. She was interested to see where this one would lead. It seemed the new Kathryn wasn't shy and unassuming like she remembered her to be.

"You're out of action for a while being pregnant and poor Claire was dumped recently? Can't you see something wrong here, or is this the norm with you people?"

Oh hell! Claire wondered if Kathryn even knew what she was saying. She'd had a lot to drink. Nervous and exposed, she became aware of Alex's fingers gently combing through her hair. She moved to sit up.

"Don't you dare move, Claire." Jess slowly rose from her chair.

Alex placed firm pressure on Claire's waist, forcing her to obey, and as uncomfortable as she felt, Claire knew they were about to witness a Supreme Court onslaught from Jess.

"I'm sorry. That came out all wrong." Kathryn raised her hands as a sign of surrender. "It's just that they're so familiar with each other. It has to worry you, surely, just a little."

"How dare you imply that anything other than honourable conduct is taking place here."

Honourable conduct? Yes, Crown Prosecutor Jessica Mercer was about to take flight. Old wounds were open now. Kathryn had stepped over the line.

"Not a damn thing has changed with you, has it? You've been the same since the very *second* I told you I was gay. Everything I ever did, you viewed tainted with the fact that you thought I was a kinky, perverted dyke."

"That's not fair, Jess," Kathryn said. "I was young. You're talking about a long time ago now."

"And you're behaving like you used to; homophobic and childish. Homosexuality is not a disease. It's not a lifestyle choice. It's as simple as two people of the same sex finding a mutual attraction. We're not perverted because we love women. Being gay doesn't make us promiscuous or incapable of monogamy or in some way more or less sexually liberated than the next person, gay *or* straight. You were incapable then, just as you are now, of understanding that it simply means that some women are attracted to women. Why, Kathryn, must you judge my family by your own small-minded archaic opinions?"

"Firstly, I'm not homophobic. This has nothing to do with sexuality, but thanks for the lecture. Secondly, you make a good point, Jess," Kathryn said. "Claire isn't your family. She's your ex-lover. Why can't *you* see the difference?"

Claire hated being spoken about as if she was invisible, but neither she nor Alex dared become involved.

Jess lowered her voice. "Claire is my ex-lover by your definition, Kathryn. By my definition, she's like the sister who never gave up on me the day I told her I was gay. I trust her with my life, and my wife. You should learn to trust *me*."

It was nearing midnight, and the stunned silence signalled an end to the evening. Jess bent to kiss Alex, then Claire, good night, both on the lips, before disappearing upstairs. Kathryn thanked Alex for dinner before she, too, disappeared in the opposite direction to one of the downstairs guest rooms.

Claire was gobsmacked. "Jesus. That was some way to end the evening. Where the hell did that come from?" She sat up at last, straightening the crick in her neck.

"Her own experience."

"Of being a lesbian?"

"No, you wally, of being complacent around people she thought she could trust."

"Oh, I see." Claire was dead on her feet. "That's why you're the shrink and I'm the nurse."

Alex sighed, rubbing her temples and yawning. "But I guess this is where you and I have quiet, sneaky, cheating sex."

"It's a tough job, but someone's gotta do it."

"Come on, kiddo, get your kit off."

Alex slapped Claire on the backside when she teasingly began undoing her jeans.

"Better still." Claire grinned wickedly. "I vote we take it upstairs and enjoy our weekly threesome."

They both rose from the couch, Alex hugging Claire good night before heading for the stairs and adding, "I'll summon the bondage chicks from the cellar."

Claire trudged toward the hall. "The slaves will just love this late hour."

"Night, Claire."

"Night, Alex."

CHAPTER FOUR

It was three a.m., and Claire woke soaked in sweat, hoping to God her screams were only in her dream. She scrambled to switch on the light. She wanted to go home. Or more specifically, she wanted to do absolutely anything to avoid sleep.

Living little more than ten minutes' drive from Jess had its advantages. She'd walked there on a couple of occasions. It had taken less than two hours, and as the thought developed from a whim to a possibility, Claire became intent on having an excuse to fill two hours with something other than sleep.

When her life was normal, Claire was like a bear with a sore head without eight hours' sleep. Even after a night shift, she could sleep soundly until mid afternoon. This last month she'd barely managed one hour without interruption. She dressed quickly and stumbled through to the kitchen and into the living room, unable to remember where she left her keys. *Fucking hell. Where are they?*

Claire hated feeling out of control. It left her heart racing and her mind floundering because of a gaping hole where order and calmness used to be. She knew anxiety originated in your head, but it was her chest that struggled under the crushing pressure. Her fuse was short and her tolerance level teetered on zero.

The cushions on the couch were the first casualties. She threw them across the room, delving her hand between the seats only to find crumbs and a few stray coins. Her head began to throb, but it didn't stop her from clambering on her hands and knees searching under the couch, the coffee table, and even the writing bureau that she'd not stepped anywhere near the entire evening.

Close to tears, she kicked the table. The pain must have jolted her memory. *The bowl!* She hopped her way into the kitchen.

"What are you doing?" Alex switched on a light and emerged from the staircase in her robe. "Bloody hell, Claire, what's happened?"

"Oh, hi, Alex. I'm just leaving." Claire used her sleeve to wipe her eyes. "Forgot where my keys were though, but I've found them now. Look, thanks for a great night." Claire's tone was impossibly chipper. It never once occurred to her that it was the complete opposite of her appearance.

"You can't drive, little one. You've had too much to drink."

"Oh, Alex, I'm not driving, silly. I feel like a walk. I'll be home in no time."

Alex stared. "Claire, it's the middle of the night. Your house is ages away, and it's not safe in your condition."

"My condition? Nonsense, Jess is the pregnant one. I don't have a condition." She attempted to laugh.

"Have you slept at all?"

Alex moved to touch Claire, but she backed away. She was on the edge and she daren't risk falling.

"Claire, when was the last time you slept?"

Claire snapped. "God damn it, Alex. Why are you so fucking interested in my sleep patterns?"

"Shoosh. Steady on. You'll wake Jess."

"Jess is already awake." They both turned as Jess entered the kitchen, moving directly to close the hall door. The last thing they needed was Kathryn joining the party. "What's going on? It's three in the morning."

Claire stood with her hands deep in her pockets, her keys firmly in her grip. "I want to go home."

"Fine, then I'll call a cab and take you." Jess smiled.

"I'm perfectly capable of catching a cab on my own."

"Are you?"

The intensity of Claire's rage increased. "It's true isn't it? Kathryn's right. Why are you even down here, Jess? Don't you trust me with your wife?" Claire spat the words like venom. "I can take myself home. I wouldn't want you to waste your time."

"Claire, you're out of line," Jess barked, but Alex gestured for her to back off.

"It's no waste." Alex's tone gave nothing away. She filled a plastic tumbler with water. "Here, you look like you could use a drink." She handed it to Claire, who had to remove her hand from her pocket to accept the drink. Claire immediately regretted doing so. Her hand shook uncontrollably. "I'll stay with you tonight, and then in the morning, Jess can come and collect me. Deal?"

"No, it's not a fucking *deal*." She threw the half empty tumbler across the counter.

Alex ignored her insolence. "You never answered the question, Claire. When did you last sleep?"

"Fuck the both of you. I don't need to hear this shit. Quit acting like my fucking parents!"

"What are you taking, Claire?" Alex asked.

"Nothing."

"Then why are you shaking?"

"I'm cold."

"No, you're not." Alex moved closer.

"What, now you're my fucking thermostat?"

"What are you taking, Claire?" Alex inched even closer and Jess manoeuvred to block Claire from the door.

"I'm fine." Claire shivered to the point of chattering teeth. "You can't keep me here. I want to go home."

"Okay, I'll take you."

"No."

"But you said you wanted to go."

"Alone. I want to go alone." Claire fought back tears as her shivering increased.

"So you can take more pills?"

"Yes. No. It's none of your business." Claire hunched over.

"What are you taking?"

"Nothing!"

"You're sweating."

Claire was a shivering, sweating mess. "God, Alex, just leave me alone."

"Why don't you want to sleep, honey?"

"Go away!"

"Claire, look at me. Why don't you want to sleep?"

Claire began to hyperventilate. "It hurts. It's awful."

Alex gave Jess a quick nod.

"Honey." Jess's tone was soft and gentle. "We need to talk about this. You need help. Please tell me why you won't sleep."

Every joint in Claire's body ached. Her head felt like it was being compressed in a vice and she was cold, so cold. They were closing in on her. Jess from behind, Alex from the front. Then there was Victoria, filling her head completely, relentlessly pounding against the vice that caused the smothering pressure. Escape seemed impossible. The room began to spin, slowly at first, then with fierce, nauseating speed. All Claire could do was close her eyes. The spinning white light turned to black, and that was all she remembered.

She woke a minute later, flat on her back, legs elevated. As Claire's eyes adjusted, an overwhelming urge to vomit swelled in her. Alex unceremoniously produced a bucket.

The contents of her satchel covered the coffee table. Two energy drinks, caffeine pills, and sinus capsules sat on the edge. Jess was slowly replacing the rest, and Claire could tell she was disappointed.

Claire sat up to sip water and explain. "Every time I sleep, I dream about her. Victoria. Every single fucking time. Not just normal dreams, but awful ones. Through something I've done, intentional or not, she dies. Either way, I wake feeling worse than the day she left."

"What was your dream about tonight?"

The horror was still so fresh in Claire's mind. "I chased her into the Yarra River and held her head under water until she drowned. Until her body went limp."

Jess sat next to her on the couch and pulled her close. "How long has it been going on?"

"About four weeks now."

"You don't want to sleep, do you?" asked Alex.

"No, it's not that exactly. I'm barely functioning. I *need* sleep, I just don't want the dreams. I thought I had it under control. It wasn't a big deal in the beginning…"

"And now?"

"I keep a diary. I've documented a total of seventy-two different ways to kill Victoria. Drowning her in the Yarra River was seventy-three. I mostly just kill her now. She doesn't get a chance to hurt me anymore. I hunt her down and don't rest until she's taken her last breath."

The nightmares were not only visually disturbing, but also each time she woke, shaking, sweating, and frightened, she was transported back to the moment Victoria left.

"Where was your head at a month ago when the dreams began?"

"I was in a good place. I remember the day clearly. It was the first time I'd woken and not been disappointed I was alone. Victoria hadn't been my first thought. It had been a good day. It felt like the first day of the rest of my life. Then it all went tits up that night."

"You killed her in your dream?"

"Not murder as such. I at least started with an accidental death."

"Building up to it eh, kiddo?" Jess smiled sympathetically.

"Something like that. I chased her on foot through Chatswood Shopping Centre, and she got run over by a delivery van when she tried to escape and burst through a fire exit onto the street."

"But the dreams have changed since then."

"In the beginning, the deaths were unintentional. I'd chase her, accidentally poison her, crash a car we were both in, or one time I clumsily tripped up and knocked her down a lift shaft." Jess suppressed a laugh. "Now they're just gruesome and disturbing. No more accidents, just psycho old me trying to end her life in the most horrendous way possible."

Alex brought her a glass of hot milk. "So, let me guess. You tried to knock yourself out with alcohol and that's what landed you in strife at work."

Alcohol hadn't been the answer. It was a recipe for disaster. Going to work stinking like a drunk with a cracking headache was unprofessional. She'd received a formal warning for having alcohol in her system after a not-so-random alcohol and drug test. It was the first time in her life she'd suffered disciplinary action at work. Claire was so embarrassed about her reprimand she hadn't told anyone, let alone Jess and Alex. Then it dawned on her. "Murray." She shook her head. "So much for patient doctor confidentiality."

"Well, technically, she's not your doctor."

"No, she's supposed to be my friend."

"Which is why she told us," said Jess.

"So how many hours' sleep are you averaging per night now you're taking all this shit?" Alex pointed to the stimulants.

"Hardly any. In the beginning, I tried to knock myself out with cough syrup or antihistamine pills, but that just sent me to sleep. I couldn't wake properly from the dreams, and sometimes I'd end up killing her twice."

"Taking all this isn't the answer, Claire." Jess waved the packet of sinus pills in her face before tossing them across the table.

"I'm trying to be grown up about this. I know feeling better will take time; I was just going to take them until I felt better and the dreams stopped."

"Oh, sweetheart, your plan is flawed." Jess kissed her cheek. "You're avoiding the root cause of the problem and only treating the symptoms. And avoiding sleep is madness. How long could you keep this up? Dealing with the dreams and what they mean will be far easier when you can think straight. Trying to walk home in the middle of the night is hardly thinking straight, my love."

"I'm sorry for speaking to you the way I did earlier. I'm such a knob." Feeling ashamed was becoming too familiar.

"Do you feel better now you've talked about it?" asked Alex.

"I do, but I didn't have to act like an idiot to get your attention, did I?"

"Well, I won't argue with that."

"And please tell me you know that I didn't mean a word of what I said? I feel like Jekyll and Hyde, but instead of good and evil, I'm more like tired and evil."

Alex left, Claire knew what for, and she returned minutes later with the spare room doona over her shoulder, and a small white pill.

"Temazepam, right?" Claire only hesitated briefly before swallowing the sleeping pill without protest.

"Got it in one. Enough kick so you shouldn't dream though. You're upstairs with us for the rest of the night. Come on."

Claire knew better than to argue, and frankly, she wanted this episode to end. "First, can you please tell me that we're okay, that I didn't ruin anything tonight?"

Alex and Jess wrapped their arms firmly around her.

"Oh, poor Kathryn will be suspicious now." Claire's sense of humour hadn't deserted her, at least.

"Fuck Kathryn," Jess and Alex replied in unison.

"And we're okay, I promise," Jess said. "Just don't do it again or I'll put you over my knee."

"Now you're talking."

Alex walked off shaking her head.

Although the main bedroom and upstairs living area were in one open space, a five-foot high wall separated the two areas, and Claire snuggled down on the couch. Jess sat with her until the sleeping pill took hold and, although frightened to let go, the sensation of being so utterly exhausted was too enticing to fight a moment longer.

CHAPTER FIVE

A t three a.m., Kathryn was tempted to see what all the fuss was about, but a dry mouth and the dull thud in her head caused her to think better of it. After all, she'd made a right arse of herself earlier in the night.

She'd heard raised voices, mostly Claire's, but unless she was called upon or it was an emergency, she thought it best to remain out of the way. By four a.m., the house was silent again and her mind was doing that jumbled half awake, half asleep dreaming before she drifted off. She was struggling to put the vision of Claire and Alex out of her mind. It had been the same with Andy and Diane, and the feeling of betrayal that gripped her then, exactly as it did tonight, was something she feared she might never shake.

However, Jess was right. Claire wasn't Diane and Alex certainly wasn't Andy. If Jess trusted them, she would, too. It was as simple as that. Plus, she liked Claire. If she was going to move to Melbourne, she and Claire might become friends, and because she'd lost touch with all her old school friends, knowing as many people as possible would ease the stress of the move.

At four fifteen, she was convinced the only thing keeping her from sleeping was an annoying need to pee. The urge nagged at her until she huffed out of bed, her eyes barely open. She stopped outside Claire's room and peered in through the small gap in the doorway. In the moonlight, she could see that the bed was empty and the covers were gone. Puzzled, she went to the bathroom and sat on the toilet, wondering where Claire was. Now almost fully awake, she returned to her own room and peered out the window. The old Ford in the driveway that must have been Claire's was still there.

What's going on?

It occurred to her that she should mind her own business and just go back to bed, but she really wanted to know where Claire was. She crept down the hall and into the kitchen. Nothing. The living room yielded more information. With the curtains open, she saw Claire's satchel on the coffee table and some of its contents next to it. She gathered the pill boxes and took them to the window for extra light. The over-the-counter pills were harmless enough, although how anyone could sleep after taking them was a mystery. But where was Claire?

The answer she was avoiding was obvious. Claire had to be upstairs with Jess and Alex. She returned to bed feeling disappointed her sister may have lied to her.

CHAPTER SIX

It was midday when Alex shook Claire. "It's time to get up. If you sleep any longer we'll have difficulty getting you back to a normal sleeping pattern, especially after a week of night shift."

Claire felt like a truck had hit her. She pulled her knees to her chest to relieve the ache in her lower back, wondering how sleeplessness somehow managed to seep into every joint and muscle in her body.

She didn't want to relive last night, but it was impossible to block out. She showered in the en suite, dressed in the pile of clothes that sat on the end of the couch, all Jess's and all too big, before facing her disastrous life.

It was only by chance that Claire and Jess rekindled any kind of friendship after she returned home from Europe. Claire had been witness to a nasty assault at the hospital and Jess was the prosecutor. She admitted to having inappropriate thoughts initially, but that was only until she met Alex. Alex changed everything for the better. Jess was happy, unbelievably happy, and when Claire hooked up with Victoria, their ex-lover relationship altered and they became best friends with a history they refused to deny.

Claire and Alex weren't close until the day Alex was summoned for a consult on her ward after a patient confused himself with a guest on the Jerry Springer show and demonstrated his frustrations by violently redecorating the waiting room. Claire had been caught in the crossfire, or more accurately, a headlock, and because Alex could do little with the crazy bloke, other than sedation, she took Claire for coffee.

That coffee turned into another coffee, then lunch, and it all made Jess happy.

"How are you feeling this morning?" Jess asked.

"Better for having slept, but I still feel like a bit of a plank. I mean, who was I kidding?"

"Come here." Jess pulled her into a tight embrace. "We'll fix it now so don't worry."

"Sorry to interrupt," Kathryn said from the kitchen, her timing impeccable. "But Alex mentioned I could use the Wi-Fi. Is that okay?"

"Of course." Claire tried to pull away and was at risk of suffocating, but Jess wouldn't let go. "The password is in the study on a note next to the computer."

Kathryn left with thanks.

Jess released her grip. "Right, you. Step this way. My beautiful wife has something for you."

Jess led Claire outside, and Alex smiled, offering them both fresh juice from a chilled flask.

"These are for you." Alex handed her a copy of the contact details for the hospital's employee assistance program, a free counselling service offered to assist staff in work and non-work related matters.

"Can't *we* work on this?" Claire wasn't sure she could face talking to a stranger about her problems.

"Trust me, you don't want to be counselled by me *and* live with me. You mightn't like what I have to say. Eventually, you'll grow to hate me and then I'll have no one to cuddle."

"I'm not staying, Alex. I appreciate everything you both do for me, but I don't think moving in here is the answer."

Alex ignored her. "So, you'll go to counselling? Talking about it and working through it is what will help you."

"I know you're right." Claire slumped, deflated.

"I've spoken to Murray, who's spoken to your boss. She's approved two weeks' leave. We'll see Murray Monday morning to get you checked out; take some blood tests, etc." She let Claire digest all this before continuing. "Now, about moving in."

"I'm not budging on this."

"If you're not here, Jess will worry herself sick. I will, too, but in her condition, I don't want her to worry at all. Do you?"

"Nice emotional blackmail." She looked to Jess for support, but nothing was forthcoming.

"Psychiatry one oh one." Alex grinned.

"Well, thanks for the lesson."

"You're welcome. Now let's go to your place and collect some of your things."

❖

First thing Monday morning, after another sleepless night, Alex took Claire to see Murray.

"Jesus, Paddy, what have you done? You look like shit." Murray rarely minced her words.

"I wish you wouldn't call me that."

"I said you look like shit, I didn't say you are shit."

"Not that. I wish you wouldn't call me Paddy."

"It's your name, well, your middle name. What's wrong with it?"

"I'm not Irish is what's wrong with it."

"You look Irish."

Claire gave up and silently cursed her mother for marrying a man with the last name O'Malley and dreamily trying to pretend they were of Irish descent. They weren't, well, not recent enough for it to matter anyway. "Can we just get on with this?"

"Get your top off and hop up there."

Claire stripped to her bra and sat on the examination table.

Murray measured her blood pressure first then frowned as she removed the cuff from Claire's arm.

"What was it?"

"It's up a bit."

"How much?"

Murray ignored her and slipped a tourniquet around her upper arm before searching for a suitable vein to take blood. "You're a little dehydrated."

Claire gritted her teeth while the needle moved inside her before finally piercing a vein. She looked away as the blood filled the syringe.

Murray listened to Claire's chest, purely routine, and then had her lie down while she poked and prodded, again routine, nothing out of the ordinary.

"So, let's talk about sleep." Murray returned to her desk. "Alex is worried, and I'm not convinced pills will help you in the long run." She eyed Claire. "What I really want to do is tell you I'm prescribing a high dose Temazepam, give them to Alex to administer, but in actual fact make them a low dose so you don't start relying on strong sedatives. You think you need a high dose?"

Claire nodded. She knew it was the wrong answer.

"Well, you don't, and I'm not giving them to you. You were smart enough to stay awake on non-prescription shit, so you're smart enough to know knocking yourself out isn't the answer either." She scribbled on a prescription. "Low dose, seven days." Her tone softened but her look remained firm. "You need the counselling, Paddy. That's what will help you sleep."

❖

Claire reluctantly made the call to book counselling. The EAP counsellor was named Jean, and she slotted Claire in at six that evening. Alex drove her and waited in the foyer reading *National Geographic*.

Jean and her office decor gave the impression that she was a breath away from chucking it all in and heading for the hills—naked. She certainly looked like she'd smoked way too much pot in her time.

As a nurse, there were only so many rear end, front end, and belly button extractions you could do before learning that judging people was a mistake. So while Jean looked like a hippie from way back, as long as she could help, she could wear her tie-dye dresses, decorate however she liked, and worship Thomas the Tank Engine for all Claire cared.

Jean was patient, compassionate, and probed gently as Claire explained her history with Victoria, the dreams, and her current sleepless situation. After crying at least a dozen times, Claire's hour was up, but she was tasked homework and a week to complete it. Her undertaking was to ask three people to tell her one or two of her better qualities and write them down.

What better qualities? Claire remained silent on the journey home, ignoring the intermittent concerned glances from Alex.

❖

Jess arrived home and stood in the doorway smiling. Kathryn glanced around her, taking in what Jess was looking at. Claire was freshly showered and in her pyjamas setting cutlery on the table, Alex sat folding washing on the couch, looking almost as exhausted as Claire, and Kathryn was cooking dinner. It was the least she could do given everyone else had been busy all day.

"Hi, Jess, what's up?"

Jess patted her stomach. "Nothing is up. I'm just smiling because my house is filled with all the people I care about."

"Is Claire okay?" She didn't want to pry, but it was the first chance she'd had to ask.

"She will be. She's taking a couple of weeks off work to sort through a few things."

Kathryn nodded knowingly. "A broken heart."

"Well, not exactly. I think she's come to terms with Victoria leaving. It's difficult, of course, four years together is a long time. But I think she might need to work on her self-esteem."

"We've all been there, poor kid."

"She's been having nightmares of killing Victoria."

"Jesus." The stimulants she found over the weekend made more sense now. "Was she trying to stay awake?"

"Yes. Stupid, I know, rubbish plan really, but she thought she was doing the right thing."

The emotional roller coaster journey Claire was enduring wasn't anything Kathryn hadn't experienced, but she knew it was a process and she knew Claire would get through it eventually. It explained why she looked like she could fall asleep standing up.

"You know I was only looking out for you on Saturday night, right?" said Kathryn.

Jess smiled. "I know. And I know what it must have looked like to you, but it was innocent. We both love Claire. Our relationship is healthy, trust me."

Jess rarely held a grudge and certainly not one against her sister when she was so clearly happy to have her back in her life.

Kathryn was relieved to finally understand why Claire had probably slept upstairs. She reminded herself that not everyone was a liar and a cheat.

Jess greeted everyone with a kiss. Kathryn could feel the warmth in the house, and she envied the life Jess and Alex had created.

Dinner was delicious, and they all looked on as Claire battled to keep her eyes open. She'd already taken paracetamol, explaining that the caffeine withdrawals were causing an insistent headache, and in the absence of stimulants, her body craved the sleep she had deprived it of for over a month now. Kathryn wanted to tell her it would be okay, but she didn't think Claire would want to hear it from her.

❖

Claire put the last of the plates in the dishwasher as Jess came over to fill her glass with water.

"Hey," said Claire, annoyed how her voice rose an octave when she felt uncomfortable. She lowered her volume. "I have some homework from the counsellor. I have to ask people I'm comfortable with to tell me one or two things they like about me. Would it be okay if I ask you?"

"Sure, honey." Jess squeezed her arm. "Don't look so worried. I reckon I can come up with more than two."

Claire grabbed her notebook, poised to write. "Okay, shoot."

Jess took the pen from her. "I'd like to write it down myself. Are you allowed to do that?" Claire shrugged. "Okay, leave it with me."

Claire was convinced she couldn't hold a conversation long enough to complete it, and her entire body felt like a lead weight. She had surrendered the sedatives to Alex, too exhausted and unreliable to administer them herself, so she went to Alex to discuss the issue. "It's only eight thirty. Perhaps you could put the sleeping pill on the kitchen bench or something. If I wake in the night, I'll come get it."

Alex smiled and gently touched Claire's cheek. "It is a little early to take it, you're right, but don't worry, one or both of us will be in to check on you. We'll leave it on the bedside table."

"Thanks, Alex. And thanks for today."

"It'll be all right, you know."

"I know. I'll just be delighted to make it past eight thirty without falling asleep."

❖

Bolt upright, shivering and naked, Claire dripped with sweat and sobbed. Everyone was in her bedroom staring at her and she guessed why.

"It was a dream, right?" she asked.

Kathryn, possibly uncomfortable with Claire's nakedness, disappeared and returned with a towel while Jess and Alex surrounded her, pulling her into protective, warm arms.

"The pill," Claire said through sobs and shivers. "I need the sleeping pill."

"What was the dream about, honey?" asked Alex.

"I don't want to talk about the fucking dream. Please, I just want the sleeping pill."

Kathryn handed over the towel before busying herself again by fetching a glass of water.

"Jean said to talk about it if you woke," said Jess.

Claire's distress intensified. "God, I don't want to talk about it. I don't want to watch her die. I just want the pill. I can't do this." Her sobbing caused her chest to heave. "I can't sleep without seeing her. I killed her with my own bare hands. I killed her."

Jess seemed to be holding back tears now, too, helplessly watching Claire. "Please, Claire, it's okay."

Claire wasn't listening. "I loved her and I killed her. That's what the dream means. That's what *all* the dreams mean. I killed her inside. I killed our relationship. How can I ever be with someone else when I don't know how to fix what I fucked up the last time? What did I do wrong?"

Kathryn's calm voice broke through the despair. "What I love about Claire O'Malley, by Jessica Mercer." Kathryn was reading from the small notebook Jess had placed on the bedside table. "I love how Claire listens to me. I'm a hard person to listen to sometimes, but Claire does so without fail."

Kathryn looked up. She continued reading when she realised the sobbing had subsided. "I love how she would never deliberately let me down. I love how she makes me laugh. I love the feeling I get inside when I know we're going to see each other—the mark of a truly great friend. I love how she loves Alex. I love her ability to be objective. I love her cooking. I love how she always sees the best in me, even when I'm not at my best. Finally, I used to be *in* love with Claire O'Malley, and now I love her. That should say it all."

Alex handed Claire the sleeping pill, kissed her forehead, and left. Kathryn replaced the notebook, gave Claire's arm a gentle squeeze before leaving also, and Jess leaned in for another big hug. "I love you, Claire O'Malley, sleep well."

Claire took the tablet and slept soundly until six the following morning.

Chapter Seven

It was difficult for Kathryn to know how much help, if any, Claire would accept from her. In her own way, she'd already gone through what Claire was experiencing, and although she was no expert, she knew the light at the end of the tunnel would eventually grow brighter.

Claire was fragile, and she saw her former self in everything she did. Claire's heart may no longer be breaking, but she was a broken woman. Kathryn didn't understand her need to help, or indeed protect, Claire, but she'd given up fighting her emotions. These days, she let them guide her.

The subtle approach was probably her best option so she remained close by while Alex and Jess went to work.

It was eleven thirty in the morning, and enough was enough. "Is this pyjama thing an all day gig, or will you dare shower and wash sometime today?"

Claire shrugged. "I'm on holidays."

"People wash on holidays, you know."

"I will. By dinner I'll be all clean."

"Dinner?" Kathryn wasn't having a bar of it. "Didn't Jean say you should exercise?"

Claire sat up warily before smiling. "Did you bug her office?"

"I'm serious. You can't just lounge around here all day, dirty."

"I'm not dirty."

"Well, you're not exactly clean."

"But you agree that I'm not dirty, right?"

"For God's sake, Claire." Kathryn was beginning to understand what it might be like to have a teenager. "I'm going to change into some gym gear and you're going to take me running. Then, after that, you'll have a bloody shower because you'll be dirty. Okay?"

Claire rolled off the couch before huffing and puffing her way toward her room. "Talk about pushy."

Kathryn laughed. "That was my subtle approach."

"Then let's pray you never have a sledgehammer in your hands," she called.

❖

That evening after dinner, Claire listened as Jess broached the subject of her flat. Apparently, Jess's colleague, a first year prosecutor, was in the market for somewhere to rent while his house was being constructed. She'd mentioned to him that she might have the perfect solution.

Claire hadn't been ready to admit she couldn't afford to stay on now Victoria was gone. Confession time had arrived.

"I have to give it up anyway. My single wage isn't enough to cover the rent."

"Not even with a few extra shifts?" asked Alex.

"Not even if I pimp myself. I've just about used up all my savings." Keeping the flat would mean permanent night shift, six days a week. Although small, her home was in an expensive suburb, and the near new flat came with a hefty price tag. "Honestly though, it would mean all work and no play. I can afford to stay until the end of next month, but that's it." She sighed. "I've been putting off thinking about it."

"Well, let's keep what's left of your savings in the bank, sublet to James, and you can stay here for the time being."

Claire rolled her eyes.

"What's the big deal?" Jess looked pleased with herself.

"I feel like a case."

"Claire, honey, you *are* a case. At the moment anyway. But that's not why you should stay. This is what friends are for. They help out. You're a bit of a mess at the moment. A good reason to stay. You can't afford your current place. Another good reason to stay, plus we have enough room here for a good few months yet. After that, this place will be a natural disaster zone and you'll be long gone and in no hurry to return."

"It just feels so pathetic."

"It's not pathetic at all. Instead of pathetic, just imagine that everyone thinks of us like Kathryn—weird, kinky, sex fiends. Nothing to do with shitty dreams and a crap time at work and Victoria leaving."

"I heard that," said Kathryn from in front of the TV. "And for what it's worth, Claire, I think you should stay."

Claire found Kathryn's input surprising, but then she had been consistently surprised by her the entire day. She suspected that Alex had asked Kathryn to keep an eye on her. She was further surprised when Kathryn made up the excuse that she wanted to get fit, and tagged along for the run. And she was unfit. Claire had to jog on the spot and wait every few hundred metres or so.

Then, after lunch, Kathryn provided some welcome company on the way to counselling. There were many great cafés and second-hand bookshops not far from Jean's office, but Kathryn wouldn't have known this unless Alex had told her. Regardless of her motivation, and although Claire remained guarded, they enjoyed a pleasant afternoon.

She had cried at counselling, and then again when she met Kathryn for coffee. Claire suspected Kathryn had done her fair share of crying when she broke up with Andy. Misery loves company, and she seemed to understand completely.

With the options now on the table, she realised she could either object to moving in with her rather average excuses, or save them all time by simply agreeing. Either avenue would lead to the same outcome. "Is Alex okay about it, too? I mean really okay about it?"

"Yes, Claire. We're all okay about it." Jess raised her eyebrows. "So, can I tell James we're all good to go?"

"Yeah, I guess." It seemed so final.

Jess took her hand. "I know it's where you set up home with Victoria. I know it's hard to leave it all behind, but I think it's the best thing for you. You'd be silly to hang on to the place, eating away at your savings, for sentimental reasons. You have to give it up sooner or later. Alex and I think sooner is the best option."

Alex had joined them. She gave Claire's shoulders a tight squeeze. "We'll get you through this, I promise."

"You shouldn't have to."

"And *you* shouldn't have to cope with what you're going through on your own. I don't want to hear another word about it."

Silent tears came again. She couldn't hold it in. It was such a big decision.

"Oh, honey, I'm sorry. I didn't mean it like that."

"I'm sorry for crying all the bloody time, and I'm not taking it like that. It's just..." She couldn't bring herself to say the words. But she didn't have to.

"She's not coming back, Claire."

"I don't want her to, honestly. I just want to know where I went wrong. She's made her choices, I respect that, but I wasn't a mean person. I thought I was a loving person. I thought I was giving her what she wanted."

"You need to stop beating yourself up," said Alex.

"You don't understand. How is anyone going to love me if I can't even work out what I did wrong?" Being alone didn't frighten Claire, being lonely did. She was questioning her capacity to love.

"You didn't do anything wrong, honey."

"Then why does it feel like I'm a polar bear who's losing her mind because she's freezing fucking cold?"

Kathryn switched off the TV and joined them at the table. "It's okay for Victoria to have fallen out of love with you."

"I know that."

"And it's actually okay for her not to invite you to go with her, not to want you there, not to want to try a separation for a while instead of breakup, and in fact it's okay for her to leave you. End of story."

"I'm not sure you're helping," said Jess.

Claire sighed and rubbed her tired eyes. "No, I get it." What Kathryn was trying to make her realise was exactly what Jean had challenged her on earlier that day. "It's okay for her to do those things because that's who she is. And because even though I wouldn't, she has chosen to and that's her decision, not mine."

"Exactly. She made her choices," said Kathryn. "Shit choices, hurtful and selfish choices, but her choices nevertheless."

Alex pushed her chair away from the table. "Right, well that's me out of a job. Who wants a coffee?"

"I think you're well rid of her and that oversized coffee machine her bitch mother took," said Jess.

Claire smiled. "She was a bitch, too, you know. I bet she thinks that because Victoria left me, she's finished with women. Plus she's too stupid to work out how to use the fucking machine."

"That's my girl."

Claire turned to Kathryn. "Thanks for today. I know it couldn't have been much fun, but I appreciate your company."

"I had a good time, actually. You have a kind heart, Claire. Any nurse worth her soul does. Perhaps you and Victoria just weren't right for each other. One day you'll realise blaming yourself is useless."

"God, I hope so."

"And it will be a great day, trust me."

Claire turned to Jess with renewed enthusiasm to move things along. "What about the lease agreement on the apartment?"

"I'm a lawyer, a damn good one, too."

"If she doesn't say so herself." Kathryn winked.

"As I was saying…" Jess frowned. "I'm a lawyer and I'll get it sorted. Don't worry about a thing."

A sense of relief settled in Claire allowing her anxiety to subside. It wouldn't last though. She gave it until the morning when she would wake, heart fluttering at the thought of taking that huge step. Giving up her home wouldn't be easy.

With the TV off, not an unusual occurrence, they all played Scrabble. Naturally, Jess won, filling the board with obscure legal terms, and eventually everyone complained and insisted a card game was more appropriate. At least if luck played a part, they'd all be in with a chance.

Pushing herself to the limit of tiredness, Claire joined in until every card resembled the one before and her eyes struggled to remain open. "I'm going for a run at seven in the morning if you're interested," Claire said to Kathryn.

"Seven?" Kathryn spat out the word like it had been stuck in her throat. "That's a bit early, isn't it?"

"I need a morning routine." Claire rolled her eyes. "Well, *Jean* says I do."

Alex scowled. "Jean's right."

"Seven isn't even that early." Claire grinned.

"Oh, okay. Or maybe we can wake at seven and go at quarter past?" Kathryn made a pathetic face and Claire gave in.

"Right. Seven fifteen."

"Excellent. Will you wake me?"

"Really? You want me to wake you?"

"Yes, please. I hate alarm sounds."

"You might hate *my* sounds."

"Maybe. We'll see. So, seven then?" Kathryn grinned.

"On the dot."

Claire dutifully collected her sleeping pill from Alex, and after bidding everyone good night, retreated to the solace of her room. She felt physically and emotionally exhausted. Her hour with Jean had taken its toll, and for the first time, she was looking forward to sleep. The feeling comforted her.

With the aid of her iPod softly filling her ears with the relaxing sound of rain, Claire drifted into a deep sleep within minutes.

At 4:06 a.m., she woke breathless and drenched after another horrendous dream. This time, she shot Victoria in the back of the head on the runway at Tullamarine Airport. She had chased her relentlessly through Melbourne and finally caught her moments before boarding a jumbo jet. The piercing gunshot woke her.

Claire grappled for the light, disorientated. The familiar surroundings gave her mild comfort before she remembered these were her new surroundings. The thought of never spending another night in her own home saddened her. Worried she may have screamed, she listened for any movement in the house.

Nothing.

Silence.

The dreams scared her like nothing she had experienced in her life, and she struggled to contain her breathing and regain her composure. She threw off her sweaty T-shirt and replaced it with a dry one. Searching for another antidote, Claire reached for her notebook. Being alone scared her, but she was relieved no one was coming. She was determined to fix this herself.

Claire concentrated on breathing steadily as she retreated under the covers and slowly read what Jess had written, as Kathryn had done the night before. Jess's words brought a smile to her face, but upon completion, she flicked the page and noticed that Kathryn had also written in the notebook:

Why I like Claire O'Malley, by Kathryn Mercer.

I like Claire because she demonstrates a loyalty to her friends that I have yet to experience. Claire taught my sister how to cook. What's not to like about that? I like Claire because, faced with a life-altering circumstance, she has the foresight to acknowledge she needs help and the courage to accept it. I also like how she sacrifices good exercise to put up with me breathlessly lagging behind. Finally, I like Claire because I think she'll put up with me long enough to become good friends. Sleep well, Claire. X

Claire did sleep well. No more dreams of Victoria haunted her, and she woke to the sound of her alarm at seven on the dot.

CHAPTER EIGHT

C laire!"
 The painful screech pulled Claire up, and she swung around to see Kathryn writhing in a heap on the ground holding her lower leg. "What happened?"

"I twisted my ankle trying to dodge that pile of shit." Her genuine wincing indicated she was in considerable pain. "Why can't people just pick up after their fucking dogs?"

Claire had never heard Kathryn swear before, and it didn't sound right, albeit amusing. Claire retraced her steps. There was indeed a pile of poo near Kathryn, now spread in a long skid configuration across the grass. Her ankle had already begun to swell. "Well, you've certainly done a job on that."

"Should I take my shoe off?" Kathryn gasped at Claire's poking and prodding.

"No, best to leave it on." Claire was almost certain nothing was broken but probably sprained. "Come on, you poor old thing, let's get you to that bench. I'll run back and bring the car to collect you."

"Hey, less of the *old*, thanks, you little upstart." Her face distorted in pain. "I know I'm old to you, but I'm not even forty. You could learn something from us more experienced ladies."

Claire removed her T-shirt, revealing a black sports bra top, and tightly bound the injured ankle as best she could with the shirt. Again, her lack of clothing seemed to make Kathryn uncomfortable. Claire wasn't sure why and chose to ignore it. "I used to date your sister, remember? I know exactly what I can learn from an older, more experienced woman."

"You cheeky brat."

Claire smiled and watched curiously as Kathryn's eyes darted from Claire's face to her chest and back again. For a brief moment, their eyes met before a flash of colour returned to Kathryn's cheeks and she looked away, embarrassed.

"I should elevate it, right?"

Claire nodded and supported the ankle as Kathryn swung her legs onto the bench next to her. "How's the pain?"

"It's fine. Nothing some paracetamol won't help."

"You're a rubbish liar."

"What? I'm hardly going to faint over a sprained ankle."

"I'm a nurse. I can tell when someone's in pain."

"All right, smarty pants nurse, it's not exactly tickling, put it that way."

"I'll be as quick as I can." Claire dashed off at a brisk pace, pleased to be blowing out the cobwebs and running with real purpose. A part of her enjoyed Kathryn's company, but another part couldn't wait until her fitness improved and she could keep up.

Claire hadn't expected anyone to be home, but Alex was about to head out the door. "Where's Kathryn?" Alex sighed. "Did you two have words?"

"She twisted her ankle." Claire headed straight to the fridge for an ice pack.

"Oh, no, is she okay? Do you want me to come along, take a look at it?"

Claire raised her eyebrows, glaring at Alex. "Are you serious? I'm a homeless, sleep-deprived nurse, not bloody useless."

"You're right, of course. I forget you're even a nurse sometimes." She leaned to kiss Claire good-bye, but hesitated, obviously thinking better of touching her sweaty face or body. "Call me. Let me know how she's getting on."

"I will, I promise."

"And, Claire, you're not homeless."

"Yeah, yeah, I know."

"Oh, and where's your top?"

"Kathryn likes it when I wear the bare essentials." Claire flashed a cheeky smile.

"Get out of here."

❖

"Wow!" Kathryn looked genuinely impressed. "That was quick." Then she looked deflated. "I really must slow you down if you can run home and drive back quicker than we ran here."

"If you were serious about running, which I'm guessing you're not, I'd be happy to train you up to speed." Claire removed her T-shirt and applied the ice pack before rewrapping Kathryn's ankle.

"Why do you think I'm not serious?"

"Well, didn't Jess or Alex put you up to this? To keep an eye on me?"

Kathryn sighed. "I will say one thing about people your age; they have an inflated sense of self-importance." Her tone was not playful. "No one put me up to babysitting you. The *entire* world doesn't revolve around you and your breakup, Claire. Bad things happen to good people every second of every day. You'd do well to remember that." Kathryn hobbled to the car.

"Here, put your arm around me."

"I'm perfectly capable, thank you. I don't need your help."

❖

One of Kathryn's biggest regrets during the aftermath of breaking up with Andy was her blind self-centeredness. She lost a good friend by not being able to think of others at a time when she was learning to rebuild her life and at a time when her friend needed her to be the strong one. She would be doing Claire an injustice if she allowed her selfishness to go unchecked.

Guilt was her weapon of choice. Kathryn refused to allow Claire to make her breakfast, and she continued to dismiss her offers of help all morning. It was nearing midday when she finally stretched out on the couch, ankle elevated, coffee in hand, freshly showered. It had been a long day already.

"I'm sorry, Kathryn." Claire gently set the newspaper on Kathryn's lap and retreated.

Kathryn looked at her watch. Claire had taken longer than she anticipated to apologise. "Hang on, don't say that and leave." Kathryn smiled. "I'm not trying to be a smart-arse, but what are you sorry for, exactly?"

"For not being able to see past the end of my own nose." Claire perched on the edge of the coffee table.

"That's a good start."

"Victoria left me. She made me miserable and she made a laughing stock out of me. I don't need to humiliate myself any more than she has already. I'm sorry I assumed you were babysitting me. I'm glad you're running with me. I enjoy the company. Well, that is until you get puffed and can't speak any longer."

"I can see Victoria left you with your sense of humour at least." Kathryn frowned. "We *poor old* things might take a little longer to get fit, but I'll get there."

"Ah, yeah, about that. I'd have called you a poor old thing regardless of your age, so I'm not apologising for that. Who cares about age? Jess is six years older than me, and Victoria was four years younger. Some of my closest friends are over fifty. In my book, if you're a twat, you're a twat regardless of your age." Claire stood and winked. "Plus, have you looked in the mirror lately? You're hardly a crusty old wench." She left.

Kathryn could feel herself blushing. She looked in the mirror all the time, well, no more than the average person, she presumed. It just never occurred to her that a thirty-one-year-old lesbian would compliment her like that. What exactly had Claire meant? Surely, Claire wasn't attracted to her. Perhaps she just found Kathryn attractive.

She shook the notion from her mind. Her entire thought process was ridiculous. Of course Claire wasn't attracted to her. She unfolded the newspaper and read an entire paragraph on the British royal family without comprehending a single word. She felt a little flutter in her stomach.

The thought that Claire might find her attractive was flattering. The fluttering grew.

She tossed the paper on the coffee table and distracted herself by hobbling outside for some fresh air.

CHAPTER NINE

With the sun beating down at a scorching thirty-six degrees, Claire retreated to the far end of the garden under the wide-reaching branches of the imposing willow tree. From the corner of her eye, she watched Kathryn recline on the sun lounge near the patio doors and switch the radio on.

It was one of those days where, further inland, it would be scorching hot. If the wind picked up, it usually signified a recipe for disaster. She assumed Kathryn was listening for any updates on bush fires. The heat was rising. After the fires of 2009, it seemed all of Victoria, and indeed the country, was watching and waiting. It hadn't rained for months, but preparations to contain scrub and dry undergrowth had been under way in fire-prone areas for a long time now.

Claire loved summer and coped with the heat better than most. She firmly pressed her iPod ear buds in and listened to relaxing forest sounds as she attempted to centre herself with t'ai chi. The heat acted as a blanket, restricting her thoughts by reducing them to tiny, insignificant fragments.

Wearing only a crop top and shorts, she attracted the attention of the old man next door who bobbed up and down near the fence, copping a look now and then.

When she turned, she saw that Kathryn had moved to sit against the trunk of the willow tree. She removed the buds from her ears. "Hey."

"Hey, yourself."

"Do you do t'ai chi?"

Kathryn laughed. "I'd always thought I'd enjoy Yoga or Pilates or anything that would empty my mind, but as with everything else in my life with Andy, I never took time for myself. I'm embarrassed to say all the best intentions in the world never got me to one single class."

Claire briefly wondered if all the time she spent running and doing t'ai chi alone contributed to her breakup. Victoria had zero interest in physical activity beyond the bedroom.

She changed the subject. "Your ankle okay still?"

"Yeah, it's good. Well, it is when I sit."

"Good."

With nothing else to say, Claire inhaled deeply and attempted to refocus. It was useless. "Are you just going to sit and watch me?"

"Do you mind? Thought I might get some tips. You look like you know what you're doing."

Claire shrugged. "Sure, I don't mind. You'll get bored though, I guarantee it." She turned her back and replaced her buds before remembering something. Shyly, she faced Kathryn again. "Thank you for writing in my notebook." Beads of sweat dripped from her neck before disappearing between her breasts. "I read it this morning at some ungodly hour. It helped." She lowered her head. "So, thanks."

"You're welcome. I knew you wouldn't ask me, so I just did it."

She was right. Claire wouldn't have asked for her contribution. Slightly embarrassed, she turned her back, replaced her ear buds, and continued where she had left off in the smothering heat.

After forty-five minutes, Claire finished her workout. Kathryn had fallen asleep, slumped against the tree trunk, breathing heavily.

Conscious of her need to rehydrate, Claire retrieved a jug of iced water and two glasses. The cool, fresh water was heavenly, and she lay flat on her back alongside Kathryn for many minutes before she, too, fell asleep.

When Claire woke, Kathryn sat sipping the iceless water, staring at her. "I bet you never snore," she said.

Claire rolled onto her stomach, stretching her back with half push-ups. "What makes you say that?"

"I admit I've rarely paid such close attention to many people sleeping before, but you looked so peaceful."

"How long do you think I slept for?"

"Not long." Kathryn smiled knowingly. "Not long enough to dream I don't think, sorry."

"Well, at least I didn't scream the neighbourhood down." Claire half laughed. "Did your husband snore?"

"Yep, the snotty bastard. I used to go to bed at least an hour before him. If I wasn't asleep, I'd pretend. Then he'd fall asleep and I'd lie awake half the night listening to him." She shook her head. "Is that normal?"

Claire laughed. "You're asking the perverted lesbo if that's normal? As if I'd know."

Kathryn shot her a warning glance. "Can we just leave that alone, please? I feel bad enough as it is."

Claire grinned, an awkward apology. "Why did you pretend to be asleep when you weren't?"

"Why do you think? You're not that naive, surely."

No, Claire wasn't that naive, and since Kathryn had asked, she answered. "So you didn't have to have sex with your husband."

"You've never had to do that, have you?"

Claire smiled. "Have sex with your husband? Nope."

"God, you're a smart-arse."

"It's my most endearing quality, but seriously, no, I can't say I've ever pretended to be asleep to avoid sex. I honestly don't understand why it's even necessary. I mean, of course I understand that you didn't want to have sex, and I can see why you might, for convenience sake, pretend to be asleep once or twice, but why didn't you just talk about it, fix it in the long term?"

"Fix what?" Kathryn's tone suggested long endured frustration. "According to Andy, the only thing to fix was me. It was *my* problem that I didn't want to have sex every night. It was *my* problem I couldn't fulfil my duty as a wife. There was something really wrong with me, or so he'd say." She eyed Claire. "Do you think there's something wrong with me?"

Claire had a few friends with marital problems, and equally as many living in wedded bliss. How was she to answer such a personal question? She swallowed hard. "Well, if you and I were together, and you avoided having sex with me, other than for the obvious reason that you're actually straight, I'd be devastated."

"Yeah, just like Andy." Kathryn sighed.

"No, hang on, no way. Nothing like Andy." Claire sat up to explain. "I'd be asking why and expecting honest answers, unless it was a casual sex thing, in which case you wouldn't have to behave that way, you'd just stop having sex with me. I think if you're in someone's bed every night, it's because you like having sex with them, or you love them, preferably both."

"But I did love Andy," Kathryn protested half-heartedly. "Well, I thought I did."

"Really?"

"I was married to him for fifteen years."

"Didn't you discuss this with your therapist?"

"Of course, at great length, but I'm interested to hear your opinion."

"Look, I'm no expert, but if you loved him so much why'd you have to pretend every night? Why couldn't you speak to him about your sex life?

"Love means different things to different people, but if that *were* us, I'd be really interested to know why you behaved that way. Was it as a result of *my* behaviour in the first place? Do we have different libidos? Is there something wrong with the sex? Would you prefer we experimented, something different? *Somewhere* different? Your happiness and enjoyment would be equally important as mine."

"God, you sound like a saint. Victoria must need her head read." Kathryn winced. "Sorry, that was insensitive of me."

"It's okay." Claire held her head high. "And you're right; she was a twit to let me go."

"Thatta girl."

They exchanged a warm smile before Kathryn continued. "It was nothing like that with Andy. We never really talked about sex or about our roles in the relationship at all. I was expected to cook, clean, do the washing, ironing, and keep the house tidy. He mowed the lawns. We only ever had sex in the missionary position."

"It sounds very traditional."

Kathryn screwed up her face. "I can't believe I'm telling you this."

"Was your orgasm important to him?" Claire gambled on prying so personally.

Kathryn huffed. "You're kidding, aren't you? Sexually inhibited women like me are apparently better at getting themselves off. It was best if I just made my own arrangements to orgasm."

Claire's eyes nearly popped out of her head.

Kathryn slumped even further down the tree trunk. "You orgasm every time, don't you?"

"Yeah, pretty much. I certainly try to make sure my partner does." Claire raised her eyebrows apologetically.

"I wasted my time with him, didn't I?"

"Not at all," Claire said. "View it as a learning curve. Now at least you know exactly what you *don't* want, and hopefully you have a good idea about what you *do* want, what you should look for in the future."

"I guess."

"My best advice." Claire winked. "Get yourself a good woman."

CHAPTER TEN

What was left in Claire's apartment was all hers. What was left. Everything trendy, modern, and technologically advanced beyond the nineties had been Victoria's, with the exception of Claire's iPod and laptop. The TV, stereo, Blu-ray recorder, home theatre system, food processor, juicer, and of course the coffee machine all belonged to Victoria.

The rest, hardly amounting to much in value, and mostly old second-hand furniture, was to be placed in storage.

Murray had kindly offered the services of her husband, Steve, to assist in the clean out. He was an engineer and drove a shiny silver 4x4 that pulled a shiny silver trailer. Within a few hours, all of Claire's worldly goods would be snugly loaded and en route to a storage location she would share with Kathryn when her container arrived after the house was sold.

It was off limits for Jess to do any heavy lifting, especially in the heat, so she dusted and vacuumed looking radiantly pregnant in linen pants and a tank top. Alex had her regular Saturday shift at the clinic so was absent, and Kathryn had insisted on helping even though her ankle still couldn't support her full weight. In fact, Kathryn was ruthless.

"Can I throw this dinner set out?" She held aloft a cup as if it were diseased, barely gripping it with her thumb and index finger. "I think the blue and white stripe look went out a while ago now."

Claire nodded despairingly, just like she continued to nod when Kathryn raised her eyebrows and asked about her glass top coffee table, her jumble sale wall clock that ticked too loudly, her bright yellow lava lamp, and finally, the plastic hand that once held the TV remote (which Victoria took), so now just sat there, empty-handed.

After living overseas with few material possessions, Claire had returned home and kept things simple. She liked living "light," as she called it. Victoria had called it living cheap. Claire loved reading, but never bought new books, only second-hand, and she never kept them, always passing them on to share the joy. Victoria hated reading anything other than real life non-fiction, and there was no way she would ever give her books away, let alone read a second-hand one.

Disillusioned by the process and the possibility of four wasted years, Claire wandered aimlessly through the space she used to call home. The tiny backyard appeared neglected already, but the contents of the shed had been taken away so James, the new tenant, would have to deal with the long grass and weeds when he arrived.

A huge part of Claire didn't want to be there packing up and driving the final nail into the coffin that was her miserable life. However, this mess was hers, and the sooner she sorted it, the better.

She stood in the kitchen where it all began to go wrong months ago. In reality, it had been wrong for a long time, but Claire remembered *that* Saturday morning with disturbing clarity. Victoria had begun her Saturday morning with a massive clean out. Her excuse—lighten the load and rejuvenate. Claire had kissed Victoria on the top of the head and left for a long run, returning to eat breakfast and read the paper in the garden. The entire time, she veiled a smug grin; after four years, Victoria was finally coming round to the concept of living "light." Claire secretly felt triumphant.

Her euphoric sense of victory was only an illusion. She failed to notice the seven boxes Victoria had carefully packed and stacked behind the study door. She failed to notice that the clothes she had left in the wardrobe—neatly packing the rest—were only enough to last two weeks.

She had been a naive fool. Her stupidity made her feel sick.

What also induced a wave of nausea every time she thought about it was the annual leave Victoria had taken for the entirety of their final two weeks together. With the exception of the odd day here or there, they had always taken leave together. This unexpected leave wasn't discussed, planned, or even mentioned, not until the Friday evening when Victoria had dined with workmates and returned home drunk, announcing she was taking two weeks off.

Now, the humiliating, gut-wrenching truth slapped Claire squarely in the face. It hadn't been annual leave, it was permanent leave, and the dinner and drinks had been her farewell.

Upsetting Claire now, more than anything, was her own behaviour leading up to that Saturday morning. She was so wrapped up in herself, her own life, that she hadn't paid Victoria enough attention. Was the fact that she hadn't even realised Victoria had packed up her belongings and resigned from her job an indication that she took her for granted?

As she was about to unplug her ancient black and tacky wood-grain panelled answering machine, Claire noticed the tiny green light flash. Victoria hated the machine, and Claire had promised to throw it away when the tape eventually wore out, but it still worked as good as gold. She rewound the tape and pressed play, hearing her own voice requesting the caller to leave a message. It wasn't until she heard Victoria's voice that she froze, riveted. "Claire, it's me. I'm settled in now. Thought you might like to know, maybe not though. Anyway, our term deposit matured. You probably didn't remember we had one. I withdrew the entire amount. Mum says I should keep it all, says you probably owe me, but that doesn't feel right, so I'll transfer half back to you as soon as I can. Berlin is great, but you already know that. Well, that's all I wanted to say, I guess." There was a long pause. "Um, I miss you."

The final words were mumbled, barely audible, but it didn't stop the growing ball of anger rising in Claire's chest. Victoria had been right; she had forgotten about the investment. To her annoyance, rage exploded with the gushing of tears and the catapulting of the vase she was holding against the kitchen door. Her mind became a jumbled mess of thoughts, conversations, and emotions. She felt Victoria's hands all over her body, but she didn't feel the love she thought they had shared. Love would have been making decisions together. Love would have been telling the truth, not lying, not hiding, not deceiving, and certainly not leaving.

Thankfully, there was no one around to witness her loss of

control. Jess went home after a gallant contribution, and Kathryn had left with Steve and the laden truck to finalise the paperwork at the storage facility.

Desperate for distraction, Claire remembered the half empty bottle of ouzo she'd thrown in the rubbish. She wouldn't normally throw out alcohol, but she had no idea how long the ouzo had been there, she couldn't recall ever buying it, and didn't really like ouzo, but neither did Victoria—although Victoria had been full of surprises lately.

The first gulp burned, but the second, now tasting more like a delicious liquorice lolly, slid down her throat as if heaven sent. Claire relaxed and her anger subsided. "Fuck you, Victoria Francis Wallace," Claire said, taking another huge swig. "And fuck your mother, too!"

She stood and raised the bottle to the empty space where the coffee machine used to live. "Fuck you, overpriced coffee maker."

The alcohol warmly saturated every cell of her body, providing her with the appealing sensation of thawing from the inside out. She loved that feeling and likened it to the aftermath of a satisfying orgasm. Claire skipped to the now empty bedroom, gulping frantically. "Fuck you, bedroom where we used to have sex."

There was little ouzo left now, but she bounced into every other room where she and Victoria had made love, and repeated the same toast, draining the bottle completely.

Claire felt as light as a feather and skipped through the house and into the garden. *Music, I need music.* The radio was gone, so she pulled her iPod and earphones from her satchel and turned the volume up nice and loud. Feeling warm and fuzzy thanks to the ouzo, she danced throughout the house, in every room and around the tiny garden. Claire dirty-danced with doorframes and dry humped the bathroom vanity. Empty toilet roll in hand—a makeshift microphone—she sang at the top of her lungs.

Ouzo was fabulously Greek, her new Greek best friend— although she didn't recall ever having had this much fun on her travels through Greece. Cheap beer, cheap gyros, and the attention of a young Greek goddess had certainly made Athens memorable though. Then, remembering the dinner set and other crockery Kathryn had culled, she dragged the rubbish bin inside, retrieved the crockery, and began smashing the plates back into the bin.

Claire was having the time of her life. Nothing on her iPod vaguely resembled Greek music, traditional or otherwise, but she seemed to smash along quite well to the beat of every song.

In her ears, where the music filled her head, her singing sounded wonderful. The taste of ouzo remained on her lips and she longed for more, but for the moment, she relished the warm buzz it sent tingling down her spine. Claire danced, smashed, and sang at full volume. *Stuff the neighbours!*

❖

Kathryn and Steve returned to the house. Given that her ankle was still painful, his help was appreciated. Kathryn froze when she heard screaming and glass smashing from within the apartment.

"Did you hear that?"

Steve unbuckled and leapt from the car. He snapped off a garden stake and marched to the front door. Kathryn already had her phone out, primed to call the police, and when Steve gave her a nod, she knew it was her cue to remain outside until he indicated otherwise. The front door was ajar, so he kicked it wide open.

"Take that, Victoria Francis Wallace."

"What the hell is that?" Steve lowered the garden stake.

They exchanged glances. "Is that Claire yelling?" Kathryn edged inside before another huge smashing sound pierced the air. "And singing?"

"If that's what you call it," said Steve.

"I hate you!"

Smash!

They crept toward the kitchen, and Kathryn was surprised to recognise the tune to which Claire was berating her ex-lover.

"Fuck off and let me go."

Smash!

Then they saw it, a sight that could only be believed if seen firsthand—Claire, dancing with the mop in one hand, a bowl in the other, singing for Ireland, before tossing the bowl into the bin, smashing it to pieces.

Steve laughed, retreating. "I'll leave you to it then."

Kathryn stared in disbelief. "She's mad."

"Either way," Steve called over his shoulder, "she's all yours."

Kathryn grinned before flicking her phone to video and pressing record. For at least thirty seconds, she remained undetected as the song concluded and Claire reached into her pocket for the iPod, obviously eager for a repeat performance.

"Hey, Kathryn, you came back. I'm just pretending to be Nana Mouskouri." She pulled the buds from her ears.

"I didn't know she covered 'No Surprises.'" Kathryn couldn't help but smile. Not entirely sure why, she propped the phone on the bench against the wall, the record function remaining active.

"You know 'No Surprises'?"

"I'm thirty-nine, Claire, not eighty. You seem to be having a good time."

"Well, it's a long story, but I found some ouzo. Then I drank it all. Oh, I should have saved you some, sorry. Anyway, I started dancing and now I'm smashing plates. But I'm out of plates now, too. I should have saved you some of those as well, sorry. Wanna dance?"

Kathryn attempted to step out of reach. "You know, normally I'd love to, but with my ankle, I don't think it's such a good idea." She feigned disappointment.

"Don't worry about that. I'll be careful." Claire took her hand.

"Really, it's still quite tender."

"You're in safe hands. I'm a nurse. And anyway, *I'm* tender."

"I'm not a good dancer, Claire."

"Nonsense."

"There's no music."

Claire took one of the ear buds, wiped it on her filthy top, and handed it to Kathryn. Bored with "No Surprises," she skipped to an upbeat track, held both of Kathryn's hands, closed her eyes, and moved in time to the beat.

"Claire, I can't keep my earphone in." Smiling, Kathryn attempted to move away.

Undeterred, Claire restricted her own movements and grinned, gripping Kathryn tightly.

"What's with the ouzo, anyway?" Kathryn resigned herself to dancing.

"I needed a drink."

"So I gathered." They were swaying more than dancing now, hand in hand. "How come?"

"Victoria rang."

"What?" Kathryn froze. "She actually rang you?"

"Well, yeah, but no. She left a message. I found a message she left." Claire wiggled her arms, impatiently encouraging Kathryn to keep moving. "She said she missed me."

"Oh, honey, I'm sorry." Kathryn watched as Claire shut her eyes again, this time holding back tears.

"She has no right to say she misses me."

"I know, sweetheart."

"I don't miss her now." Claire's eyes shot open. "The dreams have stopped." Her eyes closed again. "Now I'm just sad because I think I didn't have what I thought I had."

"I know the feeling. But it won't last. Trust me, pretty soon Victoria whatever-her-name-was will be the last person on your mind." Kathryn squeezed Claire's hands.

As if on cue, and ironically so, an eighties love ballad clicked on the iPod—"Take My Breath Away" by Berlin.

❖

At least three songs passed, and Claire's eyes remained closed. Kathryn had stopped trying to get away. Claire fancied more ouzo and wished Kathryn could have had some. The feeling of being drunk was fabulous, but she wanted to share the abandonment it provided. Kathryn wasn't as uptight as she first thought. Sure, maybe she had some weird preconceptions about what being gay was about, but that wasn't unusual. Kathryn wasn't unusual. As the song changed, Claire rethought that statement; Kathryn *was* unusual, but in a good way. She was caring, kind, and smart. Claire especially liked that she was smart.

Without thinking, without opening her eyes, and without permission, Claire stepped into Kathryn. Her cheek rested on her shoulder as she slid one hand round her waist and drew the other up so that both their hands rested between their chests.

Kathryn returned the embrace, her free hand tightly holding Claire to her. They remained this way for the duration of the song, swaying in time to the music.

"Would Andy want you back now? You know, now that you're the new you?" Claire didn't move to look at Kathryn.

"Andy liked the mothering type. He wanted to be dominated by an older woman. I'm neither older, nor the dominating type. He would hate the new me."

"Well, I like the new you. You'll find another fella in no time at all." The slow rhythm of the eighties classics ended, and techno dance music polluted their intimate moment. Claire removed their earphones but refused to release her grip.

Kathryn shrugged. "I don't want someone else. I'm enjoying being me for the first time in a very long while. I intend to live a little, do some of the things I always wanted to do."

Claire replaced her head on Kathryn's shoulder. "You'll probably find that's when you'll attract the most interest. Confident people are sexy people. You're sexy people. I mean a sexy person." She sighed. "You know what I mean."

"I guess."

"Unlike drunk, pathetic, stupid people—they aren't sexy at all."

"Stop putting yourself down. You're none of those things." Kathryn's tone was gentle.

"Well, I am pretty drunk."

"Okay, yes, you're drunk. But you're not pathetic *or* stupid."

"Just pathetic, then."

"Just nothing, Claire."

"Ha, nothing. That's exactly right. I'm nothing."

"Don't be silly. This will pass and you'll be the new Claire in no time."

Overcome with emotion, or something else she couldn't name, Claire eyed Kathryn. She moved her hand to rest on Kathryn's cheek. Her skin was soft, warm, and unbelievably smooth. She rose on her toes and kissed Kathryn's soft, glossed lips. Their mouths remained closed, their lips barely touching, but Claire lingered for a long moment and Kathryn didn't pull away.

Fresh citrus tones wafted up from Kathryn's neck, filling Claire's head. She loved expensive perfume.

It surprised Claire to realise she didn't want their connection to end. Touching Kathryn left her feeling lightheaded and vulnerable, but in a good way. It was a textbook crush, but in those moments, she imagined their entrance into a party walking arm in arm, Kathryn taking the lead wearing a smile that told the world she was in love with the woman by her side.

Claire was reclaiming her lips, just as she would eventually reclaim the rest of her body.

Kathryn's lips were now the last lips that Claire had kissed. She tingled at the thought.

CHAPTER ELEVEN

Kathryn couldn't settle. It was eight o'clock and Claire was in bed, probably sound asleep. Kathryn had a lot on her mind.

The mobile phone in her pocket felt warm and heavy resting on her upper thigh. Under normal circumstances, she would barely detect its presence, or more accurately, even have her phone on her, but this evening, since that afternoon, the secret it held in images and sound felt intrusive, demanding her attention like a nagging child.

The weather remained hot, sticky hot, and Jess had insisted the air conditioning remain off, complaining her skin was dry enough as it was. They sat in fading light, lounging in the outdoor entertainment area just beyond the house.

"Fancy a gin?" Kathryn needed something to slow her mind, and Alex's wine glass was empty.

"Sure. Why not?" Apparently, it was just the excuse Alex needed to stop rubbing Jess's feet. She joined Kathryn in the kitchen. "I'll help."

The measures were generous. "Steady on." Alex's eyes bulged, staring at the near half full glasses of gin. "You thirsty?"

"Something like that. It feels like it's been a long day."

"It will be a short night if you keep pouring like that."

Not a bad plan.

Jess lit a citronella candle and they enjoyed the slight breeze that arrived as twilight crept in. "So Claire thought ouzo was the answer this afternoon, then?"

Kathryn told herself she didn't want to talk about Claire, or even think about her, but what she wanted, even in her own mind, seemed completely irrelevant. The excitement she felt, foreign as it was, at even the mention of Claire's name, compelled her to participate in the conversation.

"Steve and I thought she was being murdered. Fortunately for us, it was just her drunk singing."

"She's never been one to hold a tune." Jess's frown indicated worry. "Did you listen to the message on the machine?"

"Yeah, Victoria was way out of line." Kathryn had taken an immediate and intense dislike to Victoria. "You can't just up and leave someone and then mumble that you miss them. Especially after you've just admitted to stealing half their money and only giving it back because you experience a pathetic twinge of guilt."

"Well," Alex said. "I think it's good for her, get it out of her system and move on. Plus it's a safe environment for her to let it all out. There's three of us here to help her."

Kathryn again felt the presence of the phone in her pocket. Was her behaviour, allowing Claire to kiss her as she did, the actions of a responsible adult looking out for a friend? If the faint throb between her legs was anything to go by, she'd failed miserably.

"I agree," said Jess. "But they were together for four years. It's difficult to get over that in a hurry."

Kathryn touched the phone in her pocket. "Oh, I don't know. In some ways, I think she's ready to move on."

Jess and Alex snapped their heads to glare at her.

"I think she's realised that she didn't have what she thought she had. I think she wants to push forward. I think she's beginning to accept who Victoria really was."

Jess looked unconvinced. "Yes, but that doesn't make you ready to move on."

"No, but it makes you less inclined to *hang* on, and that's a big step."

Kathryn sensed both Jess and Alex probably wanted to say more, but they let it go. After all, she was the expert in this field. Severing ties and moving forward was one thing, filling the void with someone new was another challenge altogether. There was no book, manual, or formula with the answers. The spark of attraction advanced stealthily, and didn't she know it.

Before she could ponder any longer, Jess and Alex changed the subject, and for the first time, they relaxed and openly discussed their babies.

"I've got one word," said Kathryn. "Australian Standards."

Jess looked perplexed.

"Okay, smarty pants, I know it's two words, but the baby equipment you buy, new or second-hand, should meet the relevant Australian Standard. Anything less and you're just exposing yourself to a life of torment if something goes wrong."

Jess shook her head as if to clear it. "I'm not being a smart-arse, but you've never mentioned kids before. For most of our closest friends, gay or not, the prospect of squeezing two babies from your vagina—the tool used for sexual enjoyment—is abhorrent. How the hell do you know so much about it?"

"IVF, four miscarriages, and no babies leaves you with nothing but a wealth of useless knowledge—unless your little sister is having twins, of course."

"Oh, Kathryn." Jess reached for her hand. "You never said. Why didn't you tell me?"

"The first time I told loads of friends I was pregnant. It was hell telling them the baby had died. I never told anyone again after that."

"I'm sorry it didn't work out for you," Alex said.

"Andy didn't really want kids anyway. Well, not kids so much, but babies. He hates babies and toddlers. Ironically, an older woman with older kids would be his dream come true." Kathryn had lived in turmoil during the failed attempts to become pregnant, and Andy had provided little support simply because he hadn't really shared her desire for a baby. Although she had desperately wanted a child, she now knew it had all worked out for the best.

"So, Australian Standard stuff then?" asked Alex.

Kathryn was grateful the focus had returned to the present. "It's the only way to go."

"Was it you or him?" asked Jess.

She should have known better than to think Jess would skim over such a huge revelation.

"Both actually. His sperm count is dismal, figures, and then with the miscarriages, it seemed I just couldn't carry to term. No one can definitively tell me why. I imagine there's more than one failing down there in all that plumbing."

"God, Kathryn, I wish you'd told me."

"Well, it's worked out for the best in hindsight. Imagine our divorce had kids been involved—bloody mess that it was." She sighed, annoyed by the whole saga. "And anyway, now that I'll be living in Melbourne, I'll have your kids to spoil."

"And they'll have a fabulous aunt as a role model."

Kathryn spluttered. "I wouldn't have been a role model a week ago." At least she was adult enough to admit she was wrong. "Do you realise you're the only openly gay person I know?"

Alex coughed.

"Sorry. Obviously, there's you and Claire now, but growing up, little sister, you were it. Jesus, if it wasn't enough that you were bloody brilliant at everything, you had to go and become a lesbian, too."

"Most people don't *become* a lesbian, Kathryn. They're born that way," said Jess.

"Oh, I know that. But all this time it's been easier for me to believe you were just trying to be different to get even more attention."

"Gee, thanks."

Alex disappeared to refill their glasses.

"But now I see how lucky and how in love you are. Alex is fabulous, and Claire still worships the ground you walk on, even after all these years."

"Claire is like my little sister now."

"Honestly, Jess. You should stop saying that. You used to screw like rabbits. It sounds incestuous."

"Well, it's the best description I have."

"We don't have to have sex, too, do we?" Kathryn teased her.

"Very funny, but you might learn something, so don't discount it."

"Anyway, your life is something to be proud of. *I'm* proud of you. God, I just watch you and Alex hang out the washing together, cook together, clean together. No arguments, no stereotypical male and female roles. It's a remarkable way to live."

"You're beginning to worry me now. Where the hell has *this* Kathryn been hiding all these years?"

"It's normal to you, I can see that. But to me, it's liberating."

"It's also one of the reasons we want Claire to stay." Jess shrugged, embarrassed. "Look, we're far from perfect, but she and Victoria had had their problems in the past. Victoria was becoming demanding and unreasonable. Claire was bending over backwards to accommodate her."

"What did she do?"

"It was Victoria who suggested Claire take on night shift, then suggested she do them more frequently, citing the money as too good to pass up on. The only problem was, while Claire was home during the day sleeping, cleaning, and cooking, Victoria was gallivanting until all hours, spending all the money. She wanted to change Claire."

Kathryn was appalled. "That's ridiculous. Claire doesn't need to change. Why didn't you say something to her? Although really, what could you have said that would have made any difference?" Kathryn thought she saw the dilemma.

"That's just it." Jess sighed, clearly disappointed. "Claire would have listened to me. She knows I wouldn't say anything without good reason. The problem was I thought she was handling it. We'd talked about Victoria at great length. I thought it was improving, not declining."

Kathryn sighed. "Christ, you have a better relationship with your friends than I ever did with my own bloody husband."

"Well, as you keep reminding me, we did once screw like rabbits."

Alex laughed. "Maybe you need to find yourself a good woman."

Why do people keep saying that? The phone in Kathryn's pocket felt like a bomb on a timer, primed and ready to explode. "That'll be the day."

❖

Kathryn's preparation for bed was slow and deliberate. Firstly, she was tipsy and her ankle had swollen over the course of the day, and secondly, because as much as she wanted to review the footage on her phone, she was enjoying the tingling sensation of restrained anticipation.

Claire's bedroom door was open and she stalled to stare through the crack. She noticed the blinds weren't drawn. Kathryn had never slept with the moonlight shining through her window, and from what she could see of Claire, she appeared to sleep naked. Even on the hottest, stickiest Queensland nights, Kathryn always wore *something* to bed. To be naked with Andy had been an invitation, and encouraging him was a mistake she had only made once.

On the bed beside Claire sat her iPod. Kathryn smiled. *She sure loves that thing.* Without consideration, she crept into the room, untangled the earphone wires from Claire's fingers, and set the device next to her notebook on the bedside table. Claire's skin glistened in the moonlight. Nothing private was exposed, but the heat of the evening left a sheen of sweat on Claire's brow, down her neck and chest, disappearing under the white cotton sheet that moulded to her outstretched body.

The room smelled surprisingly fresh, given the humid evening and the amount of ouzo Claire had consumed. Pomegranate or something sweet lingered in the oppressive air. Following her nose, Kathryn found a collection of candles, the heat causing them to emit the pleasant aroma.

A tiny strand of curly hair fell across Claire's face, but Kathryn's eyes wandered to the smoothly shaven armpit Claire exposed by resting her hand on the pillow above her head. She'd always assumed lesbians didn't shave their armpits. Silly really, because she knew Jess shaved hers. Almost unconsciously, her eyes moved to the slight rise between Claire's legs, but in the moonlight, under a sheet, she couldn't tell the state of what lay beneath. It astounded her that she wanted to know.

Kathryn gently reached for the strand of hair and settled it back in place. Claire stirred, but only slightly, and the contented moan that escaped her almost caused Kathryn to disturb her again, ever so slightly, simply to hear the sound once more.

Without hesitation, Kathryn kissed two of her own fingers before gently touching Claire's cheek. Another soft moan and Claire rolled over, her face illuminated by the full moonlight. Kathryn smiled and crept back to her own room, careful not to make a sound.

With the light on, the magic of a moonlit room disappeared. Kathryn looked around at her bedroom, or her sister's spare room. Its name did nothing to alter the emptiness she felt at that moment. She stared at her reflection in the full-length mirror and continued to do so as she slowly undressed. She lifted her arm to reveal an armpit with two day old stubble. Her breasts were sizeable and still perky. Jess often accused Kathryn of milking her mother of her entire stash of large boob genes.

Since leaving Andy, Kathryn's stomach had flattened, but she wasn't entirely sure why. She hadn't toned up in spite of him, nor to make him jealous or flaunt before him what he'd lost. In fact, she had made no conscious attempt to do anything but find herself. The naked figure staring back at her had found herself after her marriage ended, and she was comfortable with that. Her energy until that point, however, had been focused on leaving the old behind. Now it was time to look to the future, now she was lost again, and the feeling was equally frightening and exhilarating.

Without giving it another thought, she switched off the light and swung the curtains wide open. She threw her pyjamas on the chair, tossed back the doona, and slid under the sheet. The sensation of the bedding on her bare skin was best described as *new*.

The phone resting on her bedside table commanded her attention like a beacon. She had resisted for long enough and finally replayed the footage from that afternoon. She cringed at how awkward she looked, completely aware of their closeness, while Claire possessed a self-confidence that Kathryn wasn't entirely convinced originated solely from excessive ouzo.

It was one thing, Kathryn realised, to be in a moment and experience it. It was something else altogether to watch yourself hold hands with another woman, embrace her, soothe her, console her, and then let her kiss you.

Something else altogether.

CHAPTER TWELVE

Claire woke to the sound of distant chatter and the enticing aroma of a Sunday fry-up. It had been light outside for hours, but a nurse on rotating shifts could sleep under just about any condition. She hoped breakfast was nearly ready; she was famished.

"Ah, here she is. Our very own sleeping beauty." Jess cuddled her tightly as she traipsed, bleary eyed, into the kitchen.

Kathryn smiled at her before returning to the stove. Bacon sizzled in the frying pan.

"In bed before us all and the last up, you must have needed the sleep," Jess said.

Claire *had* needed the sleep, and she could have fallen asleep again, warm in the familiarity of Jess's embrace. The ever-increasing bump that would one day produce twins protruded into Claire. "I'm allowed to touch your belly when they start kicking, aren't I?"

It was obviously the first time Jess had considered that people might actually want to touch her. "You'll be the only one."

"Ah-hum?" Both Alex and Kathryn cleared their throats in unison.

"Oh, you know what I mean." She turned to Kathryn. "Of course you can fondle my belly, too. It's expected." Jess winked. "My big sister *and* my little sister, my incestuous dream comes true."

"Are we having a threesome?" Claire wasn't entirely sure what the private joke was about, but sidled up behind Kathryn, seductively massaging her shoulders regardless. She ogled the delicious looking breakfast.

"Not without me," said Alex.

Everyone laughed except Kathryn, who silently slipped from beneath Claire's hands and hobbled into the garden.

"I'm thinking of going back to work on Tuesday," Claire said. "I feel ready for the distraction, but in a good way this time. The dreams have stopped, I can get to sleep relatively easily, and that will only improve once I'm busy and occupied at work."

Silence.

Jess frowned. It was a well rehearsed and well executed barrister frown. Claire recognised it immediately.

"I know what I'm doing," she said.

"What's Jean's advice?" asked Jess.

"Not everything Jean says is right, you know," said Claire. "She's not Dumbledore." Claire remembered Jess's first rule of being a lawyer—never ask a question you don't already know the answer to. She was doomed.

"And yesterday? What was that?"

Claire looked to Kathryn, who'd returned and commenced dishing up. Their eyes met, but she wasn't sure how to read Kathryn's expression.

"Give me a break. I'm allowed to get pissed off at Victoria now and again aren't I?"

"And it simply validates my point that, given Jean's advice also, it wouldn't hurt to take another week off," said Jess.

"Kathryn and I talked yesterday." Claire looked pleadingly toward Kathryn for support. "I'm ready to move forward. I want to be *me* again. I think going back to work will help that. Kathryn, what do you think?"

Kathryn looked from Jess to Claire. "I don't know. You've been in a crisis this last month with all the dreams. This last week especially hasn't been pretty. Let's swap places for a second. What advice would you give me?"

Claire lowered her head.

"Claire?" Kathryn prodded.

Jess relaxed in her seat, a smug grin twisting the corners of her mouth as if she'd finished crucifying a defence witness on the stand. "It's the best thing, honey. You know we love you."

"Plus," said Kathryn, intervening before Claire hurled her eggs at Jess. "I was going to tackle the garden this week. I was hoping you might help."

Claire glared at Jess. "You put her up to this, didn't you?"

"Not guilty, Your Honour."

Claire's shoulders dropped. "Okay, I'll take this week off, but on one condition." Claire looked them all in the eye, although Alex had thankfully remained silent. "As of *right* now, I'm just normal old Claire again, okay?"

"Here we go," muttered Jess.

"I'm not joking, Jess."

"But you're not 'Old' Claire, though, are you? I mean, you're actually younger than all of us," Alex joked.

Claire shook her head. "And you were doing so well with your mouth shut. You lot are impossible, but I mean it. After Victoria's message yesterday, the ouzo, smashing plates, and talking with Kathryn, I don't want to dwell on any of it any longer. What happened, happened. I can't change that, so can we go back to just being us? No more mothering, okay?"

"But that's not fair. I need practice," said Jess.

"And I've always mothered you," Alex added before they both looked toward Kathryn for her contribution.

"Don't look at me. You two seem to have it covered."

Claire remembered the kiss they shared yesterday. Nothing about *that* had been motherly.

Although she would only ever grudgingly admit it, Claire enjoyed the prospect of spending the week working in the garden with Kathryn. She'd been worried that Kathryn might have felt uncomfortable about the kiss, but it hadn't been mentioned again. It had been entirely innocent at the time, but upon reflection—and she liked to reflect upon it often—it was sexy as hell.

What Kathryn had said resonated somewhere inside her, and she realised she could either go mad wondering where she went wrong with Victoria, or simply begin to let it go. The kiss symbolised a new beginning, and thankfully, Kathryn didn't appear offended.

❖

Kathryn knew Jess loved the garden. It was her therapy to counteract dealing with criminal scum on a daily basis, but since becoming pregnant, she'd been advised to take it easy, especially with twins. Kathryn was happy to help spruce up the garden, even though she'd never tended to a garden before. Andy had done all that. Regardless, it was the least she could do.

The evening was hot and humid, as usual, but the welcome northerly breeze provided some relief.

"So, where shall we start?" Claire nudged her.

"Pardon?"

"The garden. What's your plan of attack?"

Kathryn was surveying the front jungle. It looked dishevelled and neglected. If it hadn't been for the need to provide Claire with a distraction, she would have just organised for a landscaping company to come and do it all. "I've no idea. I've never touched a garden before."

"What?"

"I was under pressure. I had to think of something to deter you from work. It was the best I could come up with."

"Ah, I get it. You just love my company so much you had to think of a plan to keep me here."

"Get over yourself, Claire." Kathryn snapped out the words before she could stop herself. She knew Claire was only playing with her.

"Ah, but will *you* get over *me*?"

Until now, it hadn't occurred to Kathryn that she was under Claire, let alone in need of getting over her. What the hell was going on in her head?

"I was only joking. Sorry. No more innocent flirting with the straight girl. I promise."

Kathryn bit her tongue this time and sighed. "I'll prune and weed. You mow and tidy the edges."

"Okay, sounds fair. Will your ankle hold up?"

"Wasn't no mothering the deal?"

"Not at all. You lot aren't to mother *me*, and anyway, I'm a nurse. I'm allowed to ask medical questions."

"My ankle will be fine. I'll alternate between sitting and standing."

"Excellent. We have it sorted." Claire turned to leave before adding, "Maybe we could start early tomorrow then knock off and have drinks in the afternoon. Perhaps a bit of ouzo, slow dancing. Who knows where it could lead."

CHAPTER THIRTEEN

After a mediocre sleep, Claire rose early to run. She missed Kathryn's company, but enjoyed her solitude, pounding the leafy streets of Melbourne. She returned home to what appeared to be an empty house. Jess worked long hours and Alex's shifts were sometimes unpredictable, so they had probably travelled together, but she had no idea where Kathryn might be.

It wasn't until experiencing the calming quiet that Claire realised how much she missed her own space. Moving out of her flat had been more about her dwindling bank balance and less about herself. Now that she was slowly pushing Victoria from her subconscious, she was determined to enjoy these moments alone whenever the opportunity arose.

As much as she loved Jess, her jazz filled iPod provided background music at best. Claire slotted hers into the expensive sound system and turned it up loud.

Within moments of sitting down to eggs, bacon, mushrooms, and spinach, and even over the thumping beat of Sia, Jess came crashing down the stairs.

"Claire! Are you there?"

Claire nearly choked in surprise.

"Claire! Turn that fucking music down."

The moment Jess screamed the words, Claire hit the remote and silence prevailed. "Hey, Madam Crown, don't swear in front of the children."

"The damn children are the problem."

"Really? Not their foul-mouthed mother?"

"I need your help, please." Jess appeared in a bra with a towel wrapped around her lower half.

"Sure, but why aren't you at work?"

"Gyno appointment at ten. So, you'll help?"

"Yeah, where's Alex?"

"I'm meeting her there. Jesus, Claire. Stop asking questions." Jess rolled her eyes in frustration.

"Okay, okay. What can I do for you?"

"Come upstairs with me."

"Why? Is there a spider? You know I hate spiders, Jess. Can't you just throw something at it and I'll clean up the mess?"

"Shut up will you? What's with your onslaught of ridiculous questions?" Frustrated, Jess released the towel. "I haven't had time to go to the salon. I thought I could manage, but this fucking stomach of mine is getting in the way."

Struggling to compose herself, Claire found the sight of Jess half waxed, hilarious.

"I've done okay so far." She was barely convincing herself. "But I can't get a decent grip on the end of this wax strip to yank it off."

"Oh, you poor thing." Claire attempted to smother her laughter.

"I've tried ripping it downward, but it just hurts like hell."

Claire was near hyperventilation. "You're lucky I've seen it all before." She knelt before Jess to get a closer look.

"I'm just glad you're not Kathryn."

"Glad who's not Kathryn?" The voice came first—Claire and Jess snapped their heads up—followed by the body, the look of disgust, and then finally the hysterical yelling.

"Oh, come on. You have to be fucking kidding. You two disgust me!"

Claire shoved the towel at Jess.

"I can't believe I swallowed that bullshit the other night."

"Kathryn—"

"Alex has been gone fifteen minutes and you're at it. And in the kitchen of all places!"

Kathryn looked like her head might explode into a thousand pieces of chopped tomato.

"Kath—"

"You're a fucking liar, Jessica Mercer. How fucking convenient that Victoria moved away and how fucking convenient that Claire needed somewhere to stay."

"Just stop, Kathryn—"

"Do you honestly think fucking her is the answer, you selfish shit?"

Claire briefly wondered when Jess would yell, "Objection, Your Honour."

"Do you think it's funny to ruin the lives of the people you're supposed to care about? Are you deliberately trying to make a whore out of Claire? You make me sick, you do. I'm disgusted you're my sister."

Kathryn stormed from the room.

Jess obviously contemplated going after her, but stalled. "She'll have to wait."

Seconds later, the front door slammed.

"Well, that was fun," said Claire.

"Just get this fucking wax off me, please." Jess trudged upstairs.

Kathryn had slammed the door but remained on the inside.

The vision of Claire kneeling before Jess made her sick. She ran to her bedroom and slumped against the closed door. All she could hear was the blood rushing through her brain but to her great relief, no footsteps.

What in God's name had she just witnessed? Even as the tirade of insults flowed generously from her mouth, the little voice in the back of her mind told her she probably had it wrong. Why hadn't she listened to the voice?

Why had it felt so good to scream at her sister? She shut her eyes tightly but struggled to empty her mind. No, that wasn't it, she realised. Yelling at Jess was not the source of her satisfaction, defending Claire was.

Except now, she was pretty sure she had cocked up in monumental proportions.

She should apologise, she knew that, and she would, but was any excuse good enough?

❖

"Where's the baby oil?" Claire gazed at the neatly organised bathroom cupboard, reluctant to disturb any system Jess might have established.

"How do you know I've even got baby oil?"

"Because I know you."

Jess lay on the bed, the towel covering her. "I'll be late, won't I? It's in the bottom drawer."

"No way. This will only take a second." Claire returned with the oil and some cotton balls. The wax strip had become such a sticky conglomeration, even *she* couldn't get a solid grip. "Okay, let's fix this mess." She frowned. "Well, the wax mess anyway. I'll leave you to deal with the Kathryn mess."

"Don't even mention her name to me right now."

A fire ignited deep within Claire's belly. "You wanna hope you catch her before I do."

"Leave this to me. I'll deal with her. I don't want you in the middle of this, okay?"

"She had no right to talk to you like that."

"No, although I don't see why I copped all the shit. You were the one on your knees."

It was obvious that Kathryn's main target was Jess, but a woman in Jess's condition shouldn't have to put up with being spoken to like that. Claire was angry and disappointed. "She obviously didn't really listen the other night. I don't know who she thinks she is, but after I've had my say—"

"I mean it, Claire. You'll say nothing. Do you understand?"

Claire nodded. She really was a poor judge of character, or perhaps she wrongly took people at face value. She honestly thought Kathryn was a genuinely nice person. They were getting on so well and now it had all fallen apart. How was she ever going to trust her judgment in the future, with future partners, if she couldn't get it right now? "I really want to throttle her."

"Do you even know what that means?"

Claire thought for a second. "No. My mum used to say it. I presume it hurts."

"I'll sort Kathryn out; you just concentrate on tidying up my garden, okay?"

Claire couldn't help smiling. "I just did. One lady garden all spick and span, Madam Crown."

Jess swiped fresh air in an attempt to hit her.

"I bet you get that from your little prosecutor minions all the time."

"Get out."

❖

It was all Claire could do not to march into Kathryn's room, pack her things, and throw her out onto the street. But it wasn't her house, and Kathryn wasn't her sister. Anyway, she hoped to be around for the show when Jess gave her the bollocking of all bollockings. Until that morning, she had found herself beginning to really like Kathryn. She thought they shared a connection, both finding themselves at the dawn of a new era in their lives. And for someone who used to appear neglected and frumpy—dressing like a nun on day release—Kathryn had certainly smartened up. Her looks now matched her witty personality. Claire was disappointed and angry.

❖

The day was set to be sweltering again and Kathryn hadn't yet plucked up the courage to leave her room. Despite it being her idea, she looked on from her bedroom window as Claire began to tackle the garden. The efficiency of Claire's movements indicated she was angry.

Something about Claire sparked Kathryn's innermost protective nature. When she saw how intimate she appeared with Jess almost naked, the feeling of rage she experienced was like nothing else in her life. Even discovering that Andy was sleeping with Diane hadn't provoked as much emotion as seeing Jess and Claire. At ten thirty, Kathryn reluctantly left the confines of her room.

Freshly mowed lawn made an immediate difference, and after the edges were trimmed, Kathryn found Claire resting in the courtyard appearing to admire her handiwork. The iced water in her hand was a peace offering, but faced with the real life consequences of her earlier actions, Kathryn knew it wasn't going to be nearly enough.

As she approached Claire, her eyes became fixated on the sweat dripping down strands of hair not captured under Claire's hat. Her white tank top was almost saturated.

Kathryn cleared her throat. Not to forewarn Claire of her approach, but because she genuinely wasn't convinced she would be able to speak. "I thought you could do with a cold drink. It's getting hot out here." She pushed on even though Claire ignored her. "I'll start the weeding and pruning in the shaded areas and get to the rest later. We have all week."

"I'll get my own drink, thanks."

"There's no need to cut your nose off to spite your face. I've already brought you a drink. Please take it."

Claire turned to her but simply raised her eyebrows.

"Stop being so childish."

"That's the pot calling the kettle black. What was your outburst this morning, if not childish?"

"Can I at least explain?"

"Explain? Don't you mean apologise?"

"Yes, well that, too."

"Excellent. I'm all ears." Claire leaned back.

"I...well...look, can we just go inside, talk like adults?"

"It's a little bit late to want to start behaving like adults now, Kathryn."

"Please? I'm sorry. I can explain, Claire..."

Claire might have said she was ready to hear an explanation, but she certainly wasn't displaying the attributes of someone willing to accept an apology. Her tone grew mocking. "You don't get to speak to me like you did and get away with it. If you truly want to believe I'm fucking your sister, go ahead. You were out of line. Now get out of my sight."

"I'm so sorry." Kathryn was trembling.

"Your apology means shit to me."

Kathryn burst into tears and ran into the house. She knew she'd have to work hard for Claire's forgiveness, but she wasn't quite expecting Claire to be so hostile. For the second time that day, she found herself retreating to her bedroom.

She paced the length of the room. Frantically at first until she slowed down.

Claire's hostility had matched her own. She'd deserved every word of what Claire had said. One of them had to be the bigger person, and to date they had both failed.

She had to face Jess yet. Her day wasn't about to improve any time soon.

❖

Claire stood motionless under a cool shower, allowing the sweat and grime of her morning work to wash down the drain. She reflected on her anger. She'd never spoken like that before to someone she barely knew. The last time she'd lost her temper was when Victoria left, but she'd lost many things that day.

It was only just beginning to sink in how shaken Kathryn had been. *Surely, she deserved it?*

Claire struggled to concentrate during counselling.

Of course, Jean was pleased Jess had managed to convince her that the wisest course of action was to take the full two weeks' leave.

She studied Claire's homework, which Alex had also contributed to, and indicated she was pleased that Claire had such great friends, including Kathryn.

"Yeah, great friend she is." Claire couldn't help herself.

"You'd better explain that one."

"It's nothing."

"I'll be the judge of that."

Claire stalled. She hadn't been prepared to talk about this. "Victoria used to say that Jess treated me like a whore when we were together. Kathryn said Jess was making me into a whore this morning."

"Why do you think Victoria referred to your relationship with Jess in that way?"

"We used to be pretty wild. Jess liked to experiment; we both did. Victoria thought Jess treated me like a fuck buddy, not a proper girlfriend."

"Is that how you felt when you were with Jess?"

"No. Never."

"So when Kathryn used that word this morning, you didn't like it."

"Besides the fact that she was well out of order, no, I didn't like it."

"Did Victoria demean your relationship with Jess?"

"It felt like it. I think she was jealous. She didn't like that we were friends." No matter what, Claire couldn't hate Kathryn. "It's all a jumbled mess in my head."

"Kathryn isn't Victoria."

"I know," said Claire.

"Can you write down what happens this evening when you get home?"

Claire jotted down the homework. "What if I don't want to speak to her?"

"Then that's what you'll write down."

Claire left feeling more confused than when she went in.

Her day wasn't over yet. She trudged to meet Murray in an alley filled with coffee shops near the hospital.

Coffee with Murray was usually all talk of work, often with her amusing twist on even the direst ED situations, but today, coffee with Murray was a consult.

"Give me your hand."

"Sweetheart, we're in public." Claire winked.

Murray cocked her head and reached for Claire's hand, checking her pulse rate. Claire sighed.

"Roll up your sleeve."

"We're in a *café*."

"Well done. You've passed the observation test. Now, roll up your sleeve."

"You don't have to do this. I can tell you my pressure is fine," said Claire.

Murray ignored her, pulled the blood pressure equipment from her bag, along with a stethoscope, and proceeded to take the reading. Onlookers were amused.

"How are you feeling?" Murray sat back and sipped her short black.

"What was the reading?"

"I asked first."

"I'm better. I feel much better. The dreams are different now. I still dream of Victoria, but I'm not trying to kill her anymore. I only used four of the pills and I wanted to come back to work this week."

"So I heard."

"Alex?"

"She called with a heads-up." Murray smiled. "You had no hope of getting back to work this week, my dear."

"And my reading?" Claire asked.

"It's a little high. Something you want to tell me?"

"What was it?"

"Tell me about your day first."

"Jesus, Murray, I've had a shit day, okay? I've just come from a bloody session with Jean and I don't need this from you. A shit day won't give me high blood pressure." She lowered her voice. "Which one of us is the fucking doctor here?"

Murray frowned. "One fifty-eight over ninety."

Shit. "What was it last week?"

"Normal-ish. Still think you're ready to come back to work?" Murray ordered more coffee—decaf for Claire. "You don't realise it, but when you're stressed, you can't handle the things you can normally deal with easily."

Claire was becoming increasingly frustrated. "I know all this, Murray."

"Yes, you know it all professionally, but naturally you aren't relating it to yourself."

"Kathryn and I fought this morning." Claire saw no reason not to discuss that part of her day. "I flew off the handle. I know I'm not ready to go back to work. She was well out of line though."

"Alex mentioned Jess's sister was staying. What was the fight about?"

"It doesn't matter."

"Did you discuss the details with Jean?"

"Yes, I told Jean all about it."

"But you were mad?"

"I went berserk." Claire dropped her head in her hands. Reliving it was awful.

"Classic stress symptom. What do you think you would have normally done?"

Claire thought for a moment, struggling to push past her anger. "Just ignored her I guess. Not bothered with her really."

"But you were fired up? Do you like her?"

"*What?* No. Don't be ridiculous. She's Jess's sister, for Christ sake."

"Calm down, Paddy. I was *trying* to establish if your conflict was a personality clash, not that you have a crush on her. No wonder your blood pressure is up. How many members of the one family do you want to sleep with?"

❖

Crush. As if.

Conveniently forgetting about that morning, she recalled the kiss with Kathryn. *Who am I kidding?* A crush was exactly what it was.

Claire weaved in and out of traffic on her way home, annoyed with Murray *and* the ridiculous situation with Kathryn. Kathryn was consuming her thoughts, and she didn't intend to stop them. She had initially hoped to witness Jess tearing Kathryn apart, but now she just wished the incident hadn't happened. She didn't want it to have been Kathryn that had yelled that morning. She wanted the old Kathryn back, the one she could have a crush on without conflict.

Conflict always left Claire feeling rotten. In this instance she found herself searching for a good reason why Kathryn may have behaved the way she did. Then she began to examine her own behaviour. Yelling at Kathryn and being mean to her in return was out of character. She couldn't hold a grudge forever and she wanted to reconcile with Kathryn, but something inside was stopping her from giving in completely.

Alex was preparing dinner when Claire arrived home. Kathryn was nowhere to be seen. Claire felt exhausted. Apparently, she looked it, too.

"Hey, honey. Rough day?" Alex drew her into a tight hug.

"Apparently, I'm cheating with your wife and we're having oral sex in the kitchen." Claire sighed, nestling further into Alex's neck.

"I know, sweetheart. Are you okay?"

"Yeah, but it was rough sex this morning, you really ought to keep her on a tighter leash."

"What can I say, she likes you that way." Alex held her at arm's length. "Seriously, how are you doing?"

"I'm fine. How was the gyno appointment?"

"Good, thanks. Four arms, four legs. Just the usual."

"Have you seen Kathryn?" Claire washed her hands and selected a knife.

"I have. She's meeting Jess after work—neutral territory for their *discussion*. Plus I think Jess wanted to be in public so she wouldn't get too worked up."

"Oh, okay, probably a good idea."

"Good?" Alex looked wary. "I thought you of all people would want to see the formidable Jess Mercer in action, tearing the well-deserved Kathryn Mercer a brand new one?"

"Maybe. No, not really. Not today?" Claire diced a carrot without even looking at it.

Alex reached across Claire to remove the knife from her hands, eyeing her carefully. "Why?"

"Why what?"

Alex shrugged. "Did everything go okay with Jean?"

"Yep, fine." Claire reached for the knife that Alex moved further beyond her reach.

"And Murray?"

Claire scowled. "You *know* how it went with Murray."

Alex couldn't pretend Murray hadn't phoned her after seeing Claire. "Okay, maybe I know what Murray thinks. But what do you think?"

For a moment, Claire was annoyed. *Why does everyone want to talk about bloody Kathryn all the time?* Thankfully, before she verbalised her frustrations, she realised Alex was referring to work. "Oh, she's right. You're all right. I'm not ready to go back to work."

"And your blood pressure?"

Claire rolled her eyes. "I'll monitor it for the next few days."

Alex laughed. "*I'll* take it, thank you very much. I don't trust you."

Claire snatched the knife and some celery, chopping with precision, her eyes remaining on Alex. "And how exactly is that not mothering me agreement working out for you?"

Alex shrugged.

For a while, Alex and Claire chopped in silence. Claire was seething because her high blood pressure reading was rubbish, taken after a counselling session and in the middle of a busy café. *Damn load of crap.* But it *was* high and she was hoping to be able to chalk it up to a heavy session with Jean. Time would tell.

In a voice slightly higher than usual, Alex asked, "Did you see Kathryn at all today? I mean, other than with Jess this morning."

Claire was annoyed. The pitch of Alex's voice indicated she already knew the answer. "Come on, Alex. I'm not a child. We *are* allowed to have an adult discussion. If there's something you want to ask, then ask it."

"Where are you in your cycle?" Alex's expression was deadpan.

"What the *fuck*?"

Alex marched toward her, took the knife, and dragged her to the bathroom, shoving her in front of the mirror. "Look at yourself." Claire stubbornly eyed the sink plug. "Look!"

Slowly, Claire raised her head and took in her reflection. Her brow was creased, her cheeks bright red, but worst of all, her pupils were dilated and her usually green eyes were a dark, stormy grey.

"This"—Alex stared at Claire's reflection, giving her a shake—"isn't you. What's going on? Are you premenstrual?"

"No." Claire sucked in some deep breaths and gritted her teeth. "I don't know what's gotten into me."

"And you've been sleeping okay?"

"Yes! I already told you that. I'm falling asleep easily, not waking in the night, hardly dreaming, and feeling refreshed when I wake. Jesus, what is this?"

Alex shook her head. "And you just went from zero to ten from the moment I asked that question to the end of your answer."

Claire slumped onto the edge of the bath. "God, Alex. What's wrong with me?"

"Kathryn was really shaken when I came home. She said you'd been pretty harsh with her."

Claire glared, about to defend herself before Alex continued. "She didn't for one second say she didn't deserve it, but she thought you were going to hit her."

"*Hit* her?"

"Murray said you were on edge. Is it the message Victoria left?"

Claire realised, she hadn't given Victoria a single thought. Saturday had been a turning point. But turning where?

❖

Kathryn was nervous about seeing Claire after the events of such a long, testing day. She was nervous to the point of feeling ill.

She and Jess had met for a coffee and resolved their differences after a lengthy discussion. She'd apologised, of course, and had tried to be as honest as possible, but explaining that she was worried for Claire because she thought she was vulnerable sounded silly. She hardly knew Claire. She certainly couldn't explain her need to protect her, and on top of all that, she couldn't say how desperately worried she was that Claire would never speak to her again.

Of course, she apologised near on a million times and although it wasn't a complete lie, she cited a frustrating and disappointing call to her real estate agent as the possible cause of her agitation. It was no excuse, she had assured Jess, but it had contributed. She would make it up to Jess, she promised.

Dinner was prepared and waiting to be served when Jess and

Kathryn arrived home. Jess approached Claire reading the paper. "Go easy on her, eh? It's all fixed from my end. The rest is your choice." She kissed the top of Claire's head, and then she and Alex disappeared upstairs.

Claire wouldn't look at Kathryn as she approached. It was expected, but as long as she listened, she at least had a place to begin reconciliation. Without warning, Claire made a dash for her bedroom.

"Claire..." Kathryn sighed, straightened, and followed her.

Claire rushed down the hall and paused near the front door.

"Don't make me run down the street after you; you know I won't keep up."

Claire diverted to her bedroom.

Kathryn stood in the bedroom doorway. "If you just take a swipe at me now, get it over and done with, will that make you feel better?"

Silence. Claire perched on the edge of the bed fidgeting with the hem on her shorts, staring out the window, her back to Kathryn.

"Jesus, Claire, why won't you even look at me?"

"I don't want to hit you." Claire's voice was barely above a whisper. "I can't believe you think I'm even capable of that."

"I'm sorry, I don't really." She cleared her throat, relieved they were communicating. "Can I come in?"

Claire nodded.

"Jess has forgiven me."

"I know. I'm glad."

"But I don't have your forgiveness, do I?"

Kathryn knelt in front of Claire, gaining her undivided attention. "I can't begin to tell you how sorry I am. I was so out of line, Claire. I've felt sick all day with worry."

Claire finally looked at her.

"I have no excuse. Well, not one I understand yet, but I do know I made a monumental mistake. I know you and Jess aren't having an affair. I'm just so sorry I made you feel bad."

"I don't want you to think of Jess like you do. She's not capable of cheating, not Jess. She loves Alex."

"I know. And I love Jess."

"But the way you spoke to her, it was awful."

Kathryn wasn't sure if she could explain any of it in further detail, but Claire was engaging with her; she couldn't shut the conversation down now. "I behaved appallingly. I'm ashamed. I guess after seeing you the other day at your place, I know how vulnerable you are. I don't want you to hurt anymore." Kathryn inhaled deeply. She'd left her comfort zone and was winging it now.

"So if Jess and I were sleeping together, it's Jess's fault because she should know better and because I'm vulnerable right now?"

"Well, you should both know better, but I can't see that sleeping with Jess would be helpful right now, no."

"I can look after myself, you know. You don't have to protect me, least not from Jess."

"I know that now, but please realise that although the outcome was a disaster, I honestly was trying to look out for you."

"You called me a whore."

"No, I didn't. I would never do that, but I used the word, and I accept that what I said had the same effect. I'm so very sorry, Claire."

"Victoria used to say that Jess treated me like a whore."

"Ah, Jesus, Claire." Kathryn took Claire's hand. "I was an idiot. Please don't think I'm like Victoria. I'm not like her at all. I truly was only trying to look out for you."

Claire grinned crookedly. "Maybe don't look out for me anymore."

She knew it was a joke, but it hurt a little. "How about I just do it better next time?"

"You think there'll be a next time?"

"I don't think you pick and choose who you like to look out for. I think that just happens. One day I'll look out for you so good, you'll wonder why you ever doubted me."

"Then okay," said Claire.

Kathryn dropped her head. "Phew. Friends again?"

"Sure. Plus I'm sorry, too. I don't know what got into me in the garden."

"I got into you…"

Claire smiled fully this time.

So did Kathryn. "Okay, bad choice of words. So can we please go back to the way we were?" She laughed. "I didn't even beg Andy this much."

Claire nodded, and as soon as she smiled, Kathryn wrapped her arms tightly around her.

Kathryn couldn't be sure, but she thought she felt Claire inhale deeply. She certainly felt her relax into the crook of her neck and the arm that encircled her waist was holding her solidly, not the half-hearted embrace you'd expect from someone who only minutes ago wasn't speaking to you.

Kathryn's world appeared to have shifted on its axis. She briefly wondered if Claire felt the same.

CHAPTER FOURTEEN

Y ou're not really homophobic, are you?" asked Claire.
She and Kathryn were relaxing on a picnic blanket under
the shade of the willow tree. The garden was looking fantastic and
Kathryn sat using her laptop to update her résumé. Claire was just
being lazy reading *Rolling Stone.*

"What? You should warn someone first before you ask an
insulting question like that."

Kathryn was wearing glasses. Claire noticed she only wore them
reading for long periods or when she was using the computer. They
suited her. They especially suited her when she looked over the top,
exactly as she was doing now.

"Well, you'd hardly want to live in a house with three lesbians if
you actually were homophobic, surely?"

"I like living with you all. While I was married, I always
imagined I'd much prefer to be living with a woman. In fact, I quite
fancied the idea of living in a commune for a while."

"I suppose you are old enough to be of that hippie era."

Claire ducked an attempted clip around the ears.

"I watched *The L Word* and *Queer as Folk.*"

"Wow, well you're practically gay then."

Kathryn shoved Claire this time. "Let me finish. I think growing
up I was Jessophobic."

"I can't wait to hear this."

"I think I just got tired of being compared to my younger sister. It came as a shock when she became the golden child. I'd had that title and it was taken from me and given to her."

"But you were a child," said Claire.

"Yes, I'm explaining how this all came about if you'd shut up." Kathryn waited a moment. "When Jess came out as a lesbian, I was fifteen. She was thirteen and so damn sure of herself. It was the one thing I knew my parents weren't over the fucking moon about and I played on it. I was living in the shadow of my younger sister and at last I had some ammunition."

"But you don't think there's anything wrong with being gay?"

"Of course not," said Kathryn. "Although, I admit I don't have any gay friends that I know of, except you now, so my opinions have probably been a little tainted by Shane from *The L Word*."

"Shane? Why her?"

"Well, even this boring old accountant can tell she's hot."

Claire couldn't argue with that.

Kathryn put the computer down. "Will you read through this later, make sure I've not made any glaring errors?"

Claire nodded and put down the magazine. She was ready for a snooze.

"Would you like me to read to you?"

"Pardon?"

"Sorry, that's an odd thing to ask, isn't it? I'll just read to myself if you don't mind. Forget I mentioned it." Kathryn opened the magazine.

"No, I'd love you to read to me. I used to ask Victoria to share what she was reading all the time, but she never did, something about it being *her* time in *her* head." Claire boldly rested her head in Kathryn's lap. "Please, go ahead." She closed her eyes.

Kathryn began reading an article on Mumford & Sons. Claire was interested, but by the third or fourth paragraph, the words began to jumble in her ears, and when Kathryn rested her warm hand on Claire's shoulder, her mind began to wander somewhere else altogether. She loved that feeling only moments before sleep, and she realised she loved it even better with her body close to Kathryn. Kathryn's soft voice filled her ears, but she couldn't distinguish the words. Who needed words? Claire let the floating sensation of sleep begin to take her. She let her body sink into the blanket on the grass, her head deeper into Kathryn's lap, and her mind deeper toward sleep.

It was just like old times with Jess.

Jess?

Holy shit!

Claire sat bolt upright and the magazine poked her in the eye on the way through.

"Are you okay?" Kathryn asked.

Claire had long since been over her feelings for Jess, but this was Kathryn, not Jess. She shook her head. Nope, the feeling of attraction lingered.

It's Kathryn!

It dawned on her that perhaps Murray was only half right. Yes, Kathryn was the object of her attraction, but it was nothing like a little crush, it was full blown attraction. She was comparing Kathryn to Jess. She was a goner.

"I'm fine, but I just remembered I have to do something." Claire dashed inside and directly into a cold shower.

CHAPTER FIFTEEN

It was becoming a ritual now. Kathryn hated the word habit. It conjured up images of white powder and a runny nose, but the last thing she would do before sleep was to replay the video of her and Claire dancing. Every night.

Claire was drunk and delirious from sleep deprivation, but it couldn't take anything away from their closeness in stance and the tenderness in Claire's voice and actions. However, it wasn't Claire that shocked her the most; it was the sight of herself allowing the exchange to happen. Hundreds of times, she watched the clip to see if she flinched just once, if she looked at all uncomfortable, or if her body portrayed even the tiniest hint of displeasure. Nothing. Finally, she had to admit she liked looking at herself touching Claire and she liked Claire touching her.

Of course, it was just a silly little infatuation that would pass in no time at all, but she was conflicted. Should she enjoy the feeling while it lasted, or fight it? In those last few minutes before sleep, she chose to watch the video and enjoy every moment.

After the seventh run-through, she put her phone down and turned over, curling into a small ball. Her mind filled with thoughts of Claire. It made her smile. Claire made her smile. She was a genuinely nice person, a funny person. She knew exactly what Jess had seen in her.

Kathryn had delayed sleep for so long now, she needed to go to the toilet again. Dressed in only a long tank top, she tiptoed down the hall.

"Can't sleep either?" Claire's loud whisper made her jump.

"You frightened the life out of me." She self-consciously tugged at the hem of her top.

"It's too hot to sleep, isn't it?" Claire's old T-shirt barely covered her, and she caught Kathryn looking. "I don't sleep in this grotty thing. It's just to protect your modestly if you see me going to the loo."

"My modesty?"

"Yeah, I don't want to embarrass you."

"Me?"

"I'm playing with you."

Kathryn caught up. "You'd think I'd be used to this kind of heat. I often used to cool down with a swim before bed. Jess and Alex should really consider a pool, you know."

"I think Alex's love for the big willow tree might be the issue with that. Did you actually swim or just take a dip?"

"A dip mostly," said Kathryn.

"A skinny dip?"

Kathryn nearly choked on her laugh. "Have you forgotten our conversation about Andy?"

"Oh yeah, that's right. Have you ever been skinny dipping?"

"Only my top half and only once."

"Would you consider doing it again?" asked Claire.

"In what? The bath?"

"I'm game if you are."

Kathryn blushed but thankfully, the dull light wouldn't give that away. "I'll leave you to your bath." Kathryn returned to her bedroom.

"Hey." Claire stood in her doorway. "I know a place we can skinny dip. It's about five minutes' walk from here, but you have to be real quiet."

Kathryn's interest momentarily piqued. "I suppose we'll be breaking in?"

"Let's just say we don't exactly have an invitation. Come on, trust me on this. It'll be fun."

"You want me to come with you to a pool, break in, skinny dip, and then come home?"

"Got it in one." Claire threw a pair of shorts at her from the cupboard. "You chicken?"

The old Kathryn would have thrown the shorts back and promptly retreated to bed, but the new Kathryn pulled up the shorts and slipped on her running shoes. "Flip-flops will be too noisy."

"That's my girl."

At eleven twenty-eight, Kathryn and Claire slipped out the front door and headed toward the local swimming pool. She hadn't been a part of anything this adventurous since the time she slipped out in the middle of the night to meet Andy and her friends at a bonfire. She'd been seventeen. Running through the streets in the middle of the night would have given her a buzz except her ankle was still rather tender. She pretended her hurried hobble had the same effect.

They arrived at the pool and Claire looked decidedly chuffed with herself.

"Okay, Sherlock, how do we get in?" asked Kathryn.

Claire took Kathryn's hand and led her up the far side fence behind a thick hedge. She stopped in front of a huge pylon. When Kathryn looked up, she realised the pylon was providing support for a low section of the waterslide that jutted out over the fence. In fact, the fence had been lowered to accommodate the slide.

"The idiots measured it wrong, but because it's a council pool and this adjacent land is council parkland, they just left it on the outside of the fence," said Claire.

"Do I look like a monkey or a pole dancer who can climb that?"

Claire pushed her between the fence and pylon. "It's a good foot or two lower than the actual fence. Trust me, it's easy."

Kathryn surveyed the area. All she could see at the top of the fence was barbed wire. "Um, I just like having the one arsehole, thanks very much. That wire will cut us in two."

"Have faith." In a swift motion, Claire used the rivets on the pylon to launch herself upward. Within seconds, she was gone.

"Where the hell did you go?" Kathryn hissed toward the fence hoping Claire was on the other side.

"Just do what I did. There's no barbed wire under the slide where it goes over the fence. It doesn't look like there's enough room, but there is."

Kathryn cursed, and if she had the space, she would have paced back and forth mulling over the decision.

"Come on," said Claire. "Put your good foot up first, grab the top of the fence, and haul yourself over."

"Oh, for fuck's sake." Kathryn launched herself exactly as Claire had. Convinced she would knock herself out on the underside of the slide or rip herself to shreds on the barbed wire, she held her breath and hoped for the best. The top half of her body slipped under the slide with ease, but her legs dangled down and her middle hurt with the fence poking into it.

"You're supposed to do it all at once, not stop halfway," said Claire.

"Tell that to my sprained ankle and my poor old body."

It looked about as elegant as a hippo in the ballet, but Kathryn pulled her legs up and scrambled down the other side. "Ouch!"

Claire was laughing too much to be of any real help.

"This is breaking and entering, you know." Claire was walking off. "I doubt the police will just have a laugh with us and send us home when we get caught." She followed Claire. "I can't believe you talked me into this." Claire rounded the corner and was out of sight. "I've managed to make it to nearly forty without a criminal—"

Kathryn stopped in her tracks. Claire stood on the edge of the pool naked.

"Well? Your turn."

Kathryn gulped.

"We're just two friends going for a swim. What's there to be afraid of?"

"You have an amazing body." Kathryn couldn't help staring.

"Thank you. But it's all feeling a little one-sided right now." Claire eyed her. "Come on, get your kit off."

Kathryn hesitated. She wasn't sure she could do this, and the fact that she couldn't take her eyes off Claire was disturbing.

Claire stepped toward her. "You have a beautiful body. You have nothing to be ashamed of."

Kathryn froze.

"Is it the fact that I'm a lesbian? Because you don't have to worry about that, I see naked people all the time. We're just two girls who deserve a bit of fun in our lives, right?"

"Don't watch then." Kathryn found her voice. The urge to do

this with Claire somehow overtook her urge to flee. Facing Claire's back, she undressed then placed her hand over Claire's eyes. Together they stepped to the edge of the water. "Keep them shut until I'm in."

Claire nodded.

Kathryn slipped into the water before the desire to push her naked body against Claire's overwhelmed her. "It's beautiful." The sensation of the tepid water flowing over every part of her body was exhilarating. She watched Claire quietly glide into the water and submerge.

For many moments, Claire remained unseen before breaking the water directly in front of Kathryn. "Worth it?"

"Yes, it's worth it." They swam around each other. "I haven't felt like this in years."

"You know what? Neither have I."

The information shocked Kathryn. She imagined someone like Claire led a highly exciting and adventurous life.

"What shall we do next, then?" Kathryn was suddenly full of adventure. "Bungee jumping, skydiving, scuba diving? I've always wanted to scuba dive," Kathryn said.

"What about some of life's other bucket list items?"

"Like what?"

"Like the more accessible things," said Claire.

"Oh, you mean like making a cake mixture and eating it all before you bake it. I always wanted to do that as a child."

"Not so much."

"I know, staying up all night eating junk food and watching movies from the eighties?"

Claire sighed in frustration. "How about kissing a girl?"

"What?" Kathryn forgot to keep treading water and swallowed a gulp of chlorinated pool water as she sunk.

"It's just a thought."

"But we already kissed."

Claire looked wild with mischief. "That's not the type of kiss I'm suggesting."

"Are you serious?" Kathryn had no idea what to do, especially because the thought of kissing Claire wasn't altogether appalling. "Plus, you've kissed loads of girls. Is this my bucket list or yours?"

"*Is* kissing a girl on your bucket list?"

Kathryn didn't have a bucket list. She tried to think of a few things that she might include on it and if kissing a girl was one of them. It might not have been a week or so ago, but it probably was now. "Yeah, I guess it is."

"Then I can help you with that."

"Are you always this smooth with the ladies? How many times has this line worked for you?"

Claire looked a little hurt. "None, actually. I just feel…"

Kathryn swam toward her. "What. You just feel what?"

Claire disappeared under the water and burst through like a mutant dolphin metres away. "I feel like we should have brought a towel."

"Claire," said Kathryn as Claire disappeared again. "Claire."

Claire emerged close by. "I feel like the door is open when I'm with you. I know we'll only ever be friends, but with you I feel like I can step outside again and outside is the entire world."

Kathryn shouldn't have been surprised to realise she felt the same. Yet she was. Her eyes remained firmly on Claire's. "And about that kiss?"

Claire smiled. "It's just for your bucket list, right?"

"Right." Kathryn had no idea exactly what it was for; she just knew she wanted it.

"Tongues?" asked Claire.

"Might as well."

Before she had time to process anything, Claire swam toward her, placed her hand behind Kathryn's neck, and allowed their lips to meet gently. She daren't touch Claire, they were naked after all and her courage only extended so far. Within moments, she felt Claire's tongue enter her mouth only slightly before the kiss ended and she pulled away. Again, Claire disappeared under the water.

Kathryn swam directly to the side of the pool, arriving before Claire's head bobbed up. She was breathless and electrified all over. *What the hell just happened?*

"One more tick for the bucket list."

Kathryn tried to act cool. "Yep, ticked that big, bad baby right off the list."

Claire laughed. "Come on. We should probably head back now."

They dressed and left the pool in silence. After what had just happened, even the fence climb proved a minor obstruction. Suddenly, Kathryn was invincible.

Somewhere, in the recess of her mind, Kathryn's new invincibility would be her downfall, but for now, she loved the feeling.

CHAPTER SIXTEEN

The following Monday morning, Claire and Kathryn sat waiting for Claire's scheduled appointment with Murray. Thankfully, this time it was in her office, not a café.

Since her bold move at the pool, Claire had taken a less candid approach with Kathryn. She really wanted to be friends, and although she was only half joking about the kiss, she realised it could have backfired and Kathryn could have told her to fuck off. She couldn't put her finger on it, but something in Claire wanted to challenge Kathryn. She wanted to open her eyes to all the possibilities in the world, and since she believed it was Kathryn who was providing her with the same motivation, she was keen to repay the favour.

She had been selfish suggesting the kiss; she was at least being honest about that. She suggested it because it was exactly what she had wanted to do at the time. She hadn't recalled feeling so audacious since high school. The heady flitter in her stomach and the almost drunk-like sensation of courage left her saying things she only ever dreamed of saying. That night she had lived in the moment and she loved it. Everything with Victoria had been pre-planned and scheduled, never spontaneous.

The way Kathryn looked at her naked was a heart breaker. If she were being honest, she hadn't really believed Kathryn would want to leave the house at near midnight and break into the local swimming pool. She never once imagined they would kiss, not until it happened. The difficult part now was keeping her feelings in check. Kathryn was

Jess's sister, and she was out of bounds for anything other than their little midnight adventure. Flirting, on the other hand, was allowed. It was safe and wouldn't go any further. It certainly made her time off interesting.

Alex had taken Claire's blood pressure twice daily, and by Thursday evening, it had returned to normal. Even with the heat fluctuation and storms almost nightly, she and Kathryn worked all week to bring the garden back to its former glory. Thoughts of Victoria rarely entered Claire's mind since the dreams had stopped. Uncomfortable memories rarely surfaced, and she used the coping mechanisms Jean taught her to move forward.

Kathryn poked around Murray's stuff. "What are these used for?" She held aloft a long, slender, stainless steel set of forceps.

"Pap smears."

"Ew, really?" Kathryn quickly replaced them, wiping her hands down her smart khaki pants.

Claire didn't feel inclined to tell her they were just your normal, everyday forceps, and while Kathryn scanned the spines of the medical books on Murray's shelf, Claire found herself taking in the view.

Kathryn's sleeveless navy polo shirt was plain, but coupled with the pants and a pair of flip-flops, not to mention her dark, flowing hair, Claire liked her style.

Her eyes were focusing on Kathryn's backside when Murray charged into the room.

Very little slipped past Murray, and in the split second it took Claire to pull her gaze away from Kathryn, she knew Murray had seen exactly where her eyes were focused. "Hi, I'm Murray. You must be Kathryn."

Kathryn nodded and gripped Murray's outstretched hand. "Lovely to meet you, Murray."

"I hear you've been keeping an eye on my best ED nurse?"

Kathryn smiled warmly at Claire. "It's a hard job, but someone has to do it."

Murray grinned and turned her attention to Claire. "Righto, Paddy, off with your top and on the table."

Claire pulled her T-shirt over her head.

Kathryn rushed for the door, her eyes lowered. "I'll leave you two to it then." She disappeared.

Claire grinned and stripped off her top. "Do you enjoy ordering me to take my clothes off?"

"Maybe." Murray busied herself with the blood pressure sleeve. "What do you care?"

A quick and fruitless poke of Claire's glands justified the topless examination, and with the news that her blood pressure, pulse, and temperature were normal, Claire felt a little deflated. She was pleased everything was back to normal, but she had lost any urgency to return to work.

"How old is Kathryn?" Murray made notes on her computer.

"What?"

"Simple question, Paddy. How old is she?"

Claire calculated for a moment. "Thirty-nine, I think. Why?"

"Just curious. Your eyes were all over her arse when I walked in."

"What?"

"Look me in the eye and tell me they weren't."

"I'm *gay*, Murray. I perv on women all the time. I perv on *your* arse all the time. What's the big deal?"

"You do?"

"Of course. You're hot. What's not to perv on?"

"Should we sleep together and see what happens?" Murray's expression gave nothing away.

"I beg your pardon?"

"You heard. Should we?"

"No, of course not. I like looking at you, but you're a straight, married woman. I don't think I like you like that."

"Good. Wanna sleep with Kathryn?"

Claire's eyes nearly popped out of her head. "She's my ex-lover's sister, for Christ sake."

"I didn't ask you that."

"And she's also married *and* straight."

"Again, not the question I asked."

"We had a misunderstanding a week ago."

"Still nothing to do with my question."

"Are you insane?"

"Are you interested?"

"No."

"Yes."

Claire slumped into the chair. "Whatever."

"Look." Murray sat opposite, resting her hand on Claire's knee. "I don't want to tell you what to do or how to feel, but not so long ago you were in the midst of a breakdown, and if you wanna get laid, Claire, perhaps Jess's straight, older sister isn't the best option. And before you interrupt"—Murray raised her finger to hush any input— "I saw how she looked at you. You shouldn't mess with this, Claire. Not now. Not yet."

"How did she look at me?" Had she missed something?

"You really don't know?"

Claire shrugged.

"Just leave it, Paddy. I'm warning you."

Claire found Kathryn in the ward waiting room. She was sitting between an obese man with a worried expression and a young girl with her eyes fixated on her mobile phone. Her relief at Claire's arrival was palpable.

"So." Kathryn slung an arm around Claire's shoulders. "All good to get back to work tomorrow?"

"Yep." Claire felt an urge to numb her senses. "Let's celebrate with a drink."

"I've got an idea." Kathryn's hand slipped down to Claire's waist. "Let's head home, call into the deli, grab a wine, and I'll make you lunch."

It was a good idea because Claire was driving and it was hardly fair to expect one of them to miss out.

The drive home was subdued. Playing repeatedly in Claire's mind was Murray's warning. She had it under control, and regardless, Kathryn wasn't interested in her.

"Hey, what's up?" Kathryn had been watching her for a while now.

Claire pulled into the local Italian deli and switched off the engine. "Nothing. Just thinking about work I guess."

Kathryn eyed Claire. "Would you like to talk about it?"

"Not really."

"You don't really want to talk about work, or you don't want to talk about what's really bothering you?"

"Will you be offended if I say both?"

"Of course not. Will you be offended if I ask you again later? Just in case you want to talk then?"

The pressure that had been building behind Claire's eyes began to dissipate. "I'm fine, honestly, but sure, you can ask."

"Great. Just that question or can I ask others?" Kathryn exited the car in the direction of the deli, followed by Claire in the direction of the bottle shop.

"Do you have other questions on your mind?"

"Maybe." Kathryn shrugged.

"Then maybe you should ask them."

❖

Lunch was a smorgasbord of salads, fresh focaccia, olives, cheese, and wine.

Claire spread full length on the couch, relaxed and content thanks to the two empty wine bottles on the bench. A warm breeze whispered through the huge screen door, and Kathryn, flushed from the wine, leant against the couch marvelling at the music collection on Claire's iPod.

"I've never heard of half this stuff."

"But do you like it?"

"I do. It's a treat to find out what's coming next."

They remained silent for some time, listening to Claire's music.

"Let's play a game." Claire sat bolt upright, clocking Kathryn in the back of the head with her knee. "Shit. Sorry." She roughly rubbed it better.

"What sort of game?" Kathryn sounded wary, but Claire was already in the kitchen. "Claire?"

Claire returned to the lounge with two shot glasses and another bottle of wine.

"Oh, no. No way." Kathryn shook her head. "There's no way we're doing this."

"Come on, *old* girl." Claire knelt near Kathryn and playfully rubbed her shoulder. "What's the matter? Can't keep up with the young ones?"

Kathryn took Claire's chin in her hand. "Name the game, you little smart-arse."

"Okay." Claire winked. "Here's the deal. I play my eighties playlist. Random, of course, and you get a five-second head start to name the song. You name the song, I shoot the wine. If I name the song after that, you shoot. If I can't name it, then we're both back in, okay?"

"We're going to shoot perfectly good wine?"

"Yep. You scared?"

"I've seen you drunk on a drop of ouzo. The only thing I'm afraid of is you passing out."

"You know I'll get you up dancing before the afternoon is over," Claire threatened.

"And *you* know what happened last time." Kathryn's look was unreadable.

"Well, we're not at the pool ticking things off your bucket list, so I think we'll be safe," said Claire.

Kathryn smiled. It was a million dollar smile, and it nearly knocked Claire over. "I know you like to kiss me, but you've run out of tricks to make it happen."

Claire hesitated. It was a little bit true.

"Not such a little smart-arse now, are we?" Kathryn winked.

Claire refused to meet her gaze and busied herself filling the shot glasses before selecting her four-hundred-song strong Classic 80s playlist. She didn't want the conversation about the kiss to be over, but she didn't know what else to say. Kathryn fixed that.

"It's all right." Kathryn reached to cover Claire's hand with hers. "It was nice. I know it wasn't one of *those* kisses, but I've never been properly kissed by a woman before."

Except, it *was* one of those kisses, and nothing she could do would alter the fact that she wanted to do it again. The urge was often overwhelming, and the one annoying thing that flashed before her eyes every time she thought of it was the vision of Murray warning her off.

"A shot to begin." She held her glass aloft, so did Kathryn, and the wine slipped down. "Let the games begin."

Within twenty minutes, Claire on five shots and Kathryn on only two, it was becoming clear that Kathryn had spent a significant amount of time listening to the radio in the eighties. She guessed most songs immediately, with many others often on the cusp of five seconds. They spent considerable time arguing about who should shoot when they named songs simultaneously.

Inevitably, Claire pleaded with Kathryn to alter the rules. "Ah, c'mon, I'll be drunk soon. You don't *need* a five-second head start."

Another song began and Kathryn guessed it. "Shoot it down, baby!"

"You're a cruel woman."

"Aw, poor little smart-arse Claire, you're all cute when you're sulking." Kathryn clearly loved every second of gaining the upper hand. "Perhaps if you beg me, I'll reconsider."

"You wish." Claire manned up and took the shot. "I only beg for one thing, Kathryn, and I'm pretty sure I won't get that from you."

"Try me." Kathryn's voice was low and laced with intent, her gaze intense and unwavering.

Something in Claire snapped. She possessed courage beyond her capabilities now, and she leaned into Kathryn, dangerously close, before offering up her challenge, her words as clear and deliberate as she could manage. "Let me get this straight. You want me to beg you to make me come?"

Silence.

The iPod remained paused. Claire stared into Kathryn's eyes. Kathryn looked stunned to hear the words. After what felt like a year, Claire smiled, shook her head, and turned away.

"Uh-uh." Kathryn grabbed the neck of Claire's T-shirt. "Don't you dare say that and turn away from me." She roughly pulled Claire to her and their lips met.

At first, Claire was stunned, but Kathryn's urgency was addictive. The kiss continued chaotically, lacking synchronisation, and their teeth clashed more than once, bringing Claire to her senses.

She pulled away, breathless. "Kathryn, what are you doing? What are *we* doing?"

"You seemed to think it was okay at the pool."

A heady haze of arousal clouded Claire's mind. "We're not at the pool now."

Kathryn was leaning against the couch, and her smile melted Claire, who sat astride her. "So, this is all on your terms, is it?"

"Jesus." Claire pulled away, overcome with a wave of nausea.

"Hang on." Kathryn looped her fingers inside Claire's jeans pockets and pulled her down, her voice soft and gentle. "What's the matter?"

Claire remained speechless. This shouldn't happen.

"Look," said Kathryn, stroking Claire's cheek. "I can't name what I feel for you, and I don't particularly want to try. I know what I want, and right now that's you." She sighed. "I'm losing my battle here, Claire. You know I've never been with a woman, and I'll probably be crap at it, and while I'm being honest, I'm happy to admit I'm shit scared. But I'm going completely insane with all this flirting and innuendo. The first time I allowed myself to think of you and me in bed was the last time I remember my head not being mushy."

The soft, almost non-existent stroking on her cheek was drawing Claire in. She was thinking with her groin, and she needed something to dissolve every trace of the last four years of her life. Kathryn's admission was all the permission she needed.

She stood.

Kathryn looked mortified. "Claire, just think about it. Can we really go on like this?"

Claire held out her hand. "No, we can't. Let's fix this right now."

She hauled Kathryn to her feet, grabbed the remaining wine, and led her to her bedroom. The long walk down the passageway felt like forever.

❖

Shaking with desire, Kathryn watched Claire shut and lock the door before drawing the curtains halfway.

"You don't want to close them all the way?" Her voice was barely a crackle.

"I'd prefer to see what I'm doing, thanks."

Kathryn wasn't sure she did, but left it up to Claire's better judgement.

Claire was taking charge now. From this point on, Kathryn only vaguely knew what would happen. It was up to Claire to fill in the blanks.

"Come here."

Timidly, Kathryn moved to within inches of Claire. She was frightened about what was going to happen but not frightened enough to stop it.

"Closer," said Claire.

Kathryn had never been moved by anything Andy had said to her, sexual or not, but to hear Claire simply speak the word "closer" sent waves of arousal through her core.

Kathryn edged closer, her gaze never faltering from Claire's darkened, lust filled eyes, and their bodies touched with an electrifying jolt.

"Close enough for you, Nurse?" Kathryn's breathing was heavy and uneven.

Achingly slow, Claire stood on tippy toes and kissed her, almost innocently at first, before gently pushing the tip of her tongue into Kathryn's willing mouth. Kathryn moaned softly, encouraging Claire, who pushed her tongue deeper.

She fought the desire to rip her clothes off so Claire could be quick; she wasn't sure she needed a slow and sexy build-up. She already felt like she was about to explode, any more build-up and things might get messy.

"Do you want me to stop?" Claire asked.

Kathryn shook her head and Claire took her face in both hands, pulling back from the kiss. "This ends anytime you want, okay?"

Kathryn nodded, inhaling deeply.

"You're beautiful and I want you. Trust me, that's all you need to know right now. Just relax and let me do all the work."

Kathryn's head lowered. "That's what Andy used to say."

Claire reached for Kathryn's chin, raising it until their eyes met. "I'm not Andy, and right now my focus is getting you naked and getting you off."

"You have such a way with words."

Claire gently kissed her, tugging at her bottom lip, her hands finding bare flesh for the first time under Kathryn's top. "True. Now, let me have my way with *you*."

Their kiss intensified, and she found herself touching Claire all over. Even through clothing, touching another woman's breasts was incredible, and Claire's hardening nipples sent shockwaves directly to her clit. It had never occurred to Kathryn that a woman could react that way to her touch. Andy certainly hadn't. She slid her hands down Claire's back and forcefully grasped Claire's toned backside. It was delicious. Every squeeze left Claire moaning for more, and it was Claire's desire that fed hers. To have a woman's tongue hungrily filling her mouth was becoming unbearable. She wanted more.

"Jesus," panted Kathryn.

Claire grasped the hair at the back of Kathryn's neck and forced their lips together again. Kathryn opened for her, and the kiss was intense, addictive, like an illicit drug.

Kathryn pulled back. "I'm gonna start begging sooner rather than later."

Claire smiled as she tugged at Kathryn's top, forcing her to raise her arms to remove it. "You don't need to beg me. I'll satisfy you, I promise. But it'll be nice and slow." Claire unzipped Kathryn's pants and slipped her hand briefly inside, sinking low where her wetness seeped through her G-string.

Kathryn's legs gave way and she stumbled back onto the bed. "If you touch me like that again, you won't get a chance to go slow."

Claire laughed. "Maybe not the first time, but we've got all afternoon."

Claire yanked the bottom of Kathryn's pants and pulled them off. Kathryn lay uncovered in a simple black bra and matching G-string.

"I'm terrified, Claire," she blurted, feeling exposed and vulnerable. "Look at you, you're an expert. I won't be able to do this for you."

Claire removed her own top and jeans and stood by Kathryn. She took Kathryn's hand and pushed it inside her tight white boxers, forcing her to feel her wetness. "See? You're already doing it for me."

"I did that?"

"God, yes. You have no idea how sexy you are, do you?"

Claire allowed Kathryn's fingers to explore for another moment before tugging her hand away. "There are no rules, Kathryn." Claire joined her on the bed.

They kissed again, this time their soft lips met in perfect rhythm.

"Don't we need things?" asked Kathryn.

Claire shifted her weight onto her, positioning a leg between hers. She seductively kissed toward her ear.

"Claire, don't we need something?"

"Like what?"

"I don't know, like a dildo or vibrator or something?"

Claire nipped her earlobe, forcing her thigh snugly into Kathryn's groin. "You want to replace Andy's real dick with a plastic one?"

The pressure between her legs was excruciating. Kathryn gasped. "No. Yes. I don't know. Do I?"

Claire looked Kathryn in the eye. "I have everything you need right here." Without breaking eye contact, Claire plunged her hand down Kathryn's pants, parted her wetness, and entered her deeply, only once, before withdrawing again.

"Fucking hell." Kathryn's breathing laboured as her body jerked. "Yep, I think you have everything I need."

"I thought so. Now be a good girl and lie back and let me give it to you."

Kathryn closed her eyes and relaxed. Her fear remained as Claire rose above her, but it was impossible to compete with the overwhelming arousal she was experiencing. She let Claire slide her hands behind her back and release her bra clasp. Her eyes opened briefly to witness Claire's smile at the sight of her breasts. *I can't believe that you want me.* Andy had once mentioned she would look good with implants, but when she flatly refused, he began treating her breasts with indifference. In contrast, Claire began paying them close attention, and her nipples responded favourably. Kathryn closed her eyes again as Claire lowered her head, her tongue flicking out to lightly brush her tingling left nipple—Kathryn groaned—then her right. In a complete state of wanting, she arched forward and delved her hands into Claire's hair, gripping her tightly and pushing her open mouth over her breasts.

"Claire, I think I'm gonna pass out if you keep doing this so slowly."

Claire winked, releasing a nipple to speak. "I'm a nurse. If you pass out I'll know exactly what to do to bring you round."

Kathryn writhed as Claire reached to stroke her inner thigh. Her breathing was shallow and disjointed. "I get the feeling that what you're delaying doing to me is the same as what you'll do to me to bring me back." She drew a sharp breath as Claire's fingers danced lightly over her underwear. "Claire!"

"Open your eyes," said Claire.

"Please, Claire. Just do it." Kathryn's body had already gone where Andy could never take it. She needed release.

"Open your eyes, baby."

Kathryn obeyed, unable to control her writhing body. She clawed at Claire's bra until she exposed a breast and groped for it. Claire removed her bra, and Kathryn cupped modest breasts in her hands. "God, you're exquisite." Completely astounded that the perfect breasts of another woman could elicit such powerful sensations in her already throbbing clit, Kathryn toyed with Claire's delicate nipples for as long as she was allowed.

Claire grinned before kissing the pulse throbbing in Kathryn's neck. Kathryn exhaled in relief as she watched Claire turn her attention southward, over each breast, down the entire length of her stomach to the top of her pants, never once breaking eye contact. She pushed Kathryn's G-string over her knees, and Kathryn did the rest, kicking it off.

What followed was something Kathryn would never forget. Claire kissed up her inner thigh, slowly and deliberately toward the centre of Kathryn's passion as her fingers brushed over the tiny patch of trimmed hair.

"Please, Claire," Kathryn cried, arching her back and thrusting her pelvis. "God, I can't take this."

"Ask for it." Claire flicked Kathryn's clit with her tongue.

"What?" Kathryn pushed up on her elbows, flinging her head back as Claire's tongue circled her full and wanting clitoris.

"Ask me. Whatever it is you want, just ask." Claire's index finger played with Kathryn's dripping wet opening.

Kathryn wasn't sure what she wanted. She wanted it all—Claire's fingers, her tongue, she wanted to come. Suddenly, she knew what to ask for. "Fuck me please. Every way you can, please just fuck me. I'm begging you."

Claire smiled and did exactly what was asked of her.

Within seconds, Kathryn felt the pressure climb to an extreme oxygen-lacking height as Claire's tongue slid deep inside her. The rush of warmth and passion exploded in every cell of her body. She clutched Claire's head and pressed it to her while her entire body convulsed in pleasure.

It took a long time for Kathryn to float back to earth from her orgasm. When Claire slowly entered her again, she let out a long moan. "God, where have you been all my life?"

"Well, when you were twenty-four, I was still underage."

"Were you doing this when you were fifteen?" Kathryn could hardly breathe, let alone talk.

"Not with anyone half as sexy as you. Now hush. I haven't finished." Claire's tongue pressed firmly on Kathryn's clit.

"Jesus Christ." Kathryn spread her legs wider.

Kathryn returned to the edge within seconds, relishing a G-spot she never knew she had.

"Let it out," said Claire.

Kathryn fought to hold on.

"We can do this all afternoon. Come for me again."

Kathryn did let it out. She screamed her orgasm so loud, she was sure the old bloke next door would have a coronary.

Completely satisfied and with heightened senses, Kathryn pushed Claire off her and quenched her thirst with a huge swig of wine. "That was amazing." She reclined next to Claire. "*You're* amazing. I can't believe we just did that."

Kathryn slipped under the edge of the sheet. Post orgasm, she felt a little exposed. "I feel like I'm floating. I can't imagine any drug providing a bigger high than this."

"I'm glad you enjoyed it," said Claire.

"Women are so different, aren't they? I mean your skin, your touch, the words you say and how you say them, it's all so tender, so gentle, and so damn sexy."

"I don't want to burst your bubble, but women can be equally as cruel, calculating, and clinical as any man."

Kathryn thought about it for a moment. No, of course tenderness and kindness weren't gender exclusive, and sex with anyone you found attractive had the potential to be a wonderful experience.

Kathryn began to fidget self-consciously. Her courage was fading and she was less confident of her abilities now. She wanted to remove Claire's sexy white boxers and feel between her legs again. She needed reassurance that Claire was still turned on and wanting. Kathryn froze. *I want to get this right. What if I don't do it right?*

Claire touched her cheek and spoke softly. "It's okay. You don't have to do anything." She sounded disappointed.

"What?"

"It's fine," she reassured Kathryn with a warm smile. "You don't have to hang around. Go shower if you want."

"Shower? Do you want me to leave?" Kathryn's euphoric state was dwindling by the second.

"No, of course not. But this happens. I don't want you to do anything you don't want to do."

"Are we on the same page here?"

"Look." Claire leant on her elbows. "Most straight women love the first part but can't face the thought of the second bit. I understand."

Kathryn's eyes nearly popped out of her head. The implication that she'd had her fill and was ready to leave became a source of courage. "You think I can't do you?"

"Hmm... Well, I wouldn't have put it so crudely, but no, I don't think you want to, and I won't let you."

"You won't *let* me?"

"I'm not Andy, Kathryn. It matters to me if you're into it or not."

"And you don't think I am?"

"The look on your face tells me you'd rather be absolutely anywhere but here right now."

Kathryn had heard enough and decided Claire should stop

speaking. She hadn't waited until she was thirty-nine to experience the most amazing orgasm ever and then not finish what had started between them. She discarded the sheets, pulled off Claire's underwear—raising her eyebrow to discover she was naturally blond—before holding Claire's arms firmly above her head. "And I'm telling *you*, you little smart-arse, that I *will* make you come, and you *will* beg me to let you."

CHAPTER SEVENTEEN

Claire hadn't been smart enough to set her alarm ten minutes earlier, and now she was kicking herself. Ten minutes was all she would have needed to relive an abridged version of Kathryn's seduction the previous day.

With difficulty, she shelved the sexy thought, vowing to spend her lunch break conjuring up scenarios of a repeat performance.

Kathryn had made love to her like a woman possessed. Maybe dominating Andy wasn't her thing, but she rather quickly learned how to make Claire orgasm more than once.

The timing of Claire's return to work was ironic. Spending her days with Kathryn was a far more attractive proposition than an ED filled with sick people. The disappointment of returning to work as things were heating up between them was softened by the fact that Kathryn had job interviews scheduled for the remainder of the week.

Also softening the blow, like a stinky wet blanket, was reality. Claire was choosing to ignore this for the time being, but the fact that Kathryn was Jess's older sister couldn't be overlooked indefinitely. In fact, the thought terrified her.

Last night, things had been peculiar to say the least. Jess rambled on about work, Alex sat reviewing case notes until dinner, and all the while, Claire and Kathryn shared a secret that bound them. Claire observed how Kathryn couldn't even bring herself to look at her for the entire evening. She smiled every time she thought of their awkwardness.

Claire had attempted to wait up until it was just the two of them, but Kathryn and Alex were chatting after Jess disappeared, and her seven o'clock start the following morning demanded an early night.

Claire had sent Kathryn a text message: *Thanks for making me beg. We'll see who begs the most next time.xx*

Seconds later, she received a reply: *Sweet dreams, Claire.x*

Claire grinned, imagining the dilation of Kathryn's pupils and the subtle blushing of her cheeks as she read the message before falling fast asleep.

Now, eating breakfast across the table from Jess, Claire was beginning to wonder how she would take the news that her sister was bedding her ex-lover.

Claire backpedalled. How was Jess going to take the news that Kathryn was a lesbian?

"So, you looking forward to life back in the ED?" asked Jess, munching on toast and Vegemite.

"Mostly," Claire replied. "I guess I was getting used to being a lady of leisure."

"Well, my garden certainly benefited from your free time." She eyed Claire. "I know Kathryn's enjoyed your company this last week." Jess's expression was sincere, and Claire's heart faltered momentarily. "Thanks for tolerating her. She's too straight for her own good sometimes. I think your friendship is good for her. And you're a good friend to me, too. That's why I love you so much." Jess kissed the top of Claire's head on the way to the dishwasher.

Claire's smile faded. Deceiving Jess was hell.

Discretion was the key, and until she and Kathryn discussed an appropriate course of action, Claire's behaviour would remain in check, although she was dead keen for a repeat performance of yesterday afternoon as soon as possible. All traces of Victoria had vanished, Kathryn had ensured that, and now any residual regrets she harboured about giving up her own place had vanished, too.

Dressed in navy blue scrubs, her hair tied in a ponytail, Claire stood outside Kathryn's closed bedroom door contemplating a quick good-bye kiss. It was only six fifteen though, and Kathryn probably needed the sleep. If she were awake, Claire was sure she would have joined her for breakfast. She couldn't bring herself to knock.

With only minutes to spare, Claire zipped into the car park at the same time Murray guided her black BMW sports car through the gates. Claire didn't have the luxury of a designated parking space, so Murray waited near on five minutes for Claire to find a space and rush over.

"Jesus, Murray." Claire whistled, eyeing her in an expensive black suit, casually leaning up against her expensive black car. "You get more damn sexy every day."

"And good morning to you, too." Murray eyed her up and down. "You know, the thought of waking next to you every morning, with your cute little compliments is almost tempting."

Murray held her own where Claire was concerned, and the privilege was reserved for Claire and Claire alone. Banter of this kind between a nurse and a doctor could be professional suicide with the wrong victim. Claire was no victim.

"You only have to say the word, and I'm all yours, Doctor," said Claire.

"That's not what you said yesterday."

Claire had forgotten about their conversation yesterday. She smiled.

Murray stopped dead in her tracks. "Claire, please tell me you didn't?"

"Didn't what?"

Murray cocked her head to one side. "Remove your sunglasses."

"Huh?"

"Don't mess with me, Paddy."

"You're worse than Alex." Murray didn't scare her. She removed her sunglasses.

"Oh my God, you *did*."

"Fuck off." Claire couldn't help but smile as she nudged past Murray. "You can't tell from just looking at my eyes."

Murray grinned, catching up and nudging her back. "When are you going to learn, Paddy? It's never the answer that gives you away; it's your reaction to the question."

"Between you, Jess, and Alex, what hope have I got?"

"What about Jean?"

"I don't think I need Jean anymore. I feel completely cured."

Murray laughed and headed upstairs for a meeting. Claire headed to the front line.

It had been a quiet Monday night in the ED, and Claire only inherited four patients at handover. She was on shift with three nurses well known to her and a newer and less experienced nurse who looked like he was barely shaving.

Within minutes of the handover, another patient arrived via ambulance—a middle-aged woman with chest and arm pain. Claire worked to ease the frightened darkness in her eyes.

"Hi there, I'm Claire. Just try and relax while I get some details from this gentleman." Claire smiled, referring to Billy, the paramedic checking her in.

Billy and Claire stepped out of earshot while he relayed the appropriate information.

Claire listened before asking, "What was she doing at the time of onset?"

Billy grinned. "She was alone when we showed up, just watching TV apparently, but a whole stack of porn was piled high on the bedside table, DVDs and magazines. It looked like she'd tried to hide them with a T-shirt, but Scotty, the clumsy idiot, knocked the whole lot clean off." As an afterthought, and with a wink, he added, "No toys. Not that I could see anyway."

Claire performed an ECG, but the results were normal.

Murray arrived soon after. "What have we got, Paddy?"

"Female, forty-three, BP one sixty over ninety-two, complaining of chest pain, left shoulder pain, left arm pain, and nausea."

"It's too much to assume the ECG showed us she's had a heart attack and we can ship her off to coronary care?"

"Yep. ECG is clear."

A frown briefly creased Murray's brow before she replaced it with her caring doctor face and entered the cubicle. "Good morning, Mrs. Cleaver. I'm Dr. Murray." Mrs. Cleaver nodded her hello, clearly distressed. "I know you've been asked this many times already today, and I've read your notes, but I'd like for you to tell me how you came to be here this morning."

As per the account of events Billy relayed, Mrs. Cleaver explained that her onset of chest pain occurred while watching reruns of *Ally McBeal*. Murray nodded intently, as if it was a well-known fact that watching *Ally McBeal* could cause severe chest pain. When Mrs. Cleaver concluded her tale with the arrival of Billy and his colleague, Murray took her hand, pretending to check her pulse.

Without releasing her grip, Murray looked Mrs. Cleaver squarely in the eye and asked, "How long had you been watching TV?"

Mrs. Cleaver thought for a moment. "About two hours, I suppose."

Murray moved in for the kill. "What were you doing *before* watching *Ally McBeal?*"

Mrs. Cleaver squirmed. Claire had been about to leave but decided to stay. *This'll be good.* She busied herself tidying.

"Mrs. Cleaver," Murray said gently. "This is important information that we need to know."

"I hadn't slept at all. I'd been watching television since yesterday."

Obviously taking pity on the woman, Murray lowered her voice and changed her tact. "The paramedics who brought you in mentioned that you had some magazines and DVDs near you." Mrs. Cleaver's eyes popped wide open, but Murray continued as if talking about porn was perfectly natural. "Had you been watching those DVDs all night?"

"It's Marty Stone!" Mrs. Cleaver obviously couldn't maintain the charade any longer.

"I beg your pardon?"

"Marty Stone, you know? The famous porn star."

Claire suppressed a grin, *very* pleased she'd hung about.

Mrs. Cleaver continued. "I love him, he's just amazing, and not like those others; he cares about his women." She brushed the tears from her face. "He's considerate, too. Always making sure his partners, you know, have a good time before he does. And his girls are into it, you can tell, not like those other blokes who just thrust and thrust."

Murray took a deep breath. Claire counted the seconds before she spoke—thirteen. Murray must really have been lost for words.

"Mrs. Cleaver, what time yesterday did you begin watching movies of Mr. Stone?"

"Around lunch time. I'd just sent another e-mail to Marty." Her eyes lit up. "He answers them all personally, you know."

"Right. And do you masturbate while watching Mr. Stone?"

Embarrassed, Mrs. Cleaver lowered her head, and Murray shot Claire a death stare, knowingly indicating she knew exactly why she was lingering.

"Mrs. Cleaver, this is important." A firm tone had crept into Murray's voice.

Mrs. Cleaver nodded.

"And would you say you masturbated for the majority of the time since yesterday lunch?"

She nodded again.

"And Mrs. Cleaver, are you left-handed?"

Another nod.

Claire slipped through the curtain, struggling to contain herself. Murray followed. "Have fun examining that one."

"Me?"

"Does a romp in the hay fry your brain, Paddy? Yes, you."

"Uh-uh. No way."

"Yes way," Murray retorted smugly.

"Seriously, Murray. This woman has masturbated for nearly twenty-four hours. She hasn't washed. She needs a fucking doctor."

"Thank you, Nurse, for your insightful input, but given your expertise in all matters sexual, even as recent as yesterday, I'm asking you to examine the patient, make an assessment, and if I am required, please let me know."

Claire began to argue.

"Thank you, Nurse. That will be all." Murray grinned and headed off to see her next patient.

Claire huffed and puffed, but in the end had little choice but to offer Mrs. Cleaver an examination.

"Are you feeling discomfort anywhere else?"

"What? I don't know what you mean."

Claire hated this false modesty, and right at that moment, she hated Murray. She refused to beat around the bush, so to speak. "Your vagina, Mrs. Cleaver. Given your recent, and rather lengthy activities, are you feeling any discomfort, and would you like to be examined?"

"Oh...Um...no, thank you."

Claire breathed a visible sigh of relief.

"Well, on second thought, I do feel a little tender down below."

God no, please don't say it.

"I think perhaps I would like to know everything's okay down there." Mrs. Cleaver at least had the decency to beam bright red.

❖

Claire relaxed against the trunk of her favourite giant pine tree in the modest park opposite the hospital. She took a few moments to focus on Kathryn and not Mrs. Cleaver's sore, swollen, and completely overused vagina.

With her eyes closed, she blocked out all external distractions and fondly recalled the look on Kathryn's face the moment she realised she'd brought Claire to orgasm.

"Oh my God! I just made you come."

Claire grinned. *Jesus, you did that all right.*

Kathryn stroked Claire again.

"Whoa, hang on. Slow down." After her first climax, Claire liked to take it slow.

The shameless astonishment written all over Kathryn's face was amusing. "I can't believe how easily I make you come. I mean, I know I was easy, but you've done this before, I'm just a novice and you're almost ready to go again."

Claire couldn't believe how much Kathryn was talking.

"You, lying below me, post orgasm, is just downright sexy." Kathryn played with Claire's nipples. "And to think"—she held aloft two fingers—"I did it all with just these."

Claire didn't think Kathryn's incessant chatter was nerves anymore. Elation perhaps, but either way, she decided to put her to the test. "You sure do talk a lot."

Kathryn blushed. "Sorry."

"Don't be sorry, but I can think of something else I'd prefer you to do with your mouth."

"Really?"

"Ah-huh."

A brief look of horror flashed across Kathryn's features. Claire saw it and backtracked. "But maybe not this time."

"No, I want to. It's just that I couldn't really concentrate when you were doing it to me. I've no idea what went where or anything. I just know it felt amazing." Grinning, Kathryn lowered her voice. "Talk me through it?"

Claire frowned, unsure whether to push or not.

"Come on," Kathryn said. "I like the idea of you directing me." She kissed Claire's nipple. "Tell me how you want me to fuck you."

Claire gave in. She was only human. "Most of the time, anticipation is the key. If I kneel above you, and begin moving downward, you know where I'm going, right?" Kathryn nodded and knelt above her, eye to eye. "And there's nothing sexier than to look down at your lover's face, getting you off between your legs."

Kathryn grinned as if she knew exactly what Claire meant.

"But you don't want to rush things. Just the mere thought of you ending up down there is an immediate turn-on. If your lover's arousal is escalating, prolong any contact with your tongue until she asks nicely."

"You want me to make you beg?" Kathryn kissed the hollow of her neck.

"No. I'm helping you out here, remember? In light of that, when I ask you to make me come, I'd really just like you to focus on that."

Kathryn raised her eyebrows. "Really? Who's about to fuck who here? Sounds to me like you might need a lesson in manners, young lady."

"And I thought you said you weren't the dominating type." Claire exhaled heavily, writhing under Kathryn's seductive touch.

Kathryn sucked a nipple hard before removing her lips altogether. "Maybe I've been misdiagnosed all this time."

Claire gasped as Kathryn lightly bit her nipple. "Ah-huh. Maybe."

"Shall we find out?" asked Kathryn.

"Couldn't hurt."

"Are you always this submissive?"

Claire managed a short laugh. "Don't for one second think you're dominating me. I'm giving the lesson, remember?"

"Are you now?"

"Yep. Although it's fair to suggest you're a quick learner." Claire was ready to come again, and it was the thought of Kathryn's tongue doing all the work that was driving her to the edge.

"Really?"

"Yes. Now just fuck me already."

"You're awful sexy when you're bossy." Kathryn kissed Claire fully on the mouth—slow, passionate, and dead sexy. Her hand reached for her wetness, causing Claire to flinch in response. She pulled away. "But you do realise, I'll do exactly what I want to, when I want to. Try asking like a good girl."

Claire smiled. She had no doubt Kathryn was in control. The aching need in her clitoris was becoming unbearable. Submissive or not, she wanted nothing more than for Kathryn to taste her. "Then can you please see your way to sucking my clitoris and fucking me with your tongue?"

Kathryn flashed a warning glare.

"In your own good time, of course," added Claire breathlessly.

"Now, that's more like it."

CHAPTER EIGHTEEN

After multiple orgasms, with some unknown mind-numbing hormone still pumping through her system, Kathryn felt blissfully happy showering alone and reliving fun memories of Claire. The afternoon had been amazing. *Claire* had been amazing, and Kathryn had never come close to such intense arousal before. She was experiencing a long-overdue sexual awakening, and it drew her in like an addiction. The possibilities were endless. She imagined the toys she and Claire could play with, the positions they could explore, and the orgasms. *God, the orgasms.*

At six p.m. though, Kathryn received her first dose of reality—Alex arrived home.

Fuck!

The real world still existed beyond the four walls of Claire's bedroom, beyond her tender touch, beyond all desire and lust. Anxiety crippled Kathryn. Horror set in, intense and engulfing. *Oh, Claire. What have I done?*

Every trace of euphoria disappeared, and when her mind flashed back to the moment Claire went down on her, a moment of utter pleasure just hours ago, she ran for the bathroom and threw up. Kathryn's body and mind began fighting for supremacy about what she actually felt and what she *should* feel. Her body ached—physically ached—for more of what Claire had given her, but her mind rejected every illicit thought.

If her reaction had been disastrous upon Alex's arrival home, it was nothing compared to the moment Jess trudged up the hall, dishevelled and exhausted.

Kathryn realised—disguised by unrelenting sexual tension and selfish, obsessive behaviour—what she and Claire had done culminated in betrayal. She had slept with her sister's best friend— her sister's ex-lover. Overwhelmed, she rushed to the bathroom again and violently vomited every last skerrick of food and liquid in her stomach. Slumped against the door, she remained dry retching for a long time.

Flashback after flashback filled her head. The taste of Claire remained, in spite of the vomit. She could smell her on her fingers, even after washing them, and the pounding ache behind her eyes jabbed sharp and relentlessly.

Over dinner, Kathryn merely pushed her food back and forth. She looked between Claire and Jess, imagining them together. The thought sickened her. Jess's fingers where hers had been, Jess's tongue where hers had been, and Claire begging them both.

Jesus, I'm losing it.

She couldn't look at Claire, *wouldn't* look at Claire, and her mind became a racing mishmash of visual and sensory overload. Her only solace was gin. Alex was the only one willing to join her, and before she mixed a strong gin with tonic water for them both, she half filled the glass, drank it down—twice—then sat waiting for the numbness to overwhelm her.

Claire sent a message. *Oh, Claire.* Kathryn was trying so hard to numb her feelings, she had briefly forgotten that the reason she was in this mess, the reason she felt so damn confused, the reason she was slowly getting drunk, was Claire. The message was cute, funny even, and it sent her spiralling back through a wave of nausea, dread, and flashbacks—sex, nakedness, lust, passion, fingers, tongues, and mind-blowing orgasm after mind-blowing orgasm.

For a moment, before the final gulp of gin took hold, Kathryn experienced a moment of what it must be like to go mad. She would have sworn she felt and heard her brain short-circuit and fizzle into blackness before sound and vision returned.

It was childish, embarrassing if she was caught, but Kathryn needed that gin, and she smuggled the bottle to bed with her, hoping to God Claire was asleep.

She woke the following morning with a fierce headache, compounded by hunger and the desire to erase yesterday afternoon from her memory.

She could hear murmurings and sense movement beyond her door, but she dared not risk a confrontation with Claire. How in Christ's name was she going to face her, or Jess for that matter, ever again?

Her mind refused to let her rest. It provided a persistent visual and verbal commentary of what happened. *If you touch me like that again...Please, Claire. Just do it...Open your eyes, baby...God, please take me...I* will *make you come, and you* will *beg me.* Kathryn plunged her head under the pillow.

She had to get a grip. How in God's name was she going to portray the air of a competent accountant at her interviews if she couldn't even string audible words together? She glanced at the empty gin bottle beside the bed. *That didn't help.*

She concentrated on filling her head with numbers, accounting principles, and spreadsheets. She failed. Her mind instead focused on the number of times she went down on Claire, the number of orgasms she had—with and without Claire's fingers inside her—the number of times she took Claire to the edge, and the immeasurable times she thought she must have died and gone to heaven. She was so confused.

Then, as her anxiety reached its frantic and frightening peak, something snapped and a wave of calmness washed over her. Kathryn contemplated that tedious sex with Andy could have been avoided if she had experimented sexually when she was younger. She knew her body now, and more importantly, knew how easy it was to get off with simply two fingers and a deft tongue. Perhaps now she could finally enjoy sex with men.

There was no way on earth she was a lesbian. It was a light bulb moment. *I'm not gay. I'm liberated!* Regardless, it seemed absurd— two sisters, both gay? *I don't think so.*

Kathryn wouldn't make the same mistake with men again. Her next relationship, one she was convinced she was now ready to embark on, would be on her terms—sex when *she* wanted, sex *how* she wanted, financial equality, and importantly, emotional equality. Yesterday afternoon with Claire had set her free.

But what about Claire?

Claire was a nurse, an intelligent woman, and Kathryn was convinced she, of all people, would understand. Their infatuation had been intense and enjoyable, but it was over now. Surely, Claire was now free to live the high life of a single woman, especially as she was seeking help from Jean. If there were any residual effects from their afternoon together, Jean would iron them out quick smart—not that there should be. Claire knew Kathryn was straight, and Kathryn knew Claire was probably getting back on the bike, so to speak. Although the experience was sexually liberating, they were simply fulfilling a need in each other. *She's a good kid. She'll understand.*

Now, to set the wheels in motion, Kathryn needed a man.

CHAPTER NINETEEN

As much as Claire wanted to send Kathryn a message, make contact after their time apart, she couldn't be sure she would have finished her interview, and on the off chance she hadn't switched her phone to silent, she let it be. There was no way Claire wanted to be the one who ruined Kathryn's chance at a job by calling at an inopportune moment, simply to hear her voice.

Regardless, Claire had in mind a twilight interlude that might interest Kathryn. It wouldn't be the first time Claire had put the backseat of her car to good use, and after a romantic sunset and a bottle of wine, she fully intended to explore Kathryn's more adventurous side.

With over half her shift already a distant memory, Claire returned from her break to observe Murray in deep conversation with two police officers. After dealing with the overused vagina woman that morning, she had carefully steered clear of Murray, and fully intended to do so now. *Curiosity won't kill this little black cat. Not today.*

Claire had two patients waiting admission to wards, one awaiting surgery on an amputated fingertip—thanks to the sharp and unforgiving blade of a circular saw—and another two waiting on specialist consults. She popped her head in on all five patients, poked around with their respective monitors, and ensured everyone was as comfortable as possible given their particular circumstances.

On her way to gossip with the triage nurse, Claire was close to successfully sneaking through the heavy white door when she heard her name.

"Nurse O'Malley?" Murray's tone was all business. "Have you got a moment, please?"

It briefly crossed Claire's mind to disappear through the door anyway, pretend not to have heard in the hope that Murray would pick on someone else, but reluctantly, she released the door and slowly turned.

The two officers, one young and handsome, the other older and tired looking, towered over Murray, even when standing metres behind her.

"Follow me, please."

Claire followed, as did the officers, and they found themselves occupying a multipurpose office. With a glint in her eye and a cheeky grin, Claire leaned in close, but spoke loud enough for the officers to hear. "Really, Dr. Murray, I've told you before, I don't like doing this in front of an audience."

Murray's glare left Claire with little doubt that she should shut her mouth and keep it that way.

"Nurse Claire O'Malley, this is Officer Harvey and Officer Sayers."

Claire simply nodded, fearing a verbal greeting might antagonise Murray.

"These two officers are here to assist a patient from Hemworth who is scheduled to arrive in a few minutes."

Hemworth?

Hemworth was a high security correctional facility about forty kilometres east of the hospital. Claire was certain they housed their own infirmary.

"You and I will be the medical team making the initial assessment of the prisoner...I mean patient's injuries." She stared at Claire. "You and I alone, Nurse. Am I making myself clear?"

Claire nodded.

Officer Sayers stepped forward. "The prisoner is from the female division, fifty-three years of age, and not in the best shape. Officer Harvey and I will be on hand for the duration of her stay in the ED. Prisoners have no rights of privacy in a public hospital situation. You won't be alone with her at any time. *She* won't be alone at any time."

Murray spoke again. "Preliminary reports from the ambos suggest a severe head trauma."

Officer Sayers continued. "She has a homemade spear impaled in the left-hand side of her head, just behind the ear." The officer shrugged. "She must have pissed someone off real bad."

Claire guessed the patient probably needed surgery, a job too big for a prison hospital.

Murray eyed Claire. "You stick to the assessment and you watch yourself. Nothing fancy, Claire. Understood?"

"Got it." She knew Murray trusted her. She also knew that to have two officers attend in advance, people in high places must have thought she was dangerous. Murray would have already taken Claire offline, and the nurse unit manager would have redistributed her current workload.

On the way to meet the patient, Claire fell into step with the young Officer Harvey. "So, what's she inside for?"

"Murder." He didn't bat an eyelid. "She slit the throat of her lesbian lover."

Fuck. "You serious?"

"Of course, she claims to be innocent."

"Don't they all?" Claire wanted to murder Murray.

Sayers's phone beeped. She glanced at it briefly and eyed Murray. "Show time, Doctor."

Accompanied by two officers in uniform, perhaps prison guards, but certainly not police, Maree Black's trolley was whisked into emergency and directly into the largest and most private examination room. The two prison guards were relieved of their duty as Sayers took over.

"All right, Paddy?" Murray asked, waiting for the okay to enter and examine the patient.

"Yep. You?" Claire was imagining Charlize Theron as the serial killer in *Monster*. She was ready.

"We'll be fine. Follow my lead and remember we have an audience in there." She affectionately squeezed Claire's shoulder.

Sayers poked her head out the door. "We're ready for you now."

Claire drew a deep breath and stepped over the threshold. Prepared for the worst, she stepped around Murray, but the sight left her bewildered. The woman before them was barely larger than a child. Maree Black was slight with sharp but drawn features looking much older than her fifty-three years. She sat motionless on the bed, a white cotton blanket placed neatly over her legs. Claire thought she looked a little like Helen Mirren. Expressionless, she showed no signs of pain while the object jutting from her skull appeared menacing. Claire would have been screaming, especially given the few drugs she knew the woman had been administered. Her cuffed, blood-stained hands sat atop the blanket. It was beyond Claire how such a petite, normal looking woman required such a heavy police escort. *Talk about overkill.*

Claire spoke first, creating a sense of hierarchy and respect for Murray. "Good afternoon, Ms. Black. I'm Claire, your nurse, and this is Dr. Yvonne Murray. We'll be examining you today."

The woman barely acknowledged their presence.

Claire knew exactly what to do next, but waited for Murray's instruction. It was best to establish Murray's superiority and control immediately.

"Ms. Black." Murray's attention turned to the woman. She hadn't spoken a word and probably wouldn't unless addressed directly. Her level of cooperation was not yet clear. "Can you please tell us what happened?"

The handcuffed woman raised her eyebrows. "I would have thought that was obvious, Dr. Murray. I have a homemade—sorry, correction—prison made murder weapon lodged in my head."

"Indeed you have. We'll get to that in a minute." Murray eyed Claire. "Insert an IV line and check her BP, thank you, Nurse." She stepped back, hands linked casually at her front to let Claire work in the overcrowded room.

Taking the pair of cuffed hands in hers, Claire could have sworn a sigh, or even the slightest moan of approval, left the patient's lips. She ignored it and turned to Officer Sayers. "I'll need these off to insert the line."

Sayers glanced at Murray who gave a brief nod. She stepped forward to remove the cuffs. "Keep your hands to yourself, where I can see them, Black."

Black smiled and nodded.

Claire slipped the blood pressure sleeve up Black's arm.

"You have very soft hands, Nurse." Black smiled, but her eyes were cold and unnervingly dark.

Claire ignored her.

"You're a pretty little thing, aren't you?" said Black.

"That's enough," Sayers said firmly. Murray shifted nervously.

Black's blood pressure reading was spot on, one twenty-two over eighty, and Claire wrote it on her chart and handed it to Murray.

Claire prepared to insert the cannula into the back of Black's right hand.

"So, Nurse. Ever thought of having a lover in prison?"

Sayers stepped forward, clearly agitated. "I said that's enough. Keep your mouth shut."

The grin on Black's face turned to ice as she eyed Sayers. "I'm just making polite conversation, Officer." She frowned at Claire. "Do you think they'd give me this soft, supple little nurse to play with at Hemworth?"

Claire realised how deceiving looks could be. *She's a fucking nutter.*

"Quiet!" Sayers's commanding voice caused everyone besides Black to jump. She remained impassive. "Once more, Black. Just push this once more and this examination ends. I don't give a shit how long you have to sit around with your head split open. Do you understand me?"

Black smiled.

"Do you understand me?" Sayers gritted her teeth.

"Oh, I understand all right, Officer." Black glared. Satisfied, Sayers stepped back.

Claire waited for things to settle before continuing. Having inserted the needle, she reached behind Black to retrieve an adhesive strip to hold the cannula in place. Once this was complete, the handcuffs would be replaced and Murray could examine the wound.

Claire's small frame stretched above Black, the adhesives only inches out of reach, Claire on tippy toes.

Lightning fast, agile, and accurate, Black grabbed the hem of Claire's scrubs with one hand and firmly thrust her other under Claire's top, latching on to her breast. It all happened so quickly and Black's hand gripped Claire's breast like a vice, squeezing and twisting with an iron-like grip. Fingernails dug in, tearing and scratching her flesh, and Claire screamed, horrified at the strength of the hand that wouldn't release her.

In the time that it took Sayers, Harvey, and Murray to get to Claire, Black asked, "Wouldn't you like me to fuck you until you bleed, little whore?"

Murray pulled Claire away by the neck of her scrubs, while Harvey held Black down long enough to enable Sayers to securely replace the handcuffs. Blood oozed from the wound where the cannula had dislodged.

Murray was livid. "Officer, outside now, please?" She still had Claire by the neck, and as they entered the hall, pushed her against the wall.

Claire's chest was burning from the assault.

"Are you okay?" asked Murray. She let go and straightened Claire's top.

Claire nodded.

Murray glared daggers at Sayers, lowering her voice and stepping threateningly close. "At what stage did you feel it was appropriate *not* to divulge the information that this prisoner is a sociopath?"

"She hasn't behaved like that for some time." Sayers at least had the decency to look sorry.

"Right. And would it not have been a good idea to share this information so I could have allocated a male nurse to this case?"

"I suppose it would have."

"You suppose? Instead, I put an attractive female nurse in that situation."

Sayers's eyes slowly headed to a spot on the wall, somewhere behind Murray.

"This doesn't end here. That information was critical and you withheld it. Now, go back to babysitting your prisoner until I can assign a male nurse and doctor." Murray charged off, dragging Claire behind her.

In the privacy of Murray's office, Claire ripped off her top and bra. The bruise on her breast was already beginning to show, and the deep scratch marks, even through her bra, were bleeding and beginning to form welts. She replaced her top and dashed down the hall to a small refrigerator, grabbing an ice pack before returning to find Murray printing a wad of documents.

"Paddy, I'm so sorry."

Claire shrugged. "Distressed and disoriented patients grab us all the time. It's no big deal."

Murray slouched in her worn chair. "It shouldn't have happened. *I* shouldn't have let it happen." She glanced toward Claire's chest. "Can I take a look, please?"

"This is a sly way to get me alone with my bra off, you know."

"You do what you can." Murray winked, but her tone betrayed her.

Claire couldn't control the shaking as she placed the ice pack on the corner of the desk. Murray noticed.

Claire looked down. The bruising was spreading, and the scratches were dripping with blood.

Murray patted the small examination table, and Claire silently obliged, perching on the edge. "What happened today is unacceptable. That prisoner is a murderer and, I suspect, a sociopath. When I phoned Hemworth just now, I was led to believe that a file containing the relevant information was en route with the patient. When they realised it wasn't, the conversation was shut down."

Murray knew the process. When a patient arrives from an institution like Hemworth, the obligation sits with the institution to ensure the safety of all medical staff. Background information in this instance was imperative.

A knock at the door startled them both.

"Murray, it's just me, Ruth. Can I come in?"

Ruth was the ED Nurse Unit Manager. She had only been in the job four months, but Claire liked her.

Murray passed Claire her top to cover herself. "Sure, come in."

Ruth acknowledged Murray but spoke to Claire. "Are you okay, Claire?"

Claire sighed. "Yeah, she certainly had a grip on her, that's for sure."

"Can I get anything for you?"

"No, thanks. Murray's waited for ages to get me alone with my top off. We should get this over with."

Murray smiled at Ruth and said, "She'll have a cup of tea with sugar, thanks."

"Righto." Ruth rolled her eyes. "First day back and all, Claire. Shit luck, eh?" She disappeared.

Murray rubbed her hands together, warming them to examine Claire. "Okay, Paddy, let's take a look."

Claire lowered her top, and as Murray prepared to examine her, another knock hammered on the door.

"Jesus. What now? Who is it?"

"It's Callum. Can I have a word, Dr. Murray?"

Callum was in charge of safety. He was no pencil pusher, and the personal safety of all hospital staff was high on his list of priorities.

Murray looked to Claire, who shrugged and covered herself again. "The universe appears averse to you and my chest becoming acquainted."

She gently touched Claire's cheek and winked. "Come in, Callum."

Callum dwarfed them, but he never slouched, he simply found ways to lower himself. Today his backside occupied the corner of Murray's desk.

"I hear you two have been in the wars."

"Our arses were in the wind, Callum, that's for sure," Murray said.

Claire liked Callum. He was decent, committed, and professional. Not once did his attention focus on anything lower than her eyes, and it must have been a sight—Claire half naked on the examination table with Murray standing between her legs.

"Someone's arse needs to get kicked for this," he continued. "I just wanted to make sure you were on top of the paperwork. I was hoping to have something to correctional services this evening."

"I'll examine Claire first, and we'll write up the report immediately."

Callum eyed Claire. "Silence from you worries me, Paddy."

"If Murray doesn't get to touch me soon, I'm worried about what she'll do." Claire winked.

Callum smiled but directed his serious tone toward Murray. "I'll leave it up to you to assess if the comedian here needs counselling." Callum placed a camera on the desk. "Photos would help. It's up to you, Paddy. Murray's personal collection is one thing, but there'll be a whole bunch of old, and not so old, men looking at them, including me, so think about it." He made for the door. "Oh, and don't hold back in your report. It could have been far worse."

Callum disappeared.

Murray rubbed her hands, warming them again.

There was a knock at the door.

"Oh, for fuck's sake." Murray strode to the door, opened it, and returned with a cup of tea. "Now, hopefully, we can get started."

Claire slumped forward, head in her hands. Until Callum had mentioned it, it hadn't occurred to her that it could have been worse. The truth was it could have been dire. The tears came of their own accord. Claire felt like she was back on Jean's worn leather couch again describing dreams she couldn't control. Helplessness engulfed her. Although her injuries were mild, the fact that she had little control over someone else's actions frightened her. As a nurse, dealing with the unpredictable every day, she found this troubling. She wished Kathryn were there.

"Oh, Paddy." Murray moved to pull Claire in close.

Thankfully, Claire controlled the tears. "Come on, let's get this over with." She lowered the crumpled top from her chest, and Murray gently examined the mess Maree Black had left.

"I don't think you'll be able to wear a normal bra for a few days." Murray gently dabbed antiseptic fluid on the scratches, some of them deceivingly deep.

"I have a sports crop top. That should be fine."

"Photos?"

Claire thought for a moment. "Just take them. I'll have a look and then decide."

"I'll need a shot with your face in it. Verification that the photos and the report all match up."

The phone rang. Murray said barely five words to the caller before hanging up and addressing Claire.

"That was Ruth. She scheduled an EAP appointment first thing in the morning."

Claire sighed, annoyed at having to see Jean again. Not that it was mandatory, but everyone, including Ruth now, would be on her case if she didn't go.

By the time the reams of paperwork were completed, it was half an hour past knock-off time. Claire's head ached and so did her chest. *So much for my seaside seduction this evening.*

Claire thought of Kathryn the moment she walked out the door. She remembered how Kathryn had felt frightened and then dominant in her arms yesterday. Being with Kathryn hadn't been anything like the last time she had bedded a married woman. That encounter, an error in judgement, had been one-sided, awkward, and had left Claire wanting. Sex with Kathryn hadn't been anything like Victoria either. No, Kathryn had been something else altogether. Remembering the want in her green eyes sent a shiver down Claire's spine that ended with moisture between her legs. Although completely unsure of her attraction and abilities, Kathryn hadn't attempted to be something she wasn't, she didn't try to *be* lesbian; she simply endeavoured to make Claire feel good, feel something after Victoria, and that was the sexiest thing Claire had ever experienced.

The moment Claire reached her car, she phoned Kathryn. There was no answer, but even the sound of her voice, inviting her to leave a message, was heaven to her ears.

"Hi, it's me. I've had a really shit day. I hope yours was better. I'll see you at home soon." Claire hung up, cursing how ridiculous she sounded, but it didn't matter. In thirty minutes, she would be home.

CHAPTER TWENTY

Kathryn struggled all morning to push thoughts of Claire to the far recesses of her mind. She showered, dressed in her favourite power suit, and ordered a taxi to her interview.

The whole thing felt tedious. The interview was a success. She was sure a job offer would be forthcoming, but she had other, more important things on her mind. One thing in particular was the result of her revelation that morning. She needed a man.

Queen Street was the only place Kathryn knew to find pubs and bars in Melbourne. Where there were pubs and bars, there were bound to be men. She wasn't disappointed. Nor was she choosy.

A tall, thickset man in an expensive suit was the first to approach. He was neither handsome nor ugly with boring brown hair, but pleasant features. "Can I buy you a drink?"

"Of course you can. But don't if you're married." Kathryn didn't allow her eyes to stray from the glass of gin twirling in her hand.

"Well, I'm not married, so I guess it's okay then," he happily replied.

"Do you have a girlfriend?" Kathryn asked flatly. She didn't have the time or the inclination to play games.

"No."

"Are you gay?"

"No."

"Do you have erectile dysfunction?" This time Kathryn looked him in the eye with a faint grin.

"No. Thank you for asking. My equipment works just fine." He returned her smile.

"Then yes, please. I'd love you to buy me a drink." She turned on her stool and openly perused her victim.

The thing Kathryn realised about most men was that they more often than not required little, if any, emotional connection to prospective partners. Had she been asked similar ridiculous questions, her response would have undoubtedly been for her suitor to take a hike. Her questions clearly indicated to this man that sex was a strong possibility. *Is that really all it takes?* She wondered how appallingly she would have to behave before he walked away. Not convinced she wouldn't tire of the game well before he did, Kathryn let him do the talking while she giggled politely and concentrated on drinking.

"So what do you do?" Tony had introduced himself and pulled a stool in close.

"I'm a hooker."

His jaw nearly dislocated and fell from his face.

"Only joking. I'm an accountant. What do you do, Tony?" she asked, trying to sound remotely interested.

"I sell sound systems."

"That's an expensive suit you're wearing."

He grinned, lopsided, but nice enough. "They're expensive sound systems."

"I see."

Kathryn knew it was never a good idea for her to begin drinking so early in the day. It stood to reason that she would peak early and she did. Seven o'clock saw them both unsteady on their feet.

"My place? You interested?" Her words weren't slurring as such. She sounded more like a teenager with a new tongue piercing.

Their hands had begun exploring each other soon after the third drink. Although her approach had been crude and a little sluttish, Kathryn found herself enjoying Tony's company. It came as quite a shock to find he was genuinely charming and funny. Now it was becoming evident that they either make or break. Kathryn was excited. She fully intended to screw this man senseless until she orgasmed with the same ease as she had with Claire. She knew her body now, knew what it would take to come, and she intended to insist Tony deliver.

"Your place? Is that an offer?" Tony hesitated.

"Look." Alcohol gave Kathryn the courage for the direct approach. "Do you want to fuck me or not?"

"Jesus Christ. You put it like that, how's a man to say no?"

Tony hailed a bright yellow cab and they sat in the backseat, kissing and fondling like teenagers for the entire journey.

Thoughts of anyone or anything other than herself failed to register significance. She dragged Tony into the house and shut him in her room while she composed herself and attempted to act sober, find her sister, and request some privacy.

"Hey there." Alex beamed from the dining table. Jess was nowhere to be seen.

"Hi, Alex." Kathryn hesitated. "Look, I've brought some company home." This conversation had sounded better when she rehearsed it in her head. "I won't introduce him. Bit early for family introductions and all."

Blushing, Kathryn backed out of the room. "I'll just shut this door, eh? He won't be staying. We'll probably only talk for a while and he'll leave. No big deal, really. Okay. See you in the morning." Kathryn disappeared.

❖

At ten past eight, Claire slid her key in the front door, physically relishing the comfort of being home. Her shoulders relaxed instantly, and the throbbing headache behind her eyes retreated, if only a little.

Smiling, she slumped on her bed. *Thank God today is over.* She gently held her breast in place with one hand while she untied her runners and removed her socks with the other, flexing her hot and sweaty toes.

It wasn't until she stretched out, arms crossed on her chest providing support, that she heard what she thought sounded like a man grunting.

❖

Kathryn had teased Tony, mirroring the way Claire had teased her the previous day. She'd invited him to inspect how wet he'd made her and he promised to "Worship her body and feed her soul."

She couldn't argue with a man wanting to do that.

He went down on her, and delivered everything she asked for. He knew his way around a woman's body and he was thoughtful and attentive. He may have been a bit chubby, but he was strong and tanned with only moderate chest hair. Kathryn couldn't be with a man who was hairy all over. Andy had had a hairy back, and although she used to laugh with him about it, she hated touching it. Kathryn had the power. She felt liberated.

Tony brought her to orgasm with his fingers after apologising because he had come first.

Kathryn's day had not unfolded as planned. On the plus side, she had probably found a job and now she was naked with a man she had practically promised to have sex with within thirty seconds of meeting him. Tony was proving to be a nice man. She hated the word nice usually, but they'd only spent a short time together. She couldn't confidently say he was much more or less than that. After all, she imagined any man that picked up in a bar mid afternoon was thrilled with his day. She was hopeful he wouldn't disappoint her. Already, Tony was proving a more attentive lover than Andy. She was over Andy, therapy had made sure of that, but sometimes a wave of regret would wash over her causing her to question why she allowed it to go on so long.

There had been some comparison between sex with Claire and sex with Tony. Both were better than Andy, both were adventurous and spontaneous—less so with Tony—and on both occasions she orgasmed.

If she were to be honest, the connection with Claire was deeper, but she put that down to familiarity. She'd known Claire for years, and Tony, although genuine and seemingly kind, had been in her life just a few hours. The good news was that she wasn't a lesbian. *I'm not gay.* The relief was immense.

She understood sleeping with a man before going on at least one date wasn't ideal, but at least she knew they were sexually compatible before she wasted time getting to know him.

She was straight, and if things went to plan, she'd soon be off the shelf.

❖

Claire moved to the edge of the bed, cocking her head to listen. She was certain the grunting was inside the house, and upon reaching her doorway, was convinced it wasn't the TV, nor did it appear to be coming from the living room.

In the centre of the hall, the noises became louder.

"Aghhhh. Ohhhh. Yeah, ah, ah, ah. Oh, baby."

Someone was in Kathryn's room.

Without considering the possibility that she might interrupt anyone doing anything much, let alone two consenting adults in the throes of passion, Claire barged through the door.

The pain of the injuries inflicted by Maree Black earlier that day was nothing compared to the pain of seeing Kathryn lying naked under an unknown man. The hand of the sociopath had only grazed the surface. In comparison, Kathryn's hand broke the skin, delved deep into her chest, and wrenched out her already damaged heart.

"Oh my God!" Kathryn pulled the sheet over her.

The man, whose face was already bright red from his efforts, looked horrified before rolling off Kathryn and then continuing off the other side of the bed, landing on the floor with a thud and a groan.

Claire struggled to breathe. The dull ache that had taken residence behind her eyes engulfed her entire head. Her already bruised and battered chest now harboured a deep burning ache in the very centre. As Kathryn called her name, Claire struggled to stumble in retreat, returning to the solace of her room.

Claire lay foetal, head spinning, struggling to deepen her intake of air. She began to question what had transpired the previous day. As if on cue, her groin throbbed.

Kathryn had wanted her. They had wanted each other. Claire had given her every opportunity to escape, every opportunity to have her fill, walk out, and pretend nothing as monumental as experiencing your first ever multiple orgasm had ever taken place. Kathryn had wanted more. She had received and then willingly given. *Hadn't she?*

It was useless. Claire unfurled her tightened muscles and limbs. There was no point questioning yesterday. A more accurate appraisal would be to question herself—Victoria and now Kathryn. *Well done, Claire. You must be one hell of a catch.*

Unable to shake the feeling of pure hopelessness, Claire changed into her pyjamas and moped to the bathroom. The cold water was a welcome coolness on her burning eyes.

"Is that you, Claire?" Alex tapped lightly on the bathroom door.

Alex knew. She knew Kathryn had someone with her. "Yeah, it's me. I'll be through in a minute."

"Murray called."

Claire sighed. She knew it.

"Come talk to me when you're done."

Maree Black and her vice-like grip came flooding back, reminding Claire precisely how shit her day had been. She collected her thoughts and pushed the vision of Kathryn and the man to the far recesses of her mind. The reprieve would be short-lived and she had no doubt she would relive the hurt for days to come.

Attempting to set a light-hearted tone, Claire was as ready as she would ever be to face Jess and Alex. She burst through the hall door. "Well, thank God that day is over."

Jess hugged her carefully. "You okay, little one?"

Claire nodded.

"You know, you only have to ask for a grope if that's what you need. I can help out anytime."

"Jess." Alex growled.

"The offer's open to you, too, honey. I don't discriminate."

Claire smiled. Years with Jess had left her able to read her like a book. "You should take your wife to bed, Alex. I think she needs some attention."

"She's been like it all day."

"I am in the room, you know." Jess sighed. "Bloody hormones. I'm going to take a cold shower."

Alex patted the couch beside her. "Come tell me about the charming Maree Black."

Claire slowly sank into Alex's embrace as exhaustion washed over her. She recounted the events of the day. In a way, Claire thanked

God for Maree Black. Without her, she would have had to try harder to conjure the energy required to pretend she was okay. Alex soothed her with words for what Black had done, and Claire soaked them up, feeling soothed instead for what Kathryn was doing.

Claire was thankful—especially as Alex stroked the hair from her eyes—for having people who loved her, but being loved wasn't the same as being in love. Claire fell in love with people. Why didn't they fall in love back? Not that she was in love with Kathryn, but there had been a glimmer of something special, something she hadn't experienced since Jess, and it was alarmingly, now she had the chance to reflect, nothing she had ever experienced with Victoria. She was beginning to wonder why she had been kidding herself with Victoria all this time. She honestly thought she loved Victoria and would continue to do so until the day she died, but perhaps Victoria knew something she didn't. Perhaps Victoria knew she wasn't really *the one* for Claire. Claire was rapidly losing faith and confidence in her own judgement.

"You'd better sort Jess out before she sends for the sex slaves in the dungeons," Claire said.

"Will you sleep okay?"

"Yeah, I feel exhausted." She smiled and headed for her room. "Thanks, Alex."

"Anytime."

Claire stalled on the threshold. "You seem to be propping me up a lot lately."

"That's what friends are for," said Alex.

"Yeah, well, this friend appreciates it."

"And this friend"—Alex stalled on the bottom step—"is here for you always."

From the hall, all Claire could hear was silence. She'd heard the front door close shortly after interrupting Kathryn, so she assumed *he* had left, or perhaps they had both taken off. She decided she didn't care either way.

Her breast was bruised and tender, and although it was a warm evening, she wore a loose fitting tank top.

There was a light knock on her door. She knew it was Kathryn and ignored it.

"Claire, I know you're in there."

Claire opened the door a fraction. She didn't want to invite Kathryn in. Kathryn was wearing an old T-shirt, and Claire unabashedly looked her up and down before settling her gaze on her eyes. "If you knock and no one answers, it usually means they don't want to see you. What do you want?"

The bruising and bandages were visible beyond the confines of the tank top and Kathryn noticed them. "What happened? Are you okay?"

"What happens to me is none of your business. What do you want?" Claire's tone was neither angry nor threatening.

"I'm sorry, Claire. I don't know what to say. I guess I still like men."

"Good for you. But I already gathered that."

"Can I just explain?"

"No. You can't. Good night, Kathryn." Claire closed the door, sunk into her bed, and cried herself to sleep, a habit that was becoming all too familiar.

❖

Kathryn stood outside Claire's room for a long time. She raised her arm at least three times to knock again, but in the end, she crept back to her own room.

The bed was a crumpled mess and she went about straightening the sheets.

Claire had been hurt. She had seen bloodied bandages on her chest.

A used condom sat shrivelled in a tissue on the bedside table. She grabbed another three tissues and wrapped it tightly in a ball before pushing it to the bottom of her small waste paper basket.

Claire was hurt and she was all alone. Claire needed her.

She pulled the bin liner out of the basket and tied the corners. She placed the bag near her door to take outside when she left in the morning.

She wanted to go to Claire. She wanted to find out who hurt her and she wanted to hurt them in return.

Damn it.

She threw a pillow on the bed and marched back to Claire's closed door. She knocked again.

There was no answer, but she knew Claire was inside.

She was poised to knock again when the phone beeped in her room.

She stared at Claire's door and then at the doorway to her room. The hallway felt like a crossroads. Claire through one door and Tony through the other. Her phone beeped again.

What could she offer Claire? False hope? Empty promises and lies? She wasn't gay and even for Claire she couldn't pretend to be. No, she had to make the choice that was best for everyone. She had to be cruel to be kind. It was wrong to let Claire believe she was interested. She liked men. She liked Tony.

Kathryn closed her eyes and walked away from Claire's door.

The message from Tony was sweet. It thanked her for the most interesting day he'd had since reaching puberty. He asked her to dinner the following evening. Before replying, she stood in her doorway and took one last look toward Claire's room. She shook her head and sent a message saying she'd be delighted to finally go on a date with him.

She closed the door.

Kathryn convinced herself that closing the door on Claire and opening it to Tony was the right thing to do.

CHAPTER TWENTY-ONE

Claire had slept well, thanks to painkillers, and she woke with a sense of calm regarding Kathryn. The facts appeared clear. Kathryn had been married and was probably straight. Their coming together was simply the universe telling them both to move on. Kathryn had finally orgasmed more than once, and Victoria was no longer the last person to make love to Claire. In reality, it was a win-win situation.

"Morning, Jess."

Jess glanced up sharply as Claire entered the kitchen beaming, her singsong greeting far from what she expected so early in the morning.

"Morning, Claire. What's with you? Nothing like a little prisoner-on-nurse assault to brighten your mood. Incidentally, did you press charges?"

Murray and Claire had discussed this, but Claire was adamant she wanted to let it go. It wasn't as if Black was a danger to the wider community; she would probably be inside for the rest of her life. Claire wanted to forget it. "Nope. Life's too short to spend my precious time even thinking about that evil woman. It would serve no real purpose other than to piss me off."

"Fair call. That was going to be my advice," Jess said with an odd tone before winking.

"My God, you really do have some weird hormones going on at the moment, don't you?"

"What? Why?"

"You just gave me the wink."

"What wink?" Jess frowned.

"*The* wink. You know? The one that says let's-screw-right-here-right-now."

Jess was horrified. "I did not!"

"Really? You don't think I would know that wink after falling prey to it countless times?" Claire raised her eyebrows. "It was the wink."

"I didn't mean it, Claire. I didn't even know I'd done it."

"I'm teasing," Claire said before pouring them both more coffee. "But I think you should head upstairs. I can't risk another one of those winks."

"Oh, piss off, will you."

"Hey, hey, hey, Madam Crown, no swearing in front of the children."

Jess scowled. "I swear in front of you, don't I?"

❖

As Jess rushed out the door, briefcase in hand, Alex stumbled down the stairs, half asleep, frowning at the sight of Claire making herself a sandwich for lunch. "Are you ill?"

"What? I normally always make my lunch."

"Since when?"

Actually, Claire couldn't remember the last time she'd made a healthy lunch.

"It was just your chest she assaulted yesterday, wasn't it? Can I have a look?"

"It's just salad and turkey."

"Not your lunch, your chest. Murray said it was pretty bad." Alex pulled at Claire's scrubs.

Claire smacked her hand away, and Alex slumped on a stool, her head on her arms. "I'm sorry. I'm exhausted."

"What's with you two this morning?" Claire asked, amused. "First Jess and the wink—"

"She gave you the wink?"

Claire stifled a laugh. "Yep, straight in the eye."

"But was it *the* wink?"

"You know I know the wink," Claire said.

"Well, at least you got a wink as warning of what's to come. In the dark, there is no wink. I think winking is Jess's new idea of foreplay. Except as a warning, it's useless when you're asleep. I hated the phase she went through when she didn't want me to touch her, but this sex crazed phase is just so bloody exhausting."

It wasn't until that moment that Claire realised how lucky she was to have such great friends.

"I was being serious, if not crude. Do you want me to do anything for your scrapes?"

"How can you forget, while I'm actually standing here with the uniform on, that I'm a nurse?" Claire raised her eyebrows.

Alex shrugged. "How do you feel about work today?" She was awake enough now to play psychologist.

"I feel okay actually. A bit annoyed I guess. It could have been avoided, but other than that, I think I'm good."

"How about vulnerable? Do you have those feelings?"

Claire considered this, and her response. "Yesterday I did. But Black was one patient out of hundreds, possibly thousands, I've nursed. The pendulum swung yesterday, but it feels back to normal now. The vulnerable people are the patients, not me."

Alex smiled, nodding. "Good."

"Good? Why does that sound like a loaded 'good'?" Claire packed fruit in her cooler bag.

"Emotional trauma is personally difficult for you to deal with, your response to Victoria leaving being the obvious example. Physical trauma, on the other hand, while undoubtedly leaving you in an emotionally heightened state, remains on the surface. You process your feelings straight away. It's a good thing. Jean will want to see you more than once. My advice is to agree to whatever she suggests."

"I thought I dealt with Victoria leaving okay. It was the dreams that got me in trouble."

"Of course they're interconnected, but it was the way Victoria left that sent you on a downward spiral. I imagine you felt hopeless and out of control when it happened. I think you blamed yourself entirely and that's common when the other person has disappeared from your life. Those feelings manifested themselves in the dreams. You believed you drove Victoria away, you killed your relationship somehow and that's why she left. Your reaction, while quite normal, became complicated by the dreams. You suppressed your feelings while you were awake, exercising the only sense of control you thought you had, but one can't control the subconscious. It all came back to bite you when you were asleep. Vicious circle really." Alex poured coffee.

"So, I could have avoided it all by dealing with it immediately?"

"Well, perhaps not all of it, no. But the dreams maybe, yes."

"I should have just blurted out the whole story, shouldn't I?"

"In theory, it would have helped."

"But I couldn't even bear to say the words," Claire said, recalling her pain.

"I know."

"So, how was I going to fix it?"

"It's not easy. Why do you think I pushed you to see Jean? It was what you *didn't* tell me, Claire. What you *couldn't* say."

"Why didn't you push me to talk to you if you knew there was more to it?"

"Jess and I wanted you to stay. You can't come home to your therapist." Alex smiled.

"But you knew there was more to it?"

Alex nodded. "Much more."

"And do you think there's more to the assault yesterday?" Claire was beginning to second-guess herself.

"I doubt it. But talk to Jean." Alex stretched and yawned. "I need a shower."

"I'll say," said Claire. "You *stink* of sex."

Alex snatched a tea towel to ball up and throw at Claire as she rushed from the kitchen, bidding Alex a good day.

Claire cleaned her teeth and made a mental shopping list for the supermarket that evening. Finishing at seven made it difficult to contribute to the preparation of the evening meal, but she had volunteered for the following night and was going to make use of Jess's underutilised slow cooker.

Certainly, yesterday morning's cheeriness was for an entirely different reason—Kathryn had still been the taste on Claire's tongue—but this morning, Claire still managed a smile. Kathryn wasn't the first married, straight person that she'd lustfully fallen for. Claire knew she wouldn't be the last.

"Good morning, Claire. I understand you're upset with me, and for good reason, but can you spare a few moments to talk?" Kathryn's voice barely remained steady as she stood in the hallway.

Upset with you? For good reason? Talk?

Not unlike children's cartoons, the sound of a record player screeching to a halt, signifying the end of all happiness, rang deafeningly in Claire's ears.

Screeching.

Silence.

Who the hell am I kidding?

A dark cloud descended.

Kathryn stepped back.

Claire clenched her fists. She locked her jaw tightly shut, fearing what may spew forth if given half the chance.

She was hurt and there was no hiding it.

Sweat poured from every pore in Claire's contracted body. She could tell that the pulsing throb in her temple was visible because Kathryn stared directly at it.

Claire concentrated on breathing, but it was no use. Her mouth engaged before her brain could prevent it. "Get out of my sight," she growled, her voice low and tight.

Kathryn raised her arms in defence. "I'm sorry, okay? But someone will notice pretty soon if we can't even be in the same room together."

Claire threateningly stepped forward in response. It seemed her limbs now also worked independently of her brain.

"Okay, okay." Kathryn retreated further.

Claire laughed, bitter and evil, at the power of her threat, a mere step forward.

"Is this a joke to you?" snapped Kathryn. "Your warped idea of behaving like an adult is it? This will hurt Jess if you keep it up."

Claire became serious. "Leave her out of this. And don't you dare lecture me on behaving like an adult."

"Jesus, you're impossible. I'm so fucking sorry and you won't even let me explain."

"Explain what?" Alex leaned in the kitchen doorway glaring at them both, freshly showered and dressed in jeans and a shirt, arms folded over her chest.

Claire spun around but was too slow to hide her anger.

Alex stepped forward. "Someone had better tell me what's going on."

"It's nothing, Alex. Sorry if we disturbed you," said Kathryn.

Alex smiled. "So, which bit of this *nothing* will hurt Jess?"

And there it was. Alex's trump card. She knew Claire would crumble at even the thought of hurting Jess. Claire lowered her head, knowing exactly where Alex's attention would focus.

"Claire? You want to tell me what's going on?" Alex softened her tone.

Claire stared at a crack in the timber flooring and shook her head.

"Claire, look at me."

Kathryn stepped in. "Look, Alex, with all due respect, this really has nothing to do with you. Claire and I have had a misunderstanding. We can sort it out like adults. Alone."

Uh-oh. Claire willed the ground to open up and swallow her. Kathryn had no idea what she was messing with, agitating Alex. Claire wasn't keen to witness the result.

"Claire, honey, look at me."

Kathryn huffed in the background.

Pushing even further, Alex positioned herself between them and completely turned her back on Kathryn. "What's Kathryn sorry for, Claire?"

"Alex! I said this is between—"

"Claire?" Alex pressed on, pretending that Kathryn wasn't there. "What will hurt Jess?"

"Claire, don't answer that," said Kathryn.

"Look at me, Claire. What's going on?" Alex reached out to her. "Claire?"

Between all the yelling, the harsh tones, the threats, the implied warnings, and the constant talking, Claire heard silence. Silence was the complete absence of sound, but to Claire, it was a noise, a welcome noise that filled her ears and provided relief.

Finally, she looked up. Alex's mouth was moving, her expression concerned and tender. Kathryn's mouth was moving, too. She looked afraid, and her brow creased as her skin reddened with every passing second. Thankfully, Claire heard neither of them.

Claire turned and walked away. There was little to gain from hanging around. It seemed that everyone was upset. Explaining the situation wouldn't alleviate any of the pain.

Claire began to pack her bag for work. She guessed they must have still been talking, because now both Alex and Kathryn stood in her doorway, mouths moving.

As she approached the door, they blocked her path.

"Excuse me," she heard herself say. However, no one moved. "Excuse me, please. Can I get through?"

Alex stood her ground, her mouth moving less. Claire realised it would get physical now. She felt like she was writing the script as the scene played out in front of her.

Kathryn will try to push past. She did.

Alex won't stand for that. She didn't.

Kathryn will reach for me in the hope of dragging me past Alex. She did.

Kathryn grabbed Claire by the scrubs. Her contact was probably meant for her shoulder, but in the confusion, she made contact with her upper chest.

Not again. Pain shot through her already tender wounds, and the noise and yelling flooded deafeningly back into her ears. Alex yelled, Kathryn yelled, and the pain burned.

Everyone froze. Claire glanced beneath her top. Blood seeped from some of the deeper lacerations.

"Jesus, Kathryn! Claire was assaulted yesterday."

"Assaulted?" Colour drained from Kathryn's features.

"It's no big deal. I'm fine. Can you both just give me some space?"

No one moved. "Please." Claire raised her voice. "Get out!"

She turned her back and heard the door close. Claire removed her top and surveyed the damage. When she turned around again, she wasn't surprised to see Alex leaning against the closed door.

In the absence of the first aid kit, and knowing that leaving her room wasn't an option, Claire dabbed tissues on fresh blood seeping from her chest before replacing her top. The moment of truth had arrived.

Alex never lost out in these situations. Avoiding this conversation indefinitely wasn't an option. At least not one Claire was prepared to explore. Alex would be like a dog with a bone, especially if Jess were involved. *Especially* since Jess was pregnant.

"I slept with Kathryn." Claire's tone was neutral.

Silence.

Alex sat. Her mouth twitched and Claire guessed she was seething. "When?"

"Day before yesterday."

Realisation dawned. "Jesus. I assume it didn't go well."

Claire laughed at the irony. "On the contrary, it went exceedingly well. Want the details?"

"No, thank you. So, when did she have the meltdown that prompted her to sleep with a man to prove she's not gay?"

"I don't know," Claire said.

Alex raised her eyebrows.

"Honestly, I've no idea. First I knew of it, I walk in at the conclusion of what I can only imagine was fairly mediocre sex." Claire had no evidence to assume it was mediocre, but she wished it were.

"Jesus, Claire."

"If you keep saying Jesus, Alex, you'll be sainted."

"*Is* she gay?"

"I don't know." Alex raised her brow again. "If I hadn't seen her with the bloke yesterday I'd have thought so."

"The fact that she slept with a man, obviously *any* man, so soon, indicates that she's probably struggling with it all."

Claire glanced at her watch. Her appointment with Jean was at nine. It wasn't even seven thirty, but she needed to escape.

"Don't even think about it." She indicated Claire should sit. "From the beginning, please."

Claire relayed the events, but it wasn't until she spoke about cleansing Victoria from her entire body, and the relief she felt afterward, that Alex's expression softened. Unfortunately, at the first mention of Jess, the softness faded.

"Really, Claire. How were you expecting this to unfold?"

"I don't know."

"You keep saying that, but what worries me more than anything is that I don't think you were thinking about anyone other than yourself."

"Christ, Alex, I'm only human. Kathryn is attractive and she wanted to get screwed by another woman. I wanted to get my rocks off and forget about Victoria. Where's the harm?"

"The harm," Alex said as she gently rested her hand in the middle of Claire's chest, "is in here. If your encounter with Kathryn was simply this incredible one-off that didn't matter, we wouldn't be sitting here now, would we?"

❖

Kathryn felt like a child waiting for Alex to inevitably come to her room and have her say. She had made an error of judgement thinking Claire would understand. She imagined there would be women in the world that would find Claire's reaction flattering, but she wasn't one of them. She was hurting Claire and it felt nothing like flattery. The knock at her door caused her to jump.

"What?" Kathryn was less than inviting. She didn't need Alex to tell her she had behaved appallingly.

"Can I come in?"

Kathryn opened the door. "You should have left Claire and me to sort out our lives on our own. I mean no disrespect, but you don't need to be here."

"If you two weren't so impossible, selfish, and childish, I wouldn't be standing here at all," Alex said. "I've just come to make sure you're all right."

"Claire told you?"

"I know her better than you."

Kathryn had hoped Claire could keep their secret, but she knew she wouldn't lie to Alex. She couldn't blame Claire for her integrity. Neither of them had intended to hurt anyone. They had both behaved selfishly, but Kathryn's selfishness ran deeper. Although it wasn't her intention, she had used Claire. The guilt was oppressive.

"She told me because she's not coping and I doubt you are either," said Alex.

"I'm perfectly fine." It wasn't a complete lie. If things continued with Tony, she knew he could be good for her, but she hated hurting Claire.

"Okay, if you say so."

Kathryn was taken aback by Alex's withdrawal; she had assumed Alex would have much more to say.

"Claire isn't okay. So leave her alone please. Oh, and keep Jess out of this for the time being. I'll decide the best course of action from here. Do you understand?"

"You're going to tell her?" Panic rose in Kathryn. She already felt ill with the guilt of what she'd done to Claire. If Jess found out, she'd kill her. "It won't happen again. Do you really think it's a good idea to tell her?"

"You've put me in a very difficult situation."

"Back it up, Alex. You put yourself in this situation. You should have left it alone. This has nothing to do with you. It's between me and Claire." Kathryn put up a fight, but she knew Alex would do whatever she thought was best for Jess.

"For the time being, I won't mention it, but I'm so disappointed in both of you, not one of you gave Jess a single thought about how your little indulgent afternoon could affect her."

Kathryn stared at the ground. She had no comeback for a statement that was so completely true.

CHAPTER TWENTY-TWO

Kathryn was surprised to learn that conducting a fledgling relationship with Tony while living in the same house as Claire was easier than she expected. She was successful at her interview and commenced work immediately. Claire's shift pattern meant they were barely at home at the same time and rarely alone.

Tony quickly became her Mr. Nice Guy. She had fallen on her feet with him, but as he liked to remind her, she had played a dangerous game the day they had first met. He was right, of course. Tony could have turned out to be a sadistic creep, and although she wasn't entirely honest about her reasons for behaving the way she did, she made no apologies for going after something she wanted. Similarly, she made no apologies for her boldness in the bedroom. It was true, Claire had awakened something in her, and she was finding physical intimacy with Tony equally rewarding.

Tony made her laugh, he sent her flowers, he hung a full-length mirror in his apartment, and after two weeks dating, he gave her a front door key. It was quick, exhilarating, and nothing like she'd experienced before.

Jess was desperate to meet him. She said she wanted to meet the man that was making her so happy. She guessed Jess wanted to make sure he was nothing like Andy.

When she thought about her marriage to Andy, Kathryn calculated that they made love, on average, about once every two or three months. Even then, it was a chore she would go to great lengths to avoid. In contrast, physical intimacy with Tony was at the forefront of their relationship. It was a complete revelation for her to desire sex and initiate it.

Kathryn sat at her desk late one afternoon playing with her antique abacus. Her parents had given it to her as a graduation gift and it often provided a therapeutic distraction from spreadsheets. Today, she found herself focusing on two lines. The top line was Tony and the line below was Andy.

She flicked the beads back and forth, dissecting the similarities between them until eventually two beads remained. One was blue and one was red. She stared at those beads until they turned into four beads, then eight, and then the entire apparatus became a blur.

It had only been a month, but already she felt more relaxed with Tony than she'd ever been with Andy. Tony was a joker with a laid back personality and she liked that. Since divorcing Andy, she'd improved her looks and her self-esteem. It was difficult to tell if her confidence with Tony was related to her increase in confidence in general, or if he brought the best out in her.

She spun the two beads around and sighed.

Three weeks later, Kathryn found herself staring at the same two beads, only this time she knew what they represented and she had to face it. They symbolized what was missing from her relationship with Andy and now Tony. What disturbed her most was that she could only identify the missing piece since she'd been with Claire. Claire had unlocked a door inside her and as much as she tried, and she had certainly tried her best with Tony, it seemed that only Claire held the key to the door. If Kathryn were a coin, she was missing her opposite side. There was a real possibility that Claire was the opposite side to her coin. The thought terrified her.

That evening she spoke to Tony. In business, Kathryn rarely shied away from difficult conversations, but in her personal life, she struggled with confrontation. The look of disappointment in his eyes when she said she needed some space was distressing. She fell short of the old line, "It's not you, it's me," but the implication was the same. She agreed to keep in touch but she wasn't sure how that would work out. He said he wouldn't delete her number yet, but would wait in case she changed her mind or "worked through her stuff," as he put it. He also offered to slow things down if she thought it was moving too fast and although she thanked him for his thoughtfulness, she explained that she didn't think that was the problem.

The problem was Claire.

Tony wasn't Claire.

That was the problem.

For some people, the revelation that they had feelings for someone of the same sex could be one of the most enlightening experiences in their life. For Kathryn it was a sharp and dangerous double-edged sword. On one hand, she now at least knew why she had been struggling to connect with Tony on a deeper level. On the other hand, she wasn't ready for what it all meant. At best, she *might* be bisexual, at worst, gay. She shook her head. What a ridiculous notion. There was nothing wrong with being bisexual, or gay, she had just never imagined one of those labels would be hers.

Kathryn knew what she didn't want to be. The challenge came with becoming what she was. Right at that moment, she was utterly confused.

❖

Claire had no idea Kathryn was even home, let alone in the bathroom splashing cool water over her face, tears and mascara streaking her cheeks, which was exactly how Claire found her when she barged in to clean her teeth.

"Oh, sorry. I should have knocked." Claire turned to leave, but her compassion won out. "What happened?"

"Nothing. I'm fine." Kathryn glanced at her reflection but remained silent.

Claire rinsed a face washer in hot water before handing it to Kathryn. "Something bad must have happened to upset you this much. Is it Tony?"

"It's not Tony, it's me." Kathryn shook her head. "What the hell did you do to me? I was fine until I met you, until you touched me, until you *fucked* me. Now look at me." She sobbed into her hands.

Claire had no idea where the outburst had come from. She stood beside Kathryn, tentatively rubbing her shoulder. "I didn't *fuck* you," she said gently. "I thought we shared something special, something intimate. I'm sorry if you feel like I simply *fucked* you." She was disgusted by the implication and struggled to understand where the attack was coming from.

Perhaps Kathryn had jumped in too deep, too soon with Tony. He was the first after Andy, but that had ended nearly three years ago now. There was a small part of her that was pleased Kathryn wasn't as happy as she could have been, but that was selfish and the pang of hope it ignited was quenched when she reminded herself that Kathryn wasn't gay.

"Why do you have to be so nice, so bloody diplomatic?" blubbered Kathryn.

"You're my friend, honey." Claire pushed aside her own feelings. "Regardless of what happened between us, I care about you." Claire tried again. "What happened with Tony?"

"I really like him. What's wrong with me?" She turned to Claire, burying her face in her shoulder. "First Andy and now Tony."

"There's plenty more fish in the sea."

"That's not the point." Kathryn wiped her eyes and nose leaving a shiny glaze on the back of her hand. "What if I'm not supposed to live in the sea?"

"What are you saying?"

Kathryn shook her head. "I have no idea what I'm saying. Just forget it."

"No, hang on. What did you mean?" Claire knew what she wanted her to mean, but she couldn't allow her rising hopes to take over.

"What if I've had it wrong all this time?" Kathryn's tears returned, a little hysterically this time. "It would explain why I'm not feeling what I'm supposed to feel with Tony and why I feel like I do with you."

Claire's heart froze. She knew when she had a quiet moment to relive this conversation it would propel her back to the beginning with Kathryn, right back to wanting her and needing her. Moving on was never as simple as it seemed.

She counted to ten for composure. "Come on," she said. "Let's get you to bed."

Kathryn struggled to her feet and Claire followed her into her bedroom. She shifted a pile of clothes off the bed while Kathryn wrestled with her pyjamas, her chest convulsing with heaving sobs.

"How can you stand to look at me?" She eyed Claire. "I'm such a mess."

"You're hurting, Kathryn." Claire was struggling to keep her emotions in check, struggling not to take Kathryn in her arms and soothe her wounds. Claire wanted to take her away, fix her, and bring her back to life.

Claire held the sheet aloft and Kathryn silently snuggled low in the bed.

"What are you going to do now?" asked Kathryn.

Claire wasn't entirely sure what she meant but answered with the safe option. "Might go and watch some TV."

"Watch some with me? I don't fancy being alone."

Claire fancied being alone. She needed to digest the fact that Kathryn was probably attracted to her, that Tony was a diversion, and that she was back to square one. Like a flooding ballast tank, Claire could feel the attraction and desire return to occupy every cell in her body. It was much easier mourning the loss of a straight woman dabbling in experimental fun than it was a gay woman not yet coming to terms with her sexuality or attraction.

"Sure, why not," she found herself saying.

They settled in to watch a movie, and before long, Kathryn's head rested on Claire's shoulder.

"You're so soft," murmured Kathryn, turning slightly sideways and draping her arm around Claire's middle.

Claire attempted to concentrate on the movie.

"Do you think perhaps women are too soft for men?"

Claire thought that was absurd and wondered if Kathryn had swallowed too much Listerine, but she chose her words carefully. "I think we can be different things for different people."

"Why are some lesbians like men?"

Kathryn's emotionally strained philosophical side, while far from becoming, was at least amusing.

"Because that's who they are," Claire answered simply.

"But you're not like that."

"No, because I am who I am."

"Did you know that most people think lesbians are all butch and ugly?"

Claire saw where this was headed. "Does it worry you what the population at large thinks?"

"No, of course not," Kathryn hurried to say.

"Did you know that most people think accountants are boring?"

"Well, that might actually be true."

They laughed, genuine and easy.

"You're impossible, Kathryn Mercer, you know that?"

Kathryn suddenly looked serious. "But you know I'm probably not gay, right?"

"Well, that's open for interpretation."

Kathryn extracted herself from Claire's embrace, her voice steady and serious. "No, it isn't. I'm telling you how it is. I don't want to mislead you."

"So, what happened tonight with Tony?"

"I don't want to talk about it." Kathryn's courage vanished and her voice reduced to a whisper.

But Claire wanted to talk about it. "Did you have a fight, or worse?"

"I honestly don't want to talk about it." Kathryn fled to stand by the window.

"Is he not quite up to my standard?" asked Claire.

"You're out of line. I'm not discussing this with you, Claire. It has nothing to do with you."

Claire became frustrated. "You and I had sex, we shared something special, and it could have everything to do with me."

"We shared *nothing!*" spat Kathryn. "We shared a mistake. I'm not like you, or Jess, or Alex. I'm normal."

Claire scoffed at the word *normal*. "And that's why things are going so well with Tony, is it?"

Kathryn remained silent.

"I thought so." Claire rose to leave.

"You don't know me, Claire, and you certainly don't know what's best for me."

The vision in Claire's mind flashed back to an outstretched Kathryn on her bed, naked and beautiful. *But I know every inch of you.*

Claire's anger and frustration subsided as quickly as it erupted. "I know you like to feel wanted. I know you like knowing I want you and desire you."

"Claire, stop."

"I know you like a slow seduction. I know you like me to take away your control."

Kathryn turned, tears streaming down her face. "Please, Claire, just stop."

"I know you're frightened. I know you're struggling with your feelings."

Kathryn lowered her eyes and shook her head.

"I know you like to know that my one and only priority, when I'm inside you and I'm licking you, is to make you come." Claire stepped dangerously close. "I know you want me now."

"Claire…" Kathryn's voice deserted her as Claire tenderly touched her cheek.

"I know you want me to take away the pain."

Kathryn's eyes met Claire's for the first time.

In a ghost of a kiss, Claire allowed their lips to scarcely touch. "Tell me you want me to stop."

Kathryn whispered something, but it was barely audible.

"Pardon?" Claire kissed her again, the moisture uncomfortably building between her legs.

"I don't want you to stop."

"Will you let me take your pyjamas off, blindfold you, lay you on the bed, and make you feel incredible?"

"I really want you to do that," said Kathryn, giving in at last and pressing her lips against Claire's. "Why do you make me feel this way?"

Claire cupped Kathryn's face. "I'm not *making* you feel anything, darling. Don't you understand?" She stepped out of Kathryn's reach. "If this is so bad and not something you want, choose to make it stop."

"Claire?" pleaded Kathryn.

"More to the point, if you like this feeling so much, choose to feel it with Tony."

Kathryn pulled her back in. "You know I can't do that," she breathlessly panted. "I know I've been foolish." Kathryn kissed Claire hard.

After slowly removing her own clothes and undressing Kathryn before tying a T-shirt over her eyes, it was Claire, in the end, who lay on the bed, facing upward.

"I don't want you to think. I just want you to feel," said Claire. "Can you do that for me?"

Kathryn nodded as Claire guided her to the bed.

"I want you to ride my face, to grind into me, to let my tongue explore deep inside you, and when you can't take it anymore, I want you to come in my mouth."

Her words had the desired effect; Kathryn stumbled and had to steady herself.

With her hands guiding Kathryn's hips, Claire lowered her wetness onto her face and savoured every moment of pleasuring Kathryn.

Kathryn could deny her feelings all she liked, but the slick film of arousal that quickly spread over Claire's face told a much different story. Wanting to prolong the experience this time, Claire unhurriedly teased, ignoring Kathryn's moans of encouragement.

"We shouldn't be doing this," Kathryn said.

Claire ignored her and drove her tongue deep inside.

"God, that feels so good." Kathryn adjusted to open herself more to Claire. "I would die if you stopped now."

Claire had no intention of stopping, and if she had her way, not a day would pass when Kathryn didn't want this. Claire reached behind Kathryn and gently inserted the tip of her forefinger into Kathryn's ass.

"Oh!" It was an exclamation of surprise, not pain.

Kathryn didn't ask her to remove it, so she continued.

"A little more," moaned Kathryn.

Claire hadn't expected Kathryn to want more and she slowly pushed her finger up to the second knuckle.

"Oh God, how do you do this to me?" Kathryn was barely speaking, more so panting the words with every thrust.

In response to Kathryn's increasing tempo, Claire withdrew her tongue and concentrated on Kathryn's ass and clit. Her finger pulsed inside while she eagerly sucked, licked, and nibbled her swollen clit. As Kathryn grew closer and closer to orgasm, Claire fucked harder with her finger, now inside as far as it could go.

Kathryn groped for the T-shirt covering her eyes. She stuffed it in her mouth before violently convulsing as her orgasm gripped her.

Claire wanted Kathryn to feel the depth of her desire, so she moved her mouth to Kathryn's opening, relishing every last drop of her intense orgasm.

A part of Claire felt exhilarated. This woman that she had fought so gallantly to extinguish her desire for, now surrendered—without any real protest—to her. The need she sensed almost tangibly radiate from Kathryn was addictive. She thrived on bestowing to Kathryn exactly what she knew she wanted and needed.

Like all addictions, it came with a price. Claire knew she would pay dearly for what had just happened. Her ego and sanity would be delivered a sharp blow, but it was her heart that would unfortunately suffer yet another break.

In an unprecedented move, one even Claire wondered if she could execute, she leaned over and kissed the sated Kathryn, who had flopped beside her on the bed. "Good night, Kathryn."

"You're leaving?"

Claire nodded. "You said before we had sex last time—for the first time—that you felt no need to name what you felt or what you were. It seems to me that the name is the single thing holding you back right now."

Kathryn stuttered a failed protest.

"Let me finish," said Claire. "I don't need to tell you what has happened tonight. You have all the information and all the answers. Don't get me wrong, I can foresee the same complications you can, but I'm comfortable with my label, and my life. I have nothing to contemplate, nothing to work out, not one ounce of confusion messing with my head, and certainly no regrets. You, on the other hand, will likely experience all those things."

"So, why go? Can't you see I need you? Stay with me, please."

Claire smiled sadly. "I'm sorry. I already know the outcome of your confusion. I saw it last time, I experienced it last time, and I can't stay with you now knowing that when I go, you'll do all you can to convince yourself that Tony is the answer."

Kathryn's eyes lowered.

"See?" Claire felt it like a kick in her stomach. "It's already happening. But just try to remember this for me—nothing you have ever experienced in your life has made you feel like I do." Claire reached the door. "You deserve to be loved, Kathryn."

"You're in love with me?"

Claire didn't face her. "Maybe not yet, but wouldn't it be nice to find out if I could be?"

Claire quietly closed the door behind her.

CHAPTER TWENTY-THREE

Kathryn woke early the following morning to the sound of Claire sneaking out the front door. When she looked out the window, she saw she was wearing her running gear. Claire was nothing if not predictable. She quickly threw on a pair of shorts, scooped Jess's car keys from the hallstand, and stepped into a glorious morning. The temperature was already rising and she drove for less than ten minutes listening to the six a.m. news.

She was surprised to see so many people in the park so early and she briefly wondered if all the runners were out early attempting to shake off what happened to them last night, just like Claire.

She found the bench where she'd waited for Claire the day she sprained her ankle and she sat waiting again.

She had neither the energy nor the inclination to force uncomfortable exercise on herself to deal with her stress, and regardless, she'd barely slept last night. Why was it that soul searching was best done in the dead of night, the loneliest time of day? She had tossed and turned all night contemplating who she was and how she became that person. She didn't enjoy the process nor was she delighted with the outcome. She had orgasmed, felt as high as she believed she possibly could, and then crashed back down to earth when Claire had left her alone with her thoughts.

When she saw the familiar running gait of Claire in the distance, Kathryn stood on the path to attract her attention.

"I thought I'd see you here this morning." She gestured to the park bench.

"I'm running," Claire stated the obvious.

"We need to talk. I think away from the house is best, don't you?" Kathryn smiled. "Please? Then I'll leave you alone." Away from Jess and Alex was really what she meant, not the scene of their two sexual encounters or their endless flirting and innuendo. She hadn't forgotten about Jess in all of this, she just had to prioritise her feelings as best she could.

Claire relented. "You're up early."

"I didn't sleep much." Kathryn shrugged. "Plus, I really wanted to talk to you. I know you well enough to know that after last night, you'd try and run it out today."

"Go on."

Kathryn cleared her throat. "Thank you for last night."

"You don't have to thank me. Jesus Christ. What are you going to do next? Offer me a couple of hundred for my services?"

"Claire, just give me a break here, all right? I'm trying to explain to you what is about to happen."

Claire folded her arms.

"It's also clear to me that you and I have something going on."

Kathryn saw the look of hope in Claire's eyes. It made what she was about to say even harder.

"But it has to end," Kathryn said softly.

"Why?"

"Because I don't know who I am. I'm not who I thought I was, and that's come as quite a shock."

"But I can help you. We can do this together."

"I want to do this on my own. I don't know how long it will take, and I can't ask you to wait." Kathryn remained calm. She'd rehearsed this speech a hundred times now. "Regardless, under my sister's roof is hardly the place to find myself bedding her ex-lover."

"So, let's move out."

"I can't afford to. Not yet." Kathryn smiled sadly. "And neither can you, Claire. Plus, I want to reconnect with Jess. I want to help her as much as I can before the twins arrive, and I like living there. The timing is all wrong."

"And you won't have to deal with being a lesbian while your sister provides a constant reminder that she used to fuck me and that you are too scared to admit you have feelings for me that run far deeper that anything you have ever experienced with any man."

Kathryn shrugged. "Maybe you're right. But that's my choice."

"And you won't ask me to wait?"

"That's not fair to you, Claire. You know I can't do that."

"Do you *want* me to wait?"

Kathryn shook her head. "I'm not answering that."

"Give me some credit here, Kathryn, and let me make my own choices. Do you want me to wait?"

Kathryn hadn't expected the conversation to end this way. She had honestly thought that Claire would, at best, hear her out, but ultimately flounce off when she said she couldn't be with her. The thought that Claire might wait an undetermined period of time for her to get her life together hadn't been a consideration. "If, when the time comes that I have sorted myself out, you happen to be single and still interested, I imagine I would very much like to explore what that means."

"Fine." Claire stood. "Then I'll wait." She sprinted off into the distance.

CHAPTER TWENTY-FOUR

Not surprisingly, after a little time to absorb things rationally, Claire wondered what she had been thinking. Waiting for Kathryn to come to terms with her sexuality was probably the worst idea she'd ever had. It was a sentence to an unknown period of torture, self-doubt, and an endless string of fantasies and masturbation.

Notwithstanding every negative aspect of her decision, she actually had a plan. Well, not so much a plan, more of an ethos. Claire was determined to be one hundred percent herself. She would allow Kathryn to see her disappointment, her fears, her anger, her compassion, her love, but most of all, she refused to hide the genuine tenderness she felt for her. If Kathryn was going to turn her down, Claire wanted to make sure she knew exactly what she would be missing.

A pattern emerged where Claire would sneak into Kathryn's bedroom when the house was quiet and crawl beside her in bed, taking her into her arms. On some occasions, they would merely sleep, on others Claire would kiss Kathryn, tell her she was beautiful, and expect nothing in return. In fact, Kathryn never reciprocated any terms of endearment and she never went to Claire's room. She also never invited Claire in, nor asked her to leave. In the post-Tony confusion and with Claire's offer of time to allow Kathryn to find herself, it seemed Kathryn had become incapable of demonstrating any form of affection.

What developed became an unspoken bond of companionship,

alarmingly easy for them both, but with no actual further development until Kathryn gave the word.

Claire was fraught with concern. There was no doubt Kathryn wanted Claire around; they practically did everything together, but it was so confusing. She attempted to talk to Kathryn about her sexuality, about how Claire initially struggled with being a lesbian, and although Kathryn listened, nothing seemed to penetrate her indifferent mindset.

❖

On a Sunday afternoon, weeks after Kathryn had requested thinking space, they were finishing some household chores. Claire had been working a string of night shifts and finally had a few days off. She'd barely seen Kathryn in the last week.

She'd suggested dinner and a movie.

"It sounds like a date to me." Kathryn neatly folded her washing before carefully placing it in her drawers.

"Why?" Claire lay face down on the bed flicking through a magazine wondering what the big deal was. "It's just food and the movies."

"Because," Kathryn sighed, "that's what people who are dating do."

"That's okay. I'll ask Ruth. She might be up for it." Claire wasn't calling her bluff. She would prefer to go with Kathryn, but she and Ruth had become friends since she joined the ED, and a lazy Sunday evening out was appealing.

"You seem to be spending a lot of time with Ruth these days."

It was true. Things had progressed at work socially, and a few of the nurses went out regularly. Claire had never gone out one-on-one with Ruth though.

"I like her. She's turned out to be a good mate."

"Is that all there is to it?"

Claire grinned openly. "She's straight and I'm not interested."

"You have a thing for straight girls though, don't you?"

"No," Claire replied. "I have a thing for confused girls."

"Come on then, Casanova, where are you taking me?" Kathryn lounged on the bed beside Claire.

"Well, first, I'm taking you to a classy restaurant where you can sit and eat a kilo of raw steak while some nice little ladies jelly wrestle at your feet." Claire struggled to pull off a common Australian bloke drawl. "Then the movie will be some adult contemporary drama that will appear at first glance to be a porno, but I can assure you it's adult entertainment at its best."

"You sure know how to show a girl a good time." Kathryn left to freshen up in the bathroom and Claire pumped the air with her fist.

She had expected stronger opposition from Kathryn, but she wasn't complaining. The sheer fact that Kathryn had even equated dinner and a movie to a date was one thing, so readily agreeing to it, well, that was something else altogether. Claire hurried to prepare, not allowing Kathryn any time to change her mind.

❖

Dinner had been casual and delicious with them sharing both their main meals and dessert. Claire insisted that sharing was the only way to evenly distribute the garlic when eating Italian, and although Kathryn rolled her eyes, she didn't protest. In fact, walking to the cinema, Kathryn didn't move away when Claire looped her arm through hers and allowed the sides of their bodies to touch indiscriminately. Claire felt lightheaded.

Kathryn eyed their closeness and their entwined arms.

"I don't think we look like mother and daughter, if that's what you're hoping for," said Claire.

"No. I'm hoping we look like two friends who've had a delicious dinner and who are now off to the cinema."

Claire shrugged, allowing Kathryn to believe her own delusions. She decided to leave the conversation alone when two young men approached showing them a little more interest than necessary.

Not surprisingly, Claire felt Kathryn tense and begin to withdraw her hand. Claire tightened her grip, refusing to break contact.

As the men drew nearer, Kathryn said, "This is a bad idea."

"We're fine. Just breathe."

Almost level with them now, the men both smiled broadly as one tipped an imaginary hat and joyfully said, "hakuna matata" before going about his business.

Kathryn ripped her hand from her pocket, untangling Claire's grip. "What the hell? Can't two friends even walk down the street touching each other these days? What the fuck was that?"

"Calm down, Kathryn. They were only—"

"No! I won't calm the fuck down. They have no right to treat us that way. Well"—Kathryn stumbled on her words—"they have no right to treat *you* that way."

Claire gripped Kathryn's shoulders firmly. "Have you seen *The Lion King*?"

"What?" Kathryn frowned impatiently. "What has that got to do with anything?"

Claire took her phone from her pocket. "Google it." She proceeded to spell *hakuna matata* while Kathryn stroppily typed the letters.

Two seconds later, Kathryn stood bewildered. "It means 'no worries,'" she muttered.

Claire took back her phone. "Yes, exactly. It's not an insult. Those men thought we were together. They were probably a couple themselves, and frankly, they have every right to be pissed off that we can do what they can't—hold hands or openly touch each other. Instead, they're happy for us. That's what hakuna matata means."

Claire linked their arms again and left Kathryn to mull it over. They walked in silence to the cinema. Kathryn appeared deep in thought.

❖

"That was my worst nightmare back there," Kathryn said in Claire's ear.

The movie was yet to begin, and the seemingly endless string of advertisements would end soon. Claire simply nodded.

"I'm sorry," Kathryn said. "I don't know what else to say."

Neither did Claire. While the message from the men was one of togetherness and positivity about gay sexuality, all it seemed to do was drive the wedge deeper into Claire's heart, signifying that Kathryn might never be ready to be herself. If Kathryn wasn't ready to be herself, then she certainly wasn't ready to be with Claire.

Kathryn nudged Claire with her elbow. "Popcorn?"

Claire smiled but shook her head.

"Drink?"

Again, Claire shook her head. She simply wanted to watch the movie and pretend Kathryn was her girl. It would probably be the last time she would offer to take Kathryn out. It all felt out of her hands now, out of her reach, and Kathryn felt like she was so far away from her.

Claire felt a soft hand cup her cheek and turn her head. She looked directly into Kathryn's eyes.

"Kiss?"

"We shouldn't," Claire found herself saying, much to her own dismay. Her focus, however, remained on Kathryn's tender touch.

"I really want you to kiss me, Claire."

Claire hesitated. She wondered where her wants and needs came into the equation. "I know waiting for you was my idea, and although you haven't said anything of the sort, I know that's exactly what you want me to do. You never object to me climbing into your bed, to me kissing you, to me holding you, to our outings. I think you even want me to take you to dinner, walk arm in arm with you, and do all the things I'm doing, but what about what I want you to do for me? What you should *want* to do for me."

Claire let the question linger. Kathryn's hand dropped.

"I want *you* to kiss *me*, Kathryn. For once, give a little."

Kathryn straightened, facing the screen. Claire wasn't finished.

"I'll wait for you, Kathryn, but not like this. The rules have to change. I'm giving you space on one hand, but then when we're like this, I know you want more, but you want me to be the giver every time. In the corners of your mind, the absolution your lack of initiation for our kissing or touching gives you is false. It's allowing you to continue to pretend you're a straight woman who's simply allowing a lesbian to do things to her."

A tear fell into Kathryn's lap.

Claire continued. "You know I want you. I don't fear admitting that, but it's not enough. It's up to you now. The ball is in your court. If you want a kiss, then kiss me, if you want sex, then initiate it. If you want to hold my hand, hold it. I feel like I'm working to wear you down, to woo you into submission, and it feels all wrong. What I should be waiting for is you to decide, and from now on that's what we're going to do."

"Wasn't that what I originally asked for?" countered Kathryn.

"Yes, it was. I've taken it too far. I thought I could make you fall for me again, but you're different now, you're so closed up. I should have behaved as you asked. I'm sorry. You're not ready. I know that now."

The movie began and Kathryn remained silent. Finally, she asked, "Will you see other people?"

Claire sighed. "Maybe. I hadn't thought that far."

They watched the movie and drove home without speaking another word.

CHAPTER TWENTY-FIVE

Kathryn was tired of the struggle. The constant battle to keep her emotions in check was leaving her exhausted and short tempered. The endless debates with herself regarding her feelings and actions left her questioning her choices at every juncture.

Claire was distant. It felt like they had regressed to the day she accused her of having an affair with Jess. She had hated the feeling then, and she hated it even more now.

She longed for Claire's tender touch. The yearning was relentless, and predictably, bedtime was the worst. In the end, she would let her mind wander into thoughts of Claire just to fall asleep after fighting the desire for hours.

Her favourite new pastime, if you could call tormenting yourself a pastime, was sitting in the busy coffeehouse near her work and staring at the men walking by trying to decide if she fancied any of them. Of course she did, she wasn't blind, she knew even Jess could spot a handsome man in a crowd, but the thought of anything other than looking at them was far from appealing.

Kathryn considered joining a salsa dancing class, joining a clay pigeon shooting club, learning golf, or perhaps her best idea to date was to learn sports massage so she could rub down some footballers after a tough game. Eventually, she seriously considered the possibility that she was going insane. The thought was both frightening and charming.

There was nothing she could do to erase her thoughts of Claire. Nothing.

Claire had been right, she'd been deluding herself all this time and now that Claire had removed herself from Kathryn's life almost completely, the loss was inexplicable.

During a late evening stroll after a particularly tough day, she devised a plan. Claire had gone with Ruth for drinks yet again, and Jess and Alex were on a date night. Kathryn had cooked dinner, but Claire didn't have time to eat. She couldn't even be annoyed about the effort she'd gone to cooking, because Claire had already told her she might not be home. Faced with a huge pot of curry she no longer had the appetite for, Kathryn dished out lunch sized portions into plastic containers and left them on the bench to cool while she took a walk.

The evenings were cooler now, and autumn was slowly draining colour from the urban landscape. She liked a place where the seasons had a distinct look and required distinct clothing for the conditions.

The streets were littered with evening walkers, and she briefly enjoyed being part of the little "after dinner walkers" subculture, albeit anonymously, until she realised she was possibly the youngest person out walking without a dog. Perhaps older people saw more merit in utilising every minute of the dwindling daylight. Everyone greeted everyone else in a kind manner and she vowed to walk again the following evening.

When there was no one around to nod at or say good evening to, she was again left with her own thoughts. They were reaching the desperate stage and she had to move forward, she had to get a decent night's sleep, and she had to stop snapping at her assistant because the chocolates she was continually buying as an apology were sending her broke.

Step one on her road to recovery came to her while she watched a teenage boy chase after a dog that had obviously absconded. The dog loved the game. He probably wondered why he hadn't tried it before, especially as he was now being bribed with treats. Step one was all about perception. She realised she had to change hers.

Her idea was groundbreaking and simple; she would no longer fight her attraction to Claire. There was no way she was acting on it again, that was a certainty, but all the effort required to hold it at bay was punishing. Finally, the dog willingly allowed the boy to pick him up. Game over.

Her relief at just making that one decision was enormous.

That night, Kathryn went to bed early, touched herself while imagining a fantasy involving Claire and her in the back alley behind a nightclub, orgasmed once and slept soundly until her alarm sounded at six thirty. Nine hours' sleep and she woke feeling fantastic.

Step one was a keeper. It astounded her that she hadn't thought of it earlier.

She ran into Claire at breakfast.

"Morning," said Kathryn.

Claire eyed her from head to toe. "You sound chipper today. Is it Saturday? Have I forgotten to sleep in again?"

"Nope. It's only Friday, sorry to disappoint you." Kathryn held a mug aloft, silently offering a coffee.

Claire shook her head. "No, thanks. I think I'm nearly late."

"Okay. Maybe next time."

Claire frowned. "Maybe, sure."

"Oh, by the way, how many times have you forgotten it's Saturday and not slept in?" asked Kathryn.

"A few. But nothing beats the time I showed up to work when I wasn't even rostered on. See you later." Claire disappeared.

Kathryn heard a beep and saw Claire's phone by the sink. "You forgot your phone," she called.

"Damn that thing." Claire ran back to fetch it. She looked at the screen. "Holy shit."

"What is it?"

"You've got to be kidding me."

"What's wrong, Claire?"

"Victoria's thinking of coming back."

"For good?" Kathryn's heart flipped inside out and her coffee threatened to resurface.

"I'm not sure. It just says she wants to see me."

"Do you want to see *her*?"

Claire's silence was all the indication Kathryn needed.

"I gotta go. I'm late."

Kathryn didn't want her to leave. "Claire, stay and talk about it."

Claire was already out the door.

Kathryn tipped her half finished coffee down the sink. She

couldn't understand why Claire would even entertain the thought of seeing Victoria. What was Victoria playing at? She didn't know her personally of course, but Jess and Alex did and they were more than a little disappointed in the way she treated Claire.

Kathryn rushed to the front of the house to stop Claire, but there was no sign of her. *Shit!* She paced the length of the hall. Her heartbeat gained momentum and sweat dampened her armpits. She wasn't sure if it was fear or panic, but she at least had the smarts to recognise that it wasn't only worry regarding Victoria's possible return, it was jealousy. As she sat on the edge of her bed with her head between her knees, she realised she was shit scared of losing Claire.

It occurred to her that you couldn't lose someone you didn't have, and that was Kathryn's light bulb moment. She'd only ever experienced one other moment like this, and that was when she realised Andy needed to stay out of her life forever. As far as second light bulb moments went, she felt underprepared.

She wanted Claire and needed her. *Great timing, Kathryn.* How the hell was she going to tell Claire her feelings were reciprocated, if that was what she decided to do, with the threat of Victoria's return looming?

CHAPTER TWENTY-SIX

Claire pulled into the car park and read the message again. If it weren't for the fact that she liked her phone and that it was not the phone's fault Victoria had messaged, she'd have thrown it under a semi trailer on the way in.

She'd composed at least one hundred replies, all unsuitable and all beginning with the line, "If by chance you don't have a single vehicle accident on the way to the airport…" Months ago, she may have wanted to see Victoria, if for no other reason than to tell her how deplorable her behaviour was, but now she liked not thinking about her. One bloody text message and she was consuming her mind.

Murray tapped on her window. "You glued your arse to the seat, Paddy?"

It scared the daylights out of her and she ran to catch up. "Read this."

Murray took the phone without breaking stride. "You're showing me a message about buying milk on the way home."

Claire snatched the phone back. "Not that one, this one."

She stopped dead. "Is she fucking serious?"

"I've no idea."

"Just ignore it." Murray marched on.

"What and risk her just showing up?"

"Yeah, fuck it. What do you care if she shows up? Let her waste the cash on the plane ticket if she's stupid enough." Murray stopped short of the entrance. "Nothing sends a clearer message than being ignored."

Claire wasn't sure Victoria received those types of messages as loud and as clear as others might. She shoved her phone in her pocket vowing to think about it later.

Later came sooner when Victoria messaged again. *Tickets are a lot of money, Claire. Do you want to see me? x*

Murray laughed when she read it.

"You're not helping."

"Of course I'm helping," she said. "This is what good friends do. We mock something like this so we can leave you in no doubt that your ex is a complete shithead."

Claire rolled her eyes and continued with her day.

Two hours later, her phone beeped again. She reluctantly looked at it. *I hope your day is going ok. I was wondering how you were doing after hearing from V? X* Kathryn hadn't messaged her in weeks. Not since the incident at the cinema. It was a nice gesture. Maybe Kathryn was finally coming out of whatever rock she'd been hiding under this last while.

She replied, *I'm ok. Thanks for checking on me. It's nice of you to think of me. x*

Barely five minutes after she flushed a foreign object out of a carpenter's eye, her phone beeped again. This time she was less surprised. It read: *I can't believe you're ignoring me. I suppose it could be the shock, but give me a break here Claire. X.*

Murray leaned over her shoulder to read it. "Stay strong. She'll give up soon."

"Which ex-girlfriend called Victoria are you remembering, Murray, because I'm quite sure she won't just *give up*."

"Can I call her?" Murray snatched for the phone.

"No. Don't be daft."

"So, wait it out. I promise you she'll give up."

Claire knew how persistent Victoria could be. She wanted to trust Murray's judgement, but she knew Victoria best, surely. But then, she had walked out on Claire in the most unexpected fashion. Maybe she really didn't know her at all. Her phone beeped again. Murray was successful in her snatch this time.

"Whoa, that one is definitely for you and probably shouldn't be ignored."

Claire read a message from Kathryn. *I think about you often, but especially when I know you're hurting. Call me if you need anything. Kx*

Murray had shot off toward her office and Claire followed.

"No way, Claire. I'm staying out of this one," said Murray when Claire caught up.

"You gotta help me with this. I'm going mad."

Murray looked her in the eye before opening the office door and ushering Claire in. "What's going on?"

"I think Kathryn's gay."

"Gay for real, or just flirting with the gay girl kind of gay? Big difference, Paddy."

"She's gay."

Murray gave her the "say no more" look.

"I like her."

"You liked her sister years ago, too."

"That's true."

"Does she like you?"

"She likes what I do to her."

"Jesus, Paddy, is that all you ever think about?"

Claire picked a spot on the floor to focus on. "I think she likes me, but I think she's scared."

"Of Jess or the fact that she's banged her prize ex-girlfriend?"

Claire's eyes shot up. "Am I Jess's best ex?"

Murray threw a prescription pad at her. "I can't see how the title fits, but yes, I believe so."

"Seriously, Murray, I can deal with the Victoria stuff, it's not a problem really, but what should I do with Kathryn? I really like her and I think she really likes me." Claire explained the conversation at the cinema and how they'd both given each other space. "I can't talk to Jess or Alex about this."

"It sounds like you made it pretty clear you would let her work it out. How long that takes is up to her. Perhaps talk to her tonight and tell her there's nothing to worry about with Victoria. I think that's a good start. I can't see how you can move forward unless she makes the first move though, Paddy."

Murray was right, of course. Bloody woman was always right. Claire agreed and was about to leave when her phone beeped again. The message from Victoria read. *Look, you win. I'm already in Australia. Been here since last week. I had to come back because of my fucking visa. I'm getting a different one. Can we meet up or not?*

Claire allowed Murray to take the phone this time. After a few taps, she passed it back with a message on the screen. All she had to do was press send. It read. *Please stop contacting me, Victoria. I don't want to see you. We have nothing to say to each other. Good-bye.*

Claire pressed send. Murray squeezed her shoulder and she switched off her phone and returned it to her locker.

CHAPTER TWENTY-SEVEN

With four women in the house and all great cooks, it was rare to eat takeaway, and even rarer to consider it on a weeknight. Most kids Kathryn's age grew up with parents who might consider fish and chips on a Friday or Saturday night, but even then it wasn't a regular thing. In those days, it was the cheapest takeaway and their local shop had the best chips in Australia, according to her dad.

Tonight was one of those nights where the thought of cooking was akin to suggesting they all chop off their little finger, and besides Jess, every one of them moaned about their rotten day. Claire and Kathryn nearly knocked each other over trying to reach the fresh glasses of wine Alex poured.

"How about Thai?" Kathryn sipped her drink wondering what Claire had decided to do about Victoria.

"How about it indeed. I'm in," Claire said.

Alex fished around in the bottom drawer for a menu. "Claire and I will pick it up. You phone ahead."

No, no, no. Kathryn had wanted to talk to Claire before Victoria came back, assuming she was coming back, and suggesting takeaway seemed like the easiest way to spend time together alone. *Shit!* She really needed to know what Claire had replied to Victoria. She could ask her outright now, but it seemed so out of context when they were talking about dinner. Also, she wasn't sure she was prepared if Victoria was coming to see Claire. She wasn't sure she was prepared if she wasn't. She was scared to jump either way and the crippling fear rendered her useless.

"Claire and I will go, Alex. You stay at home and look after your wife."

Jess pulled her head out of her briefcase long enough to say, "Actually, Kathryn, I wanted to pick your brain on some accountancy stuff. I'm working on an embezzlement case, and I could do with a deeper understanding of what this bloke appears to have gotten up to."

In the end, Kathryn had to agree to stay with Jess. She calmed herself with the thought that she'd mention the topic of Victoria later. She vowed that by the end of the evening she would know what Claire felt, if anything, for Victoria.

❖

"She did *what*?"

Claire had just told Alex that Victoria had wanted to see her. She was relieved Alex wasn't driving; they would have spun off the road by now.

"I know. The cheek of her, right?"

Alex sat reading the messages. "And she's bloody well already here. She's a piece of work, Claire. I know I try to be neutral in these instances, but you're so much better off without her."

Claire appreciated the affirmation, but no longer needed it. She knew Victoria leaving was the best thing that could have happened; now she just wished she and Kathryn could work themselves out. Besides a message earlier that day, Kathryn had shown no signs of caring either way if Victoria returned or not. Even though Claire replied, the conversation seemed over. Of all the things that could have jolted Kathryn into action, surely the threat of the ex-lover returning should be at the top of the list.

"How's Kathryn these days?" asked Alex.

Claire frowned.

"Oh, I know I could ask her myself, but we kind of have an unspoken agreement that I'll stay out of her love life."

"She's not seeing Tony anymore, you knew that?"

Alex nodded. "I figured it all went pear shaped."

Claire felt awkward speaking about Kathryn behind her back.

Especially concerning sensitive topics she knew Kathryn wouldn't openly share. She kept it vague. "I think she might be confused."

"Oh, I see. So, it wasn't just a passing phase?"

Claire couldn't stop now she'd begun. "I think Tony was a lovely bloke, on the whole."

"But he just wasn't enough?"

"No. I don't think so."

"And perhaps you're enough but she doesn't want to admit that."

Claire pulled up at the row of shops to collect dinner and more wine. She turned to Alex. "What would it mean if I was enough? If she admitted I was enough."

"If it's that important and something happens between you, then you have to come clean and tell Jess."

Claire nodded. She knew that would be the answer. She just needed to hear it. Kathryn would struggle with telling Jess almost as much as she was struggling with her sexuality. "Come on. Wine shopping then dinner?"

"Sounds perfect to me."

Claire branched off in one direction searching for red, while Alex perused the white. She always ended up buying the same wine, but liked the process of looking before selecting. Time management wasn't one of Claire's most outstanding qualities while shopping.

After selecting her favourite bottle, she became distracted in the spirit section and saw ouzo on the shelf. Although packing up her house had been difficult, she remembered how Kathryn had made her feel during her ouzo induced bout of self-pity. It had been the first time she'd felt anything real since Victoria had left and the dreams had begun. The significance of the day made her smile.

She grabbed a bottle from the shelf on a whim and was walking quickly toward the checkout when a thick tattooed arm clamped around her neck.

CHAPTER TWENTY-EIGHT

Jess was talking, a lot, but Kathryn couldn't focus. She didn't care that a well known insurance executive had forged signatures and had effectively raised invoices for works not undertaken, nor requested, to the tune of six million dollars. She found herself discussing standard practices, and she drew a flowchart to demonstrate the movement of funds, but ultimately, she just wanted Claire to come home.

If Victoria was returning to Australia, she needed to make her move first.

"There's more to it, I know there is." Jess removed her glasses and rubbed her eyes. "Ivan can't find the proof, that's all."

Ivan was the detective on the case. Another useless snippet of information Kathryn didn't want to know.

"Do you think Claire will want Victoria back?" It was out of the blue, she knew that, but she couldn't hold it in a moment longer.

"What? Are you mad? She's well rid of her."

She'd put her foot in it. "She messaged Claire today asking if she could come and see her."

"Fucking hell." Jess shut her folder. Six million dollar embezzlement apparently had nothing on Claire's private life. "What did Claire say?"

"I've no idea. I haven't had a chance to talk to her."

"What exactly did the message say?"

Kathryn relayed the message as best she could remember.

"She wants to fly halfway round the world to see Claire?" Jess whistled. "Is she insane?"

Kathryn could only think of Victoria as a bitch. Insane wasn't nearly harsh enough for the way she treated Claire.

"She must want her back."

Kathryn cringed at the thought. "Claire wouldn't have her back now, surely?"

Jess laughed. "No way. A while ago I thought she was seeing someone else. It was the happiest I'd seen her in ages. You know, a bit of a spring in her step and all."

Kathryn felt her chest deflate.

"But it must have fizzled out because no one's been around. I don't mean to sound crude, but I hope she had some good old-fashioned sexy fun before it ended. I think she needed something after Victoria."

Kathryn felt like her brain had been replaced with an expanding lump of goo representing guilt. "It was me." She blurted the words before she could think twice. She experienced a brief moment of relief before panic set in.

"What?"

"I'm so sorry, Jess. It was me."

"What?"

"I slept with Claire."

"You're straight!"

"Not so much. Apparently."

"You had sex with Claire?"

Kathryn nodded.

"The same Claire I used to have sex with?"

She nodded again.

"Holy Jesus." Jess paced the kitchen. "There are certain rules that should never be broken, Kathryn, and you've just broken all of them." Jess was livid. "How could you after you accused me of sleeping with her? Honestly, Kathryn, how did you think this would pan out?"

"I wasn't thinking. We'd had a bit to drink. It was silly the first time, but—"

"The first time? How many times have there been?"

"Just twice." Kathryn could feel the onset of tears. She didn't want to hurt Jess, but she didn't want to lose her chance with Claire either.

"Twice? Two separate instances and not once did you think the respectable thing to do was tell me?"

Kathryn stood eye to eye with Jess. "She's not yours anymore."

Jess stopped dead and inhaled deeply. "No. She's not mine." She poured a glass of water for herself and the remainder of the wine for Kathryn. "Does she feel the same about you?"

"I've treated her badly. I pushed her away. She used to want me. I don't know if that's the case anymore." Kathryn recounted the series of events for Jess right from the beginning.

"And here we are." Jess shook her head. "You've made a right mess of this. She might want you, but we don't know. You want her, but she doesn't know, and bloody Victoria is probably on her way to fuck it all up as we speak." Jess reached for Kathryn's hand. "We'll get it all sorted tonight, okay?"

Kathryn nodded.

"So you think you're a lesbian now?"

"I don't know. I really liked Tony."

"Was that his name?"

Kathryn realised she'd never spoken of Tony to Jess. That in itself spoke volumes. "He was a nice man, but he wasn't Claire. There was something missing with Tony that was never missing with Claire. When I was with him, I was with a really lovely man. When I'm with Claire, though, it's as if I'm with my soul mate. Does that make sense?"

"It makes sense. Alex is going to have a field day with this."

Kathryn took a deep breath. "Alex knows."

"Ah, give me a break, Kathryn. Am I the only idiot in the house that didn't know?"

"She said she was going to tell you. She knows you better than you know yourself, so I'm sure she was only waiting for the right moment." Kathryn looked her in the eye. "But I'm glad I got the chance to tell you myself."

"I imagine it's been tough for you. Would you have talked to me about it if the other woman wasn't Claire?"

"I wanted to talk to you about it a million times, but I wasn't sure I deserved your understanding."

Jess punched her shoulder. "You're the worst fake homophobe I've ever met."

"But you still love me, right?"

"Maybe."

Kathryn took her in her arms and squeezed. "And you're okay about me and Claire."

"No, I'm not bloody okay, and I swear to God if you hurt her you'll have me to deal with."

Kathryn smiled. "And what if she hurts me?"

"I'll fucking kill her."

❖

Claire thought it was a joke, but as the arm around her neck began to tighten and her breathing became restricted, she realised it was no laughing matter.

The look on Alex's face suggested it was very serious indeed.

"Everyone get the fuck down or I'll stick her."

Claire couldn't be sure, but she thought she'd heard the term "stick her" about a million years ago in a Hollywood movie.

Her ridiculous thoughts didn't detract from the fact that the man holding her had a knife. The man holding her could end her life. Claire couldn't breathe. Whether it was panic or the actual constriction of her throat, she couldn't be sure.

She fought to release the arm around her.

The man holding her stood on her foot. "I've got this." A manky old fishing knife entered her vision. He spoke so only she could hear. "Please, just stay still. I won't hurt you."

She stopped struggling as clarity overtook her panic. The man holding her sounded young, and the voice he addressed the shop owner in was nothing like his voice when talking to her. The hand holding the knife had been shaking. He was scared. Stupid and scared.

"Empty the fuckin' till in a bag or she gets it."

She felt pressure on her side. The hand holding the knife was resting near her ribs. Something told Claire that this man was telling the truth when he said he wouldn't hurt her. She considered talking to him, but it had gone too far already. He had a knife and he was holding up a liquor store. His fate was sealed whether she talked him down or not.

"I'm not fucking joking."

Claire briefly wondered how this would end if he didn't get out of the shop soon. The thought of a skilled police officer with a high powered rifle lining him up from a reasonable distance wasn't appealing.

The man made a sudden movement toward the counter, and Claire hadn't been ready. She stumbled and their feet became entangled, causing them both to fall forward.

Claire registered heat and pain in her side and she wanted to double over, but the man was holding her upright. The look on Alex's face told the story.

The knife had pierced her skin. She couldn't bring herself to think that she'd been stabbed, she didn't want to be a victim of a stabbing, but she could feel warm blood oozing down her side. The pain was excruciating.

"No! Claire." Alex stepped forward just as the shop assistant threw a bag onto the floor.

The tight grip on Claire disappeared, leaving her unbalanced and unsteady on her feet. Before she understood what was happening, the man rushed from the shop, scooping up the bag of cash on the way.

From that moment on, everything seemed to happen simultaneously.

Alex ran to Claire and helped lower her to the ground. "You're going to be fine." She pulled a promotional beach towel from a shop display and pressed it to Claire's side after briefly looking at the wound. "I think it's more of a fleshy slice than a deep stab."

"Is that a technical term, Doctor?" Claire began to shiver. Fleshy slice or not, it hurt like hell. She wished someone would turn the lights off. Umpteen bright strips beamed on her from above causing her to squint, intensifying her distress. She was the centre of everyone's attention. If she had her way, she'd get up, walk out, and drive to the hospital. As it was, she could barely move without flinching in pain.

Alex took the fluorescent jacket the shop assistant offered and placed it over Claire. He came back a moment later with another beer beach towel. "It's all I have to keep her warm, sorry."

"Have you called the police?" asked Alex.

"I tripped the distress button the moment I saw the knife. They should be here soon. I called an ambulance, too. Don't worry."

"Are you okay?" Alex asked him.

He began to tear up when another shopper, who'd cleverly remained at the rear of the shop, took him by the shoulders with comforting words.

It felt like Claire had been on the floor forever when the cavalry arrived. In reality, it had only been five minutes.

One of the paramedics, Michael, put an oxygen mask over Claire's face and after a quick inspection, placed a massive wad of gauze over her injury.

"She'll be fine. The oxygen's just to help her while she's in shock. Few stitches at the hospital and she'll be right as rain."

Alex smiled. "She's a nurse. I'm sure she'll let you know if she needs anything else."

"Like painkillers?" said Claire.

"Coming right up, madam," said Michael.

The moment they were in the ambulance, Alex called Jess. Claire just hoped the news wouldn't induce labour.

❖

Kathryn knew it would take Jess a long time to come to terms with the fact that she and Claire had slept together. She wasn't expecting miracles, but at least their conversation had been a step in the right direction. They were discussing the issue further when Jess's phone rang.

"It's Alex. I bet she's forgotten what we ordered."

Kathryn looked at her watch. Claire and Alex had been gone nearly an hour. The shops were only fifteen minutes away. "Surely they're on their way home."

Jess answered and Kathryn listened.

"Alex, slow down. Bloody hell. Where are you now?" Jess stood and colour drained from her face.

Fear rose in Kathryn. Her immediate thought was a car accident. "What's happened?"

Jess waved at her to be quiet. "She's in good hands, Alex," she said into the phone.

"Jess, is it Claire?" Kathryn was becoming agitated.

"Okay." Jess was nodding now. "But no vital organs or anything?"

Vital organs?

"Well, I doubt it tickles." Jess ran her fingers through her hair. "We'll be there as soon as possible." She put the phone down.

"What is it, Jess? Is it Claire?"

"Claire was involved in a hold-up at the store."

"Fucking hell, is she okay?" Kathryn broke into a sweat.

"She's fine, but she was stabbed."

"Stabbed? Someone stabbed her?" Her head pounded with fear.

"They're taking her to hospital for stitches, but she's going to be fine." Jess gulped water. "God." She steadied herself with the back of the chair. "I can't believe it."

Kathryn couldn't believe it either. "But she's all right?" Her brain struggled to move past the fact that someone had stabbed Claire.

Jess squeezed her shoulder. "Alex assured me it's just a flesh wound."

It was becoming clear what Kathryn needed to do. Fear was a powerful motivator. Fear gave her clarity. It was now clear that she loved Claire O'Malley and she needed to tell her. "We'll meet them there then?"

Jess nodded.

"Is Alex okay?"

"Shaken and upset, but not hurt. She saw it all happen. She saw the bloke grab her. She said there was nothing she could do."

Kathryn switched to autopilot. She locked the back door, collected Jess's phone and wallet, grabbed her bag, locked up the house, and helped Jess into the car.

It wasn't exactly a mercy dash to the hospital, but she had things to say and she needed to say them sooner rather than later.

CHAPTER TWENTY-NINE

"Ah, Paddy, you've had your fair share of bad luck lately." Murray was there when they arrived at the ED. "They say it comes in threes, you know?" She smiled a greeting at Alex. "First, Maree Black, now this. What's the third thing, I wonder?" She peered around the side of the nurse who removed the gauze pad from Claire's side. "Nasty, but not too bad. A good clean and some stitches will sort you out. A dickhead with a knife; it could've been a whole lot worse."

The comment hit Claire like a truck.

She vomited the entire length of the bed. Her life had hung in the balance while some imbecile wannabe gangster used her to steal someone else's hard-earned money. Nurses hurried to clean up the vomit. Some were only in the vicinity after calling on Claire to wish her well, but all remained untroubled by the volume of rancid smelling vomit.

Murray returned and waited for the commotion to die down.

"There's a police officer waiting to see you. Shall I show him in? Get it over with?"

In fact, the police officer had some good news. They apprehended the man, who turned out to be a seventeen-year-old boy, shortly after the hold-up. He didn't make it past McDonald's in the adjacent street. Staff saw blood on his arm and they called the police because they thought he'd cut his wrists. The police officer said he'd seen enough assholes—he apologised for his language—and hold-ups in his time to know the kid was genuinely remorseful. He had asked after Claire and insisted he hadn't meant to use the knife at all.

Alex held her hand. "That's some good news at least."

"He didn't intend to hurt me." Claire spoke the words aloud to help them sink in.

"He's about to learn the hard way that you can't go wielding a knife at innocent people," the officer said.

Claire supposed not. "He told me he wouldn't hurt me if I stayed still."

"It was probably the truth, love. Unfortunately, when you break the law and you're a dumb arse, you get into all sorts of bother."

"I know he didn't mean to hurt you, honey, but he did. There are consequences for those actions," said Alex.

Murray showed the officer out, leaving Claire and Alex alone.

"Are you okay?" asked Claire. She might have been the one high on morphine, but Alex had been there, too. It was a harrowing experience for everyone concerned. She was wishing they'd ordered pizza.

"What? God, I'm fine." Alex waved a dismissive arm. "I'm not the one with fifteen stitches in my side."

"No, I know. But you were there. You saw it happen."

Alex lost colour.

Claire handed her the bucket and turned away while she dry retched.

"It's a weird realisation, isn't it?"

"It was awful," Alex admitted. "I don't know if I'll ever get the image out of my head. Seeing you like that was—"

"It's okay. I'm okay."

Alex pulled herself together. "I know. It all happened so fast."

Murray barged in holding two pill bottles—antibiotics and painkillers. "Merry Christmas, Paddy."

CHAPTER THIRTY

Kathryn knew there was no need to run, and Jess struggled to keep up, but rushing to see Claire was instinctive. Even Jess lumbering behind didn't slow her down.

Jess's phone beeped. She pulled up breathless and checked the message. "She's being stitched up. We'll wait until that's over. Poor thing. She'll be sore for a few days."

Kathryn finally stopped.

Jess caught up and leaned on her. "Can we please go slowly now?"

Partitioned to optimise space and accommodate vending machines, the waiting area was busy. Kathryn sat at a chair closest to the triage desk. She felt like the kid in the front row at school, but she didn't care. She needed to be as close to the door as possible.

They heard Murray's voice before they saw anyone coming. Jess recognised it immediately, and she and Jess rose to greet Alex and Claire.

"I deliver to you one stitched up Paddy." Murray greeted Jess with a kiss on the cheek, and Kathryn shook her hand.

Claire looked pale as if she'd seen a ghost, and when she began to sway, everyone except Jess lunged to keep her upright and steady.

Everyone including Victoria.

"Where did you come from?" Jess was obviously not intending to use her manners.

Victoria reached up to touch Claire's cheek. "Poor baby, are you okay?"

Kathryn flinched as if someone had jabbed her violently in the ribs. It was heartbreaking, watching Victoria so naturally touch Claire, as if she belonged with no one else. She scolded herself, wondering what she had expected. She didn't trust Victoria; she would let Claire down again. No one could change that much. But then *she'd* also let Claire down? Hadn't she gone some way to breaking her heart and using her, just like Victoria?

Claire backed off. "I told you I didn't want to see you."

Kathryn took a double take.

She locked eyes with Claire. She couldn't read her expression, but in such a brief moment, she wanted to convey so much. Her intense stare couldn't possibly let Claire know she had finally come to her senses. Her eyes had no way of telling Claire that she wanted her.

Victoria took a step back. "I thought I'd surprise you."

Murray interrupted. "Let's not do this out here."

"Victoria's leaving, Murray. We're fine out here." Claire raised her chin and addressed Victoria. "I'm not surprised you're here. I doubt anything you do could surprise me again. You're predictable, Victoria. You never listened to what I wanted and you're still not listening."

Kathryn's stomach turned somersaults with pride. She stepped forward. "It's time for you to leave."

"And who are you?"

Kathryn looked to Claire, then Jess, then Alex. "I'm the person that can give her everything you can't."

For a split second, Kathryn was sure the entire ED went silent.

The words came as a surprise to her as much as everyone else.

Jess beamed with pride and Alex looked stunned.

Claire responded by vomiting all over the floor.

Kathryn had to admit, she didn't see that coming.

Murray pushed a wheelchair behind Claire, forcing her to sit down. "Show's over, folks." She wheeled Claire back through the triage doors.

Victoria looked down to her leather boots now sprayed with Claire's lunch.

Kathryn stood her ground. She could have sworn she'd grown six inches and developed an Olympic swimmer's shoulders.

Jess and Alex followed Claire. "Don't be too long," said Jess.

She was nearly done. "Claire's moved on and she's made it clear she doesn't want to see you. I know you've flown a long way and it's probably cost you a small fortune, but please, for her sake and mine, respect her decision for once."

Victoria gave nothing away. "I'm home to upgrade my visa for Germany. You can't know her very well if she didn't even tell you I've been in Australia for over a week now."

"And you don't know Claire at all if you think your lies are acceptable to her." Kathryn couldn't believe she'd been worried sick all day about nothing.

"My mother told me I was wasting my time."

"From what I've heard, you'd do well to listen to your mother less and learn to stand on your own two feet." Kathryn wondered if Victoria ever did any of own her dirty work.

Victoria turned and left.

When Kathryn woke that morning, she wasn't expecting such an eventful day. She inhaled deeply. Now that she'd induced vomiting in the woman she loved, a first in her book, her life was complete. With trepidation and excitement, she hurried to discover the aftermath of her revelation.

❖

The triage nurse said she thought Victoria had arrived at the hospital by chance, thinking that Claire might be working a night shift. The nurse apologised because she let slip that Claire was there as a patient, not on shift. Claire guessed Victoria probably went to their old apartment first and the hospital was naturally the next place she'd look.

Regardless, she had more important things to worry about; Kathryn had just outed herself to everyone, including Jess. She briefly wondered if more morphine would improve the impending conversation. *Fuck it.* Surely, the most recently stabbed person in the room deserved some slack.

After speaking to the triage nurse, Murray whisked them to her office. She was pushing Claire in the wheelchair and it was the worst ride of her life.

"Jesus, slow down. I won't be stitched up for much longer if you keep taking corners so fast."

As Murray's door shut behind them, Claire looked to Jess. "I can explain." She wanted to save Kathryn the torture of having to walk into the office alone and face a barrage of questions.

"There's no need. Kathryn and I spoke earlier tonight."

"She told you?"

Jess nodded.

"And?" Claire was both relieved and terrified. Jess's expression gave nothing away.

"And if you do anything to hurt my sister you'll need more than bloody stitches when I'm finished with you." She smiled.

Just at that moment, Kathryn came crashing through the door. She obviously caught the last half of Jess's little speech. "Oh, I see she's giving you the same pep talk. Thank goodness it's not just me."

An odd silence prevailed as everyone looked at everyone else. Murray let out an audible sigh, and Claire quickly caught a glimpse of Jess smiling at Alex before she turned her attention to Kathryn. "Thank you for doing that just now."

Kathryn had tears in her eyes. "Can Claire and I have a moment, please?"

Jess, Alex, and Murray all patted Claire on the shoulder before leaving, and Jess kissed Kathryn on the cheek.

"Are you okay?" asked Kathryn when Murray closed the door behind her.

Claire nodded. "Please don't ask me about what happened at that place right now."

Kathryn nodded.

"Later, okay, when it's just me and you?"

"Of course, honey."

"I'm glad you're here," said Claire.

"I've been such an idiot."

"You're here now. That's all that matters."

"And so was Victoria. I've been worried all day because I wasn't sure if you wanted to see her or not, then she tells me she's been here all week."

Claire cocked her head and winked. "That's my girl. Full of shit to the brim."

"But she's not your girl now."

"Well, no, this is true. I'm kind of hoping that after tonight I'll have a new girl. How do you rate my chances?" She reached for Kathryn's hand.

Kathryn kneeled before her and rested her hand on Claire's knees. The wheelchair began to move backward, and Kathryn lost balance, pushing Claire into the examination table and knocking a tray of clean instruments onto the floor with a clangour. Claire shot her hands up to cover her head, but nothing else came crashing down. Her nerves felt like they were dangling by a thread. She held it together.

The door swung open and the others rushed through the door.

Claire raised her arms. "It's okay. Bloody Murray forgot to put the brakes on."

Everyone laughed.

"Have you finished your special moment?" asked Alex.

"Not quite, just another couple of minutes please."

They filed out again.

"Where were we?" Kathryn knelt again.

"You were about to tell me that you're my girl."

"Oh, yeah. That's right." Kathryn's expression turned serious. "I want you to know, though, that I came to the conclusion I wanted to be with you before this happened. You can ask Jess if you don't believe me."

"I believe you."

Kathryn sighed. "Of course you do." She rested her head in Claire's lap.

Claire instinctively ran her finger through her hair and gently massaged the tense muscles in her neck. "Kathryn, look at me."

Kathryn lifted her head. Claire leaned forward until their foreheads met. She let the tears out. "You've made a disastrous day into a wonderful day." Claire felt like a time bomb ready to explode, but she feared losing control if she let out her pain now. "Can you please kiss me and then take me home?"

Kathryn pressed her lips gently to Claire's. If Claire thought they shared chemistry before, it was nothing like now. She opened her mouth and felt Kathryn's tongue gently caress her lower lip. The contact was exquisite and surpassed any painkilling drug received that evening. There was no need to hide and there was nothing stopping them being together. The kiss felt pure and it was all the antidote Claire needed after a truly rotten day.

"Come on then," Kathryn said. "Let's get you home and to bed."

Claire raised her eyebrows. "You don't waste any time."

"I didn't mean it like that." Kathryn's eyes widened, horrified.

"Oh, so you don't want to sleep with me?"

"No. Yes of course, but no." Kathryn was stammering.

"I'm kidding."

"I'll get used to your sense of humour, won't I?"

Claire just grinned. She hoped Kathryn would come to know her inside and out, but she hoped they'd never tire of each other.

In the car park, Claire used Kathryn for support as she lowered herself gently into the passenger seat.

"I feel like I could sleep for a week," she said.

"See that you do," said Murray. "You'll need all the energy you can get for therapy."

"I was wondering who would mention that first." Claire sighed.

"I've got one word, Paddy, PTSD."

"That's not a word, Doctor; it's an acronym."

"And you're still a smart-arse, so that's a good sign."

"He didn't mean to hurt me, but I concede I'll be back in Jean's office. Don't worry."

"Damn straight," said Murray. "And the quicker the better."

Claire rested her head against the seat. It felt so good to be going home. "So, what's for dinner?"

CHAPTER THIRTY-ONE

Although it was amazing that she and Claire were finally together, nothing could change the fact that Claire and Alex had been involved in a terrifying experience. Jess had taken Alex to bed immediately, taking toast and a cup of tea with them.

Kathryn was sleeping in Claire's room. She hadn't asked permission, but there was no way Claire should be alone.

She heard the shower running. It had been nearly ten minutes now. She changed the bed sheets and slipped under the covers. She surveyed the room. A solitary candle was burning on the windowsill, and a toasted cheese and tomato sandwich sat on the bedside table with a coffee. She'd taken a large T-shirt from Claire's drawer and placed it on the pillow. She knew Claire usually slept naked but wondered if, this evening, that would leave her feeling vulnerable.

Another five minutes passed before Claire padded in, a towel wrapped around her and her eyes puffy and bloodshot from crying. Claire dropped the towel and struggled to raise her arm high enough to dress herself.

Kathryn leapt out of bed. "Here, let me help you with that. You're not completely dry. Can I?" She held the towel aloft and waited for Claire's nodded consent. Kathryn tenderly dried Claire's back, stomach, chest, and arms. Claire sobbed silently.

Kathryn gently dressed her in the T-shirt then hopped into bed. "Come on," she said, holding the covers back. "You're safe now." Claire gingerly lowered herself onto the soft sheets. Kathryn handed her more painkillers and the coffee. Claire ate half the sandwich before Kathryn switched off the light.

"Would you like me to hold you?" asked Kathryn.

"Yes, please."

"I don't want to hurt you," said Kathryn, shifting closer. "Tell me if it hurts, okay?"

Claire remained on her back while Kathryn drew her close, resting a protective arm around her shoulders. Unsure of what to do with her other hand, she let it fall on her own waist until Claire searched for it and entwined their fingers, drawing both hands up to her chest and under her chin.

When the sobbing subsided, she felt Claire's body relax into hers. "Tonight was terrible. I just want to forget about it."

Kathryn softly kissed her hair, savouring the fresh apple scent of shampoo, and invited her to sleep. "I'm here and I'm not going anywhere. I'll hold you as long as you need me."

Claire mumbled her thanks, moments from slumber, as she snuggled deeper into Kathryn's protective embrace.

EPILOGUE

It was difficult for Claire to remember life before Kathryn. She knew it existed of course, and at particular moments—often fleeting—certain smells, words, and places would spark a pang of pain that reminded her Victoria had certainly existed in her past life. Sometimes at work, a patient might possess similarities to Maree Black, or she might detect a waft of the distinct reek of cheap aftershave the boy in the bottle shop had worn, but overall, it was Kathryn who existed for her now.

Life felt remarkable. Sure, it had been good in the past, but with Kathryn, Claire felt complete, and the world was brimming with opportunities.

Her recovery after the incident had been speedy. A couple of weeks off for her wound to heal, followed by another four on light duties. Now she was back in full flight.

The dynamic in the house had changed, too. Alex and Jess graciously stepped aside while Claire became the focus of Kathryn's life. The transition from one couple to two was smooth, but it had a limited shelf life.

"My settlement should be through any day now." It was late on a Friday evening and Kathryn returned naked from Claire's old room, which they had long since turned into their walk-in wardrobe.

Claire was in bed, busily tapping away on their iPad. Jess was due in four weeks and it was critical they find a place of their own.

"What are you doing?" asked Kathryn.

"I'm looking at rentals. This place will be hell when the babies arrive."

"Oh, I don't know, I kind of liked the idea of helping out with the babies."

Claire glared at her. "It's not the babies that worry me; it's Jess."

"Good point."

The evenings were cool, and Kathryn slipped under the doona keenly eyeing some of the properties Claire was perusing. "Can I borrow the iPad for a moment?"

"Sure. I need a bathroom break anyway." Claire raced down the hall to the bathroom. The scar on her side tingled. She lifted her T-shirt and gently rubbed a finger over it to calm whatever it was sparking the nerves into action. She liked the scar. It signified the day Victoria disappeared from her life, the day Kathryn came into it, and the day she realised she wasn't immortal. From that day on, she had vowed to live the life she wanted to live, not just settle for second best. She returned to bed and stole a glance at Kathryn. She smiled.

"Can I show you something?" Kathryn handed her the iPad.

On the screen was a lovely house with a handsome porch and charming front garden. "Ha, see. I knew you'd catch the real estate bug sooner rather than later." Claire kissed Kathryn's cheek. "How much?"

"Eight hundred thousand."

Claire whistled. "That's a lot. Where is it?" Disappointment washed over her. She couldn't even begin to think of what kind of repayments would come with a mortgage on that sort of property.

"It's just the other side of that park you run to."

Claire knew it would be brilliant to live so close to Jess and Alex, but the prices of property were high. Travel another thirty minutes into suburbia and they would be half that. Living in the same suburb as Jess and Alex was an impossible dream.

"Maybe we need to work out how much we can afford." Claire felt deflated. Her head dropped. "I barely have a savings account, baby. I don't have anything," she quietly added.

"I went and took a look at it after work today." Kathryn sat up, squarely facing Claire. "It's a beautiful house. Do you like it? At first glance?"

Claire clicked on the slideshow and stared in awe at the fully refurbished home—quaint and leafy on the outside, modern and light on the inside. "It's stunning. Is this the type of place you'd like?"

"It's the type of place I'd like to buy for us to live in."

"What?" Claire was only just beginning to understand what Kathryn was implying.

"My house in Brisbane is sold. It will settle any day now."

"You can afford this house?" Claire was amazed.

"Yes, I believe so. We'll need a mortgage, but not substantial. We can afford the repayments. I'm an accountant; I've already crunched the numbers." Kathryn looked decidedly pleased with herself.

"I don't know what to say."

"Just say you'd like to come and take a look at it tomorrow first thing."

"Of course, I'd love to."

Kathryn cupped her chin. "Things moving too fast, baby?"

"No. I just feel like a bit of a freeloader, I suppose."

"You'll love the house. I promise."

"As much as I love you?"

Kathryn kissed her gently. "Don't get carried away. It's only a house."

Claire kissed her deeply. "You're amazing," she said. "And with a house like that, what a catch."

Kathryn pinched her backside. "So now you only love me because of my money?"

Claire had no idea her property in Brisbane had been worth so much. "I like having a rich girlfriend."

"I'm hardly rich."

"But you are my girlfriend."

"Yes, and you're mine. All mine." Kathryn kissed her. "You *are* okay about no longer being footloose and fancy free, right?" Kathryn lowered her voice. "Because I don't like sharing my things."

Claire experienced sensory overload as Kathryn's lips connected with hers again, her tongue gently forcing its way deep into Claire's mouth. Claire was alive with a million sensations of love, want, desire, and passion. Never in her life had she experienced such a physical reaction to a psychological need. She felt moisture between her legs and an aching grip of desire clenched tightly in her lower abdomen.

"I want you to be mine. I want you to belong to me. And what I really want tonight is to make love to you," murmured Kathryn between kisses.

Hearing those words, knowing that Kathryn wanted her and was on the verge of taking her, exhilarated Claire.

"Close your eyes, baby." Kathryn smiled as Claire frowned. "Just for the first time, close your eyes and feel me make love to you."

Claire was deliriously aroused, and with this new Kathryn, the one that was so capably seducing her, she found herself entirely at her mercy. She closed her eyes as Kathryn's warm and supple lips kissed near her scar.

"I just want you to relax and enjoy." Kathryn slowly parted Claire's legs.

Convinced she was in the gentlest of hands, Claire visibly let go, sinking further into the mattress.

The subsequent sensation caused Claire to jolt. Kathryn's tongue scarcely touched her clit, but her response was instant and intense. Then she let out a desperate moan and squirmed involuntarily as she felt Kathryn's insistent tongue.

Claire fought to hold back the orgasm that was building at an alarming rate. "Please make it quick, baby."

Kathryn moved her tongue back to Claire's clit and slowly pushed two fingers deep inside her.

"Oh, *God*." Claire couldn't remember ever feeling anything quite so exquisite. She longed for satisfaction.

Kathryn began a long, deep rhythm. She angled her fingers to ensure every thrust stroked Claire's G-spot, bringing Claire to the edge in seconds. The more Claire wanted, the more Kathryn gave her. "Come for me, baby."

Claire writhed. She was so close to the edge.

She pumped harder. "Let it out, Claire."

Forgetting where they were, Claire let out a cry before Kathryn quickly clasped her hand over her mouth. Gently, as Claire's body shuddered through her orgasm, Kathryn replaced her hand with her mouth, kissing Claire with unbridled affection. Her fingers remained inside.

"I think I've waited for you all my life," Claire quietly gasped as Kathryn moved to hold her close and kiss her forehead.

"You've waited for a suppressed lesbian all your life?"

"No, smart-arse." Claire eyed her. "I've waited for someone to make me feel like this."

Kathryn choked back tears. "How do I make you feel?"

"Complete. You complete me. It's the most remarkable feeling that I never knew was missing until I found it. Found you."

Kathryn looked pleased with herself.

"I would never have believed in a million years I could orgasm like that," said Claire.

"What?" Kathryn tilted Claire's chin so their eyes met. "Never like tonight?"

"No, baby." Claire smiled bright and wide. "It's the sum of us that makes it all so spectacular. It's not experience, not notches on the bedpost, not a shit marriage, nothing like that. It's just us— uncomplicated and pure."

"It sounds so simple when you put it like that."

"It *is* that simple, trust me. This type of feeling doesn't happen every day, straight or gay."

Kathryn smiled. "I still can't believe you're here every morning when I wake."

After many long minutes enjoying gentle kisses and the sheer closeness of their bodies, Kathryn went to remove her fingers.

"Don't, not yet." Claire couldn't bear to have Kathryn leave her so soon.

Kathryn grinned wickedly, pulsing the tips of her fingers against Claire's G-spot.

Claire closed her eyes again, basking in sweet sensations as they flooded back through her even stronger than before.

"Is that what you want, baby?" Kathryn moved her mouth to whisper in Claire's ear. "Do you want to be a good girl for me again?"

Claire couldn't speak.

"Like this?" Kathryn used her thumb on the outside for added stimulation.

"God, yes. Exactly like that."

Kathryn took a nipple in her mouth. "I adore every part of you, Claire. I want to make you feel like this forever. *I* want to feel this way forever."

Kathryn increased the speed of her probing fingers and kissed her, hard and passionately, muffling Claire's moaning. Claire came, stronger and more intensely than before.

❖

"Where's the damn keys?" screeched Claire.

Kathryn looked at the tidy space around her. She'd left Claire to unpack the living room boxes while she concentrated on the bedroom. The bedroom was spotless while the living room still looked like a bomb of packing paper and boxes had exploded. Moving with Claire had certainly been an experience. She wondered how Claire could be a nurse; she was distracted so easily and was so damn messy.

"Kathryn!"

Grinning because she knew precisely where the keys were and because she knew Claire only used her full name if there was a spider or if Claire was frustrated to the point of uselessness, Kathryn swiftly locked the back door and hurried to put Claire out of her misery.

Kathryn stepped aside to dodge flying bubble wrap before pressing the palm of her hand firmly, but lovingly, in the middle of Claire's chest. "Calm down." She patted Claire's bulging left jean pocket. "The keys are here, baby."

"Bloody hell, I'm so rubbish!" Claire's hysteria wasn't subsiding.

Kathryn's phone beeped. She glanced at it for a moment. "Ah, false alarm."

"What?" Claire threw her arms in the air before slumping heavily against the wall and sliding to her backside. "A false alarm. Thank God." She wiped her brow and took some deep breaths. "I don't think I'm ready for this aunty caper."

Kathryn remained standing and leaned against the wall peering at Claire. "What makes you say that?"

"Look at me." Claire was beginning to lose some of the redness she had developed over her face and throat. "I'm a mess."

Kathryn laughed. "It's been a stressful day. Moving can be a nightmare."

Claire sighed.

"You're a capable nurse and a great friend to Jess and Alex. You'll make a fabulous aunty to those lucky kids."

"You think?"

"I know." Kathryn held out her hand. "Come on, let's go."

"Go where?"

"To the hospital, of course." Kathryn kissed Claire passionately. "I love you, baby, but sometimes you just need to chill out. That message was from Alex telling us everything is fine and not to hurry because it might take a while."

"You said it was a false alarm."

"Yes, I did."

"You lied to me?"

Kathryn rolled her eyes. "It was for your own good."

"You're not going to apologise?"

"Nope." Kathryn ushered Claire from the house.

"Well, now I'm seeing the real you, aren't I?"

Kathryn sighed dramatically. "Yes, darling."

"What else have you lied about, Kathryn Frances Mercer?"

Kathryn held the car door open. "Just get in, will you."

"Okay, but I'm not happy about it."

"Your protest is noted."

"Good."

"Incidentally, what would make you happy?" Kathryn stared into the most beautiful blue eyes and thanked her lucky stars for bringing Claire into her life.

Claire paused and she developed a frown.

Kathryn wondered what she was thinking.

"Marry me?" Claire turned to her, grinning.

"Pardon?"

"I'm the happiest I've ever been," said Claire. "When you asked what would make me happy, that was all I could think of. You and me forever would make me complete."

Kathryn couldn't speak. She could barely breathe. "Yes." Tears welled in her eyes.

"Yes? You mean it?"

"Yes."

Claire pulled Kathryn close, tears of elation streaming down both their faces.

"Holy shit, we're engaged!" Kathryn fumbled with the key in the ignition.

"And we're going to be aunts soon, too," Claire added.

Kathryn's phoned beeped again. She read the message. "Better get a wriggle on."

"Why?"

"The false alarm is no longer a false alarm."

Claire grabbed the phone from her. "Step on it!"

Kathryn reversed the car out of the driveway and sped off toward the hospital. Fifteen minutes later, the phone beeped again. "What's it say?"

"It says don't rush."

"Jesus, false alarm again?"

"Nope," said Claire. "It says Thomas Leo and Charlie Matilda Mercer were born just two minutes ago and both babies are perfect. They're all doing well."

Kathryn pulled over. "They're okay?"

Claire took her hand. "That's what it says."

Kathryn couldn't hold back the tears. "Our little niece and nephew were born on the day we became engaged?"

Claire smiled. "I wonder when we have kids, will someone we know get engaged."

Kathryn wiped the tears from her eyes to focus on Claire. "You want kids?"

Claire kissed her. "I do if you do."

"I'd love to make a baby with you." Kathryn said. She'd given up hope of some day becoming a mother.

"Shall we go and see these kids first, perhaps get married, and then maybe find some sperm?"

Kathryn smiled and pulled back into traffic.

"Sounds perfect."

About the Author

Michelle is Tasmanian born and resides in the UK with her wife, just north of London. She's a fair-weather golfer, a happy snapper, and a lover of cafés and bookshops.

2015 has been an exciting year for Michelle so far. Her debut novel, *Getting Lost*, was released in March, and *Keep Hold*, a romantic comedy, is her second novel. However, it doesn't stop there. January 2016 will see the release of the controversial *The Fifth Gospel*, her third novel.

For now, however, let Michelle take you to a sweltering hot summer in Melbourne. Escape to a leafy inner suburb and meet Claire and Kathryn. Laugh with them, cry with them, and jump into bed with them.

Some rules should never be broken, but where's the fun in that?

Books Available From Bold Strokes Books

The Time Before Now by Missouri Vaun. Vivian flees a disastrous affair, embarking on an epic, transformative journey to escape her past, until destiny introduces her to Ida, who helps her rediscover trust, love, and hope. (978-1-62639-446-9)

Twisted Whispers by Sheri Lewis Wohl. Betrayal, lies, and secrets—whispers of a friend lost to darkness. Can a reluctant psychic set things right or will an evil soul destroy those she loves? (978-1-62639-439-1)

The Courage to Try by C.A. Popovich. Finding love is worth getting past the fear of trying. (978-1-62639-528-2)

Break Point by Yolanda Wallace. In a world readying for war, can love find a way? (978-1-62639-568-8)

Countdown by Julie Cannon. Can two strong-willed, powerful women overcome their differences to save the lives of seven others and begin a life they never imagined together? (978-1-62639-471-1)

Keep Hold by Michelle Grubb. Claire knew some things should be left alone and some rules should never be broken, but the most forbidden, well, they are the most tempting. (978-1-62639-502-2)

Deadly Medicine by Jaime Maddox. Dr. Ward Thrasher's life is in turmoil. Her partner Jess left her, and her job puts her in the path of a murderous physician who has Jess in his sights. (978-1-62639-424-7)

New Beginnings by KC Richardson. Can the connection and attraction between Jordan Roberts and Kirsten Murphy be enough for Jordan to trust Kirsten with her heart? (978-1-62639-450-6)

Officer Down by Erin Dutton. Can two women who've made careers out of being there for others in crisis find the strength to need each other? (978-1-62639-423-0)

Reasonable Doubt by Carsen Taite. Just when Sarah and Ellery think they've left dangerous careers behind, a new case sets them—and their hearts—on a collision course. (978-1-62639-442-1)

Tarnished Gold by Ann Aptaker. Cantor Gold must outsmart the Law, outrun New York's dockside gangsters, outplay a shady art dealer, his lover, and a beautiful curator, and stay out of a killer's gun sights. (978-1-62639-426-1)

The Renegade by Amy Dunne. Post-apocalyptic survivors Alex and Evelyn secretly find love while held captive by a deranged cult, but when their relationship is discovered, they must fight for their freedom—or die trying. (978-1-62639-427-8)

Thrall by Barbara Ann Wright. Four women in a warrior society must work together to lift an insidious curse while caught between their own desires, the will of their peoples, and an ancient evil. (978-1-62639-437-7)

White Horse in Winter by Franci McMahon. Love between two women collides with the inner poison of a closeted horse trainer in the green hills of Vermont. (978-1-62639-429-2)

Autumn Spring by Shelley Thrasher. Can Bree and Linda, two women in the autumn of their lives, put their hearts first and find the love they've never dared seize? (978-1-62639-365-3)

The Chameleon's Tale by Andrea Bramhall. Two old friends must work through a web of lies and deceit to find themselves again, but in the search they discover far more than they ever went looking for. (978-1-62639-363-9)

Side Effects by VK Powell. Detective Jordan Bishop and Dr. Neela Sahjani must decide if it's easier to trust someone with your heart or your life as they face threatening protestors, corrupt politicians, and their increasing attraction. (978-1-62639-364-6)

Warm November by Kathleen Knowles. What do you do if the one woman you want is the only one you can't have? (978-1-62639-366-0)

In Every Cloud by Tina Michele. When Bree finally leaves her shattered life behind, is she strong enough to salvage the remaining pieces of her heart and find the place where it truly fits? (978-1-62639-413-1)

Rise of the Gorgon by Tanai Walker. When independent Internet journalist Elle Pharell goes to Kuwait to investigate a veteran's mysterious suicide, she hires Cassandra Hunt, an interpreter with a covert agenda. (978-1-62639-367-7)

Crossed by Meredith Doench. Agent Luce Hansen returns home to catch a killer and risks everything to revisit the unsolved murder of her first girlfriend and confront the demons of her youth. (978-1-62639-361-5)

Making a Comeback by Julie Blair. Music and love take center stage when jazz pianist Liz Randall tries to make a comeback with the help of her reclusive, blind neighbor, Jac Winters. (978-1-62639-357-8)

Soul Unique by Gun Brooke. Self-proclaimed cynic Greer Landon falls for Hayden Rowe's paintings and the young woman shortly after, but will Hayden, who lives with Asperger syndrome, trust her and reciprocate her feelings? (978-1-62639-358-5)

The Price of Honor by Radclyffe. Honor and duty are not always black and white—and when self-styled patriots take up arms against the government, the price of honor may be a life. (978-1-62639-359-2)

Mounting Evidence by Karis Walsh. Lieutenant Abigail Hargrove and her mounted police unit need to solve a murder and protect wetland biologist Kira Lovell during the Washington State Fair. (978-1-62639-343-1)

Threads of the Heart by Jeannie Levig. Maggie and Addison Rae-McInnis share a love and a life, but are the threads that bind them together strong enough to withstand Addison's restlessness and the seductive Victoria Fontaine? (978-1-62639-410-0)

Sheltered Love by MJ Williamz. Boone Fairway and Grey Dawson—two women touched by abuse—overcome their pasts to find happiness in each other. (978-1-62639-362-2)

Death's Doorway by Crin Claxton. Helping the dead can be deadly: Tony may be listening to the dead, but she needs to learn to listen to the living. (978-1-62639-354-7)

Searching for Celia by Elizabeth Ridley. As American spy novelist Dayle Salvesen investigates the mysterious disappearance of her ex-lover, Celia, in London, she begins questioning how well she knew Celia—and how well she knows herself. (978-1-62639-356-1).

Hardwired by C.P. Rowlands. Award-winning teacher Clary Stone and Leefe Ellis, manager of the homeless shelter for small children, stand together in a part of Clary's hometown that she never knew existed. (978-1-62639-351-6)

The Muse by Meghan O'Brien. Erotica author Kate McMannis struggles with writer's block until a gorgeous muse entices her into a world of fantasy sex and inadvertent romance. (978-1-62639-223-6)

No Good Reason by Cari Hunter. A violent kidnapping in a Peak District village pushes Detective Sanne Jensen and lifelong friend Dr. Meg Fielding closer, just as it threatens to tear everything apart. (978-1-62639-352-3)

The 45th Parallel by Lisa Girolami. Burying her mother isn't the worst thing that can happen to Val Montague when she returns to the woodsy but peculiar town of Hemlock, Oregon. (978-1-62639-342-4)

Romance by the Book by Jo Victor. If Cam didn't keep disrupting her life, maybe Alex could uncover the secret of a century-old love story, and solve the greatest mystery of all—her own heart. (978-1-62639-353-0)

A Royal Romance by Jenny Frame. In a country where class still divides, can love topple the last social taboo and allow Queen Georgina and Beatrice Elliot, a working-class girl, their happy ever after? (978-1-62639-360-8)

Bouncing by Jaime Maddox. Basketball coach Alex Dalton has been bouncing from woman to woman because no one ever held her interest, until she meets her new assistant, Britain Dodge. (978-1-62639-344-8)

All Things Rise by Missouri Vaun. Cole rescues a striking pilot who crash-lands near her family's farm, setting in motion a chain of events that will forever alter the course of her life. (978-1-62639-346-2)